In These Streets

Also by Shelly Ellis

Chesterton Scandal series

Best Kept Secrets
Bed of Lies
Lust & Loyalty
To Love & Betray

Gibbons Gold Digger series

Can't Stand the Heat
The Player & the Game
Another Woman's Man
The Best She Ever Had

Published by Dafina Books

IN THESE STREETS

SHELLY ELLIS

KENSINGTON PUBLISHING CORP.
www.kensingtonbooks.com

DAFINA BOOKS are published by

Kensington Publishing Corp.
119 West 40th Street
New York, NY 10018

All Kensington titles, imprints, and distributed lines are available at special quantity discounts for bulk purchases for sales promotion, premiums, fund-raising, and educational or institutional use.

Special book excerpts or customized printings can also be created to fit specific needs. For details, write or phone the office of the Kensington Sales Manager: Kensington Publishing Corp., 119 West 40th Street, New York, NY 10018. Attn. Sales Department. Phone: 1-800-221-2647.

ISBN-13: 978-1-4967-1895-2
ISBN-10: 1-4967-1895-X
First Kensington Trade Paperback Printing: December 2018

eISBN-13: 978-1-4967-1896-9
eISBN-10: 1-4967-1896-8
First Kensington Electronic Edition: December 2018

10 9 8 7 6 5 4 3 2 1

Printed in the United States of America

To Andrew and Chloe, you make it all worth it.

Acknowledgments

If you've read my previous books—both the Gibbons Gold Digger series and Chesterton Scandal series—you know that I like to write about the world of the rich and privileged. Both series were set in the affluent, fictional town of Chesterton, Virginia. I wrote about rich black folks not just because it's fun to talk about people who have servants, drive expensive cars, and own yachts. It's also the type of life for African Americans that isn't usually shown in books nowadays. (*Hey, we need escape fiction, too!*) But the truth is the glamorous life is far, *far* removed from my own life. (*Surprise! I know you're so shocked. LOL*)

I was born in Washington, D.C., before it went through gentrification and renewal, back when it was still called "Chocolate City" and also called, unfortunately, the "Murder Capital of the World." I lived there when Marion Barry was the infamous mayor who was busted by the FBI and caught on tape smoking crack cocaine. From the seventh floor of my family's apartment building in Southeast, D. C., I remember seeing search helicopters at night and hearing the occasional boom that you weren't sure was a car backfiring or gunshots.

But the D.C. of my childhood wasn't all crime and chaos. I remember a lot of joy, fun, and laughter, too. I remember go-go music playing loudly on car stereos and blasting from boom boxes during family cookouts. I remember going to the corner store with my grandmother who went to "play her numbers" and how she would buy me and my cousins scratch-off tickets and maybe a honey bun, if we were good. I remember trips uptown to see the Smithsonian museums and the Capitol building and feeling so special because so much history and knowledge was only a train ride away from my home.

The Branch Avenue Boys series (and its precursor, the MacLaine Girls series) are my special ode to my hometown and my youth. It's my special thanks to Washington, D.C., for the memories. I hope I did it justice.

I also want to say thanks to my parents who made my childhood seem ideal even if the world in which it took place wasn't perfect.

I want to thank my husband, Andrew, and my daughter, Chloe, for making my adulthood such an interesting and enlightening adventure. I hope I reciprocate by being the best partner and mommy I can be.

I want to thank my editor, Esi Sogah, and my agent, Barbara Poelle, for their continual feedback and support.

Also, I want to thank my street team members and my Facebook page coordinator, Shawnda, as well as all my Facebook page members. You guys have pretty lively conversations, and I'm fascinated by your takes on my characters and their stories.

Thanks to my fellow authors for commiserating. You guys share freely—expressing your fears, hopes, and self-doubt—and I appreciate your vulnerability and honesty.

And thanks to all my readers. Without you guys, I'd still be typing this stuff on my laptop—and it would stay there. You make this journey come full circle.

Chapter 1

Derrick

Derrick was throwing his satchel over his shoulder and slamming shut one of his file cabinet drawers when he heard the thump. He paused and squinted at his office wall where a white board, family photos, and his framed college degrees hung.

"What the hell," he murmured.

Thump! Thump!

This time the picture frames clacked and rattled against the drywall, like they had received a seismic jolt from the ground two stories below.

Thump! Thump! Thump!

Derrick then heard a muffled chorus of male shouts. They sounded like they were coming from farther down the hall.

"Whup that nigga's ass!" someone shouted.

"Get 'em Nico! Get 'em!" another boy yelled.

Derrick closed his eyes. "Damn," he muttered, finally realizing exactly what he was hearing.

It sounded like a fight had just erupted at the Branch Avenue Boys' Youth Institute—a *big* one. And as the

Institute's director it was his job to help break it up, which meant he wouldn't be heading home yet despite the long ass day he'd had.

"Shit," he murmured as he yanked his satchel off his shoulder and tossed the leather bag into his rolling chair.

Derrick had sat through a half dozen meetings today. One had been with a carpentry instructor who'd announced he would be leaving the Institute at the end of the month for a better, well-paid job, leaving Derrick in a lurch to find his replacement. Another meeting had been with a mother who had begged Derrick to let her sixteen-year-old son, Cole, into the Institute's rehabilitation program because she was terrified of what would happen to the teen if the city sent him to the local detention center for his drug charge. When she started crying and literally dropped to her knees on the linoleum floor, Derrick finally caved. He'd told her yes; he'd find a spot for her son—even though the Institute already had a waitlist twenty deep. He didn't know where he would find space for the boy, but he would make it work, somehow—like he always did.

But once the clock on his wall struck five, Derrick had felt his shoulders sink with the weight of exhaustion. He'd just wanted to go home, have dinner with his fiancée, Melissa, and meet up with his boys, Ricky and Jamal, for drinks later. It was a monthly ritual they'd had for nearly a decade and he had never skipped out on them before.

But it looked like he wouldn't be able to do any of that anytime soon thanks to the brawl in the office hall.

Derrick grabbed his walkie-talkie and jogged around his desk, grumbling to himself as he whipped opened his office door.

"Otis! Otis!" he called into the walkie-talkie. "Otis, we need help on the second floor! Can you send someone up?"

He got only static in response.

Guess I'll have to do this all by myself then, he thought with exasperation.

Derrick clipped his walkie-talkie onto his belt and quickly undid the cuffs of his shirt. He rolled his sleeves up to his forearms, revealing a series of tattoos and a few brands from his younger days.

He ran into the corridor, and the muffled shouts became a full roar. It was hard to see exactly who was fighting because nearly a dozen boys were huddled in a tight circle, not far from the door leading to the stairwell. They jumped and shoved to get a better view. As he ran toward them, he noticed the bedraggled-looking counselor standing in one of the classroom doorways. Her pale, wrinkled face was crumpled like she was about to burst into tears.

"I tried calling Otis!" she shouted to Derrick. "I really did, but he's not answering."

"I did too," he said.

Otis was the head security guard on staff at the Institute. He'd been a burly, intimidating corrections officer back in the day, but now he was just fat and lazy. Even the boys liked to call him Officer Twinkie behind his back. Otis was content to hide in the rec room, stuffing his face full of donuts while he watched talk shows on the staff flat screen. He would increasingly turn down the volume of his walkie-talkie so the static wouldn't interfere with his TV watching during the day, which would explain why he hadn't responded to the emergency call about the fight in the hallway. But considering that Otis was responsible for supervising all security, this was unacceptable.

Guess it's time to finally replace Otis, too.

It was yet another task he'd have to add to the growing list for the week.

Derrick nodded at the counselor. "Don't worry. I've got it! Just stand back, okay?"

She didn't look convinced, but shrank back into the classroom anyway when another thud ricocheted down the hall.

Derrick had a better view now. He could see that only two boys were tussling while the rest were cheering them on. Their T-shirts were ripped. One had the other in a headlock. The shorter of the two, who was in the headlock, was punching the other in the gut. Blood poured from the corner of the taller boy's mouth. They slammed against the drywall again, knocking down one of the Institute's plaques and sending it crashing to the floor.

Derrick took a deep breath and plunged forward like a man diving into an Olympic-sized swimming pool.

He yanked one boy back, a fat one who was nearly his size. The boy turned with his fist raised and then lowered it when he realized who was standing beside him.

"Oh, hey, Mr. Derrick!" he shouted as Derrick shoved another boy aside, then another. Finally, he was in the center of the circle.

"Stop this shit, right now!" he shouted, reaching for the two boys.

The shorter one was no longer in a headlock. His fists were up. He looked prepared to take a swing.

"I mean it! Don't make me have to—"

Derrick's words were stopped short by a punch to the face.

"Hey, baby!" Melissa called out as Derrick opened the apartment door. "You got home just in time! Dinner's almost done."

Their Calico cat, Brownie, greeted him as he closed the door behind him. The chubby cat rubbed its head and body against Derrick's pant leg and he leaned down to rub her back in return, then dropped his satchel to the floor. Despite the tissue stuffed up his nose, Derrick caught a whiff of the stir fry his fiancée was cooking. He could hear it sizzling in the kitchen too.

"How was your day?" she shouted to him as he walked down the short hall leading to their eat-in kitchen.

He passed their hallway mirror and winced.

Even though some of his shoulder-length dreads were hanging in his face, he could still see bruises blooming on his nose and his left cheek just a few shades darker than his mahogany skin. They would probably be purple by to-morrow. Blood was on his shirt, near the breast pocket.

"It was a little rough," he mumbled to Melissa as he tugged the bloody tissues from his nostrils, sighing at his reflection. "Just glad it's over."

He then rounded the corner and saw Melissa standing at their stove, wearing a tank top, yoga pants, and no shoes, slaving over dinner and looking as beautiful as ever. Her long, elegant neck and smooth, brown shoulders were on full display thanks to her braids being piled atop her head in a colorful kente wrap. She hummed absently to Jill Scott on their stereo as she cooked, tossing a cup of snow peas into the stir fry.

She had been humming when he first met her almost twenty years ago at the Boys' Institute. That day he'd been sweeping the foyer—one of his daily chores during the two years he'd served at the Institute for his assault charge. Melissa had been on her way to visit her father, the Institute's then director, Theo Stone or Mr. Theo. She had been hum-ming a tune by Aaliyah and bobbing her head to the music. Her eyes had been closed. She'd stopped short when she bumped into Derrick.

"Oh, I'm sorry!" she'd said, pulling her headphones from her ears and smiling bashfully up at him. "I didn't see you there."

But he had seen her. He had been staring at her as she un-knowingly walked straight into him and he hadn't moved an inch to stop the collision, too amazed by the lovely creature in front of him.

"I-I'm D-D-Derrick," he'd blurted out in response, making her smile widen. "You can call m-me Dee, though. E-e-everyone here c-c-calls me Dee. B-but my name is r-really Derrick."

"Hey, Dee! I'm Melissa," she'd replied—and he had been in love with her ever since.

Today, she was smiling again as he leaned down and kissed her bare shoulder, making her giggle. She turned away from the stove to face him and pointed toward the refrigerator with her wooden spatula. "Can you grab the wine I have chilling in the . . ."

Her words drifted off. Her smile instantly disappeared.

"What the hell happened to you?" she screeched, dropping the spatula to the granite counter and turning off the oven burners. She reached up for his face and gently touched the bruise on his cheek, grimacing. "*Who* did this, Dee? Did you get mugged or somethin'?"

He shook his head and exhaled. He then turned slightly to toss his bloody tissues into the kitchen waste bin. "No, I broke up a fight between a couple of the boys today. That's all."

"*That's all?* That's all?" She slowly shook her head. "If you were breaking up the fight then how the hell did you end up being the one who got stomped?"

"I didn't 'get stomped.'" He tugged her hand from his face. "The boys were swinging and accidentally hit me a few times. It happens. Neither of them meant to do it. They apologized when they settled down."

"Oh, they apologized! Well, I guess that makes it okay then!" she exclaimed sarcastically before crossing her arms over her chest.

"Look, I took care of it. That's all that matters." He grabbed one of the ceramic plates on the counter and peered down into the wok on the stove. "You didn't put too much sriracha in here, did you? You know I don't like it too hot, baby."

He raised his gaze when she stomped her bare foot.

"Derrick Miller, are you really asking me about some damn chili pepper sauce when you walked through the front door with a bloody nose, a ripped shirt"—she said, fingering his torn shirt collar—"and a busted face like you just stumbled out of a boxing ring? This is not cool! It's not right! You shouldn't have to—"

"And what exactly do you want me to do about it? Huh?" he asked, not having the energy or patience to mask his irritation. "It's part of the damn job. You of all people should know that!"

She fell silent and pursed her lips.

He hadn't meant to lash out at her, but he didn't come home to start an argument. He just wanted to eat dinner and spend some coveted alone time with his girl. Was that too much to ask? Besides, Melissa had grown up knowing how the Boys' Institute operated. Her father had been at the helm of the place for more than thirty years before he retired four years ago, and Derrick had taken over as director. She'd had a front row seat to the horror stories that came with running a place like the Institute, but she also knew the highs and the joys you experienced seeing children that society had basically thrown away get a second chance.

"Look, baby, it was a bad day." He sat down his plate, reached out, and wrapped his arms around her. "But I handled it." He forced a smile. "Trust me, the bruises look worse than they feel."

But his soothing words weren't working their magic. She still stubbornly shook her head. "Enough is enough, Dee. I'm a teacher who loves my kids too, but there is no way—*no way* I'd put up with half the shit that you do.

They *accidentally* hit you today. What if they *accidentally* stab you or shoot you tomorrow?"

He sucked his teeth in exasperation.

"I mean some of those boys are hard-core criminals. Some of them—"

"—are just like who I was twenty years ago," he finished for her, dropping his arms from around her waist. "Come on, Lissa. You want me to be a hypocrite?"

"They are *nothing* like how you were. Don't give me that shit! You guys were in there for petty crimes—getting into school fights and shoplifting from corner stores. Some of these boys are facing first-degree-assault and drug smuggling charges, Dee. The city is making that place the dumping ground for kids everyone else is too terrified keep in their classrooms!"

"Which is exactly why I want them with me. I know who they are. I've been where they are. I won't give up on them the way everyone else has. Theo wouldn't have given up on them either!"

She stiffened. He watched as she narrowed her dark eyes. "Are you really going to bring him up?"

"Why shouldn't I? What I said about your dad is true. You know he loved those kids. He still does."

"Oh, yeah, he loved them. He loved them so much that he was willing to sacrifice his marriage, his family, and his life for them. He made it clear to me, Mama, and everyone else that the boys at the Institute were the most important things in the world to him—even more important than *us*. And then, when he was ready to retire and we thought we finally had him all to ourselves, he went gay and ran off with some dude!"

Derrick winced. Maybe he shouldn't have brought up her father after all.

She looked Derrick up and down. "So is that what you're trying to tell me? You really want to be *just like* my daddy? Because if it is, I can give you this ring back right now." She held up her hand and pointed to the solitaire diamond on her finger.

At that, his shoulders slumped. All his rising anger dissipated. "Baby, you know that's . . . that's not what I meant. I love you. I do! It's just . . . I love my job too, and the boys need me . . . and . . . and . . ."

He couldn't find the right words so he let the sentence drift off into silence and raked his fingers through his dreads in frustration instead.

"Enjoy your dinner. I didn't put any sriracha in it this time, so you should like it," she muttered, wiping her hands on a dish towel, tossing it aside, and stepping around him.

"Come on, baby, don't be that way." He reached out for her and tried to draw her close again, but she pulled out of his grasp.

"Tell Ricky and Jamal I said 'Hey,' when you see them tonight, okay?" she called over her shoulder as she walked out of the kitchen and down the hall to their bedroom. She then bent down and scooped their cat into her arms. "Come on, Brownie. Let's go grade some papers."

Derrick heard their bedroom door slam shut seconds later.

"Shit," he said before roughly scrubbing his hand over his face. "Oww, shit!" he said again, wincing reflexively at the pain in his cheek.

Chapter 2

Ricky

"Mr. Reynaud?" someone called out then knocked at his office door. "Mr. Reynaud?"

Ricky didn't answer. He was three minutes away from getting his rocks off—maybe two. Anyway, he was pretty damn close and he didn't want to lose the momentum.

"Give it to me! Give it to me, baby," Kia groaned.

He'd recently hired Kia—a pretty, young college grad and Instagram model who'd moved to D.C. three months ago. She still hadn't learned the menu and he'd had to comp meals at least twice a week because she kept screwing up orders, but she had a nice smile, big tits, and an amazing ass. She'd been flirting with him for weeks, shamelessly rubbing up against him in the prep area or sitting on his office desk and giving him a perfect view of her thigh-highs as she talked about her roommates and living in the big city. Though Ricky generally preferred not to get down and dirty with the wait staff at his restaurant because it could get messy, tonight he'd made an exception.

Ricky squeezed one of her breasts, rubbing his thumb over the hard, brown nipple. She arched her back and moaned. He watched as she gripped the edge of the desk while he steadied her bottom, and she met him stroke for stroke, raising her hips off the wooden surface.

"Come on! Keep goin'!" she urged. "Don't worry, daddy. I can take it!"

Daddy?

He cringed inwardly.

Some women thought it was a turn on when they called you that, but it always ruined the mood for him. He didn't want to imagine this chick's father right now, or wonder if she was playing out some Electra complex with her boss on his office desk. But he shoved those thoughts and the word out of his mind and pumped even harder, making her writhe and groan.

"Oh, God!" she whimpered. "Oh, God!"

"Uh, Mr. Reynaud, are you . . . are you in there?" He heard another knock. It sounded more frantic this time.

"I'm . . . busy!" Ricky shouted between breaths. "Come . . . back . . . later!"

"You have someone waiting out here, and they said they have to speak with you *now.* Mr. Reynaud, did you hear me?"

"Almost done. Almost done. Almost done," he chanted, feeling his heart thud in his chest, hearing his blood whistle in his ears.

A stapler clattered to the floor. A rattling mug filled with pens tipped over and the pens went rolling across his desk.

"I'm sorry . . . what did you say, sir?" the voice called out to him through the closed door.

Kia fell back against his desk calendar. Her groans and moans turned into yells and Ricky quickly clamped his hand over her mouth to stifle the noise. He didn't want the rest of the staff on the floor to hear.

She must have mistaken it for some kinky gesture because she shifted his hand from her mouth to her throat and began to squeeze his fingers, like she wanted him to strangle her. He didn't take her up on the offer. He was an open-minded dude but erotic asphyxiation wasn't his kink. Instead, he gripped her shoulders, spread her legs even wider, even throwing one high-heeled foot over his shoulder. He increased the tempo yet again. Her eyes rolled to the back of her head. She began to pant and whine.

And then, finally, he came with a euphoric rush that made him see pinpricks of stars, and that made him convulse and collapse on top of Kia's bare chest and gulp for air.

After a few seconds, he raised his head and gazed down at her.

"That was amazing, baby," Kia said breathlessly, trailing a finger along his chin.

He gave her a quick peck on the lips before pulling out of her with a grunt. He then staggered into his office bathroom, pulled off his condom, knotted it, and tossed it into the trash can. He grabbed a wash cloth, soaked it with hot water, and began to wipe himself down with the efficiency of a man who had done this many, *many* times before. Ricky stared at his reflection and noticed the bright red lipstick on his sienna-hued cheek, just above his beard.

Can't have that, he thought, reaching for a tissue near the sink.

He had a face that most women would consider handsome—full lips, soulful eyes, and high cheekbones—and he used it to his advantage. The broad shoulders, toned build, and imposing height didn't hurt either in winning over the ladies. Ricky hadn't had a serious relationship in years, but he didn't have to worry about a cold bed at night either.

After he finished wiping off Kia's lipstick and cleaning himself up, he tugged his boxer briefs from his knees back up to his waist.

"Wanna meet up for a second round after my shift is over?" she asked.

He could see her in the reflection of his bathroom mirror. She was still reclining on his desk, like a cat sunning itself in a window.

"I would, but I've got somewhere to be later. Gonna have to take a raincheck."

"A raincheck?" She frowned and pushed herself up to her elbows as he raised his pants' zipper. "What? What do you mean, 'You've got somewhere to be'? Where is that?"

He forced himself not to roll his eyes.

Well, that didn't take long, Ricky thought. He'd smashed her for the first time literally five minutes ago and she was already asking him about his business? He had been too focused on her body to notice the big, dewy brown eyes and the trembling bottom lip, but he noticed them now. This was a girl who got easily attached. He should have known better. He'd have to be a little more gentle than usual with this brush off.

"I've just . . . uh . . . gotta meet some old friends. That's all."

It was the truth. He was meeting his long-time friends, Derrick and Jamal, later tonight for drinks.

Ricky made some final adjustments to his clothes, stepped back into his office, and reached into one of his desk drawers. He removed a bottle of Gucci Guilty and sprayed a bit onto himself and then into the air before glancing down at her again. "Fix your clothes, honey. It's almost seven and we open up soon for the evening service."

Kia's glossy lips formed a comical pout as she pulled up her bra cups and dragged the straps back onto her shoulders. "Wait a minute! Are you saying you just expect me to—"

She stopped when the frantic knocking started up again, making Ricky grouse with annoyance.

"The fuck . . ." he muttered as he strode toward the door.

"Ricky, don't you walk away from me!" Kia yelled.

"Just go in the bathroom and get dressed," he hissed over his shoulder at her as the knocking continued.

Her brow wrinkled and she pushed back her shoulders. "Don't talk to me like that! Don't just tell me to get dressed like I'm some . . . some hooker! Who the hell do you think you are?"

"Mr. Reynaud?" the person on the other side of the door shouted. "Mr. Reynaud, this guy says he *really* has to—"

Ricky whipped open his office door, making Kia let out a "yip" that sounded a lot like a kicked puppy. She hopped off his desk and ran to his office bathroom, pushing down her pencil skirt and tripping over the lace thong trailing from one of her stilettoes.

The door knocker turned out to be one of the floor waiters whose knuckle was still raised and poised to knock again. He jumped—startled, like he hadn't expected Ricky to actually answer this time.

"*What?*" Ricky asked. "What the hell is so important that you had to beat my damn door down? Is the kitchen on fire?"

The bespectacled waiter hesitated, pushed his glasses up the bridge of his nose, then pointed to something down the hall.

Ricky leaned into the hallway to see what the waiter was pointing at. When he did, his jaw tightened.

"What's up, Pretty Ricky? I've been lookin' for your ass!" the young man called out as strolled toward them. "I was about to bust in on you if you had me waitin' out here any longer."

The young man was wearing a sweat-stained tank top and black skinny jeans slung low on his hips—definitely not proper attire for Reynaud's, the upscale restaurant that Ricky owned and managed. If he were the average person, the maître d' would have turned him away at the door. But he wasn't the average person—and he knew it.

"What are you doing here, T. J.?" Ricky asked, waving off the anxious waiter who quickly nodded and gave T. J. a wide berth before hastily making his way back down the hall to the restaurant floor.

"Stop callin' me T. J.," T. J. snarled, baring his buckteeth like some feral dog. "It's Big T now! The only person I let call me T. J. is my mama—and you ain't her."

Ricky leaned against the door frame. "Fine, *Big T*. Why the fuck are you here?"

"Why the fuck do you think I'm here? Dolla Dolla sent me."

Dolla Dolla was Ricky's business partner and investor. Ricky had known the D.C. drug kingpin since the early days when he'd finished serving his time at the Institute with Derrick and Jamal, but still had to hustle to take care of his grandmother and little sister. Dolla Dolla had given him a few jobs every now and then—some above board, some not. When Ricky got older and decided to put that life of crime behind him, Dolla Dolla had given him his blessing. He had even loaned Ricky the money to start his own restaurant, with the prerequisite that Ricky become co-owner of Club Majesty, a strip joint Dolla Dolla had started downtown.

Ricky figured the deal had some strings attached. Dolla Dolla liked him, but he wouldn't just give Ricky money and make him co-owner of one of his businesses out of the kindness of his heart. He just didn't comprehend *how many* strings were attached until it was too late. By then, he'd figured out that the strip club was a front for several of Dolla Dolla's criminal operations.

In a locked storage room at the club that was supposed to be used for toilet paper and hand soap were shelves upon shelves of stolen designer purses and electronics.

And though Ricky wanted to hire an accountant, Dolla Dolla insisted he already had his own. Ricky noticed after checking receipts one day that the numbers didn't match the ones the accountant had recorded that previous month. He realized the accountant was cooking their books, likely to hide something from the feds. And on top of all that, on any given night, Dolla Dolla's men would roll up to the strip club's service entrance loaded down with duffel bags and suitcases, and head straight to the club's basement. The suitcases would sit there for days undisturbed, and then mysteriously disappear a week later.

Ricky didn't ask any questions about the mysterious suitcases, or anything else for that matter. He knew who his business partner was, and as long as Dolla Dolla let him do his thing as manager and co-owner of Club Majesty, he'd let Dolla Dolla do whatever he wanted behind the scenes. But the restaurant was off limits. That was the implicit agreement they'd had for years. Dolla Dolla didn't bring that shit here, which is why he wasn't happy to see T. J. standing in front of him right now.

"Look, I told y'all if you needed to reach me, call me," Ricky said, towering over T. J. and dropping his voice to a whisper. "Don't just show up at my place and ambush me like this. I don't play that shit!"

"Man, I don't give a damn what you said! Dolla Dolla told me to give you a message in person. *He's* the one I listen to, not you, nigga."

Ricky gritted his teeth so hard the molars might crack.

T. J. had to weigh less than one hundred and twenty pounds. Ricky could easily whip his little ass up and down the hallway for talking to him like this. But he knew T. J. was one of Dolla Dolla's prized emissaries. The little punk also carried, which meant a fight with fists could devolve into bullets flying. So Ricky took a deep breath to steady himself.

"Then just spit it out and be on your way," he said in a measured voice. "I've got a fuckin' business to run."

T. J. shook his head. "Nuh-uh, I'm saying this shit in private. Not with no other people standing around."

"What other people are standing around? Nobody else is here!"

"Then who the fuck is that?" T. J. asked, pointing over Ricky's shoulder.

Ricky turned to find Kia standing timidly in his bathroom doorway. He'd forgotten she was back there. She was dressed now, at least, though she had a confused look on her face.

"Uh, Kia, can you give us a sec, honey?" Ricky asked.

She quickly nodded. "S-sure, Ricky. I-I think my shift is starting anyway." She then walked toward the office door and squeezed between the two men. When she did, T. J. looked her up and down. He licked his lips and leered hungrily at her like she was one of the many dishes on Reynaud's house menu.

"Damn, you got some good taste in bitches." He turned back to Ricky, grinning ear-to-ear. "Her pussy good too?"

Ricky didn't answer him. Instead, he motioned T. J. into his office and shut the door behind him. He watched, infuriated, as T. J. strolled to one of the arm chairs facing his ebony desk. The young man flopped back into the chair and rubbed his palms over the smooth leather like he was caressing a woman.

"Nice," he mused. "I need to get me one of these. Where you get it from? Marlo Furniture or some shit?"

"Look, just give me Dolla's message, all right?" Ricky snapped, stepping behind his desk and facing T. J. "I don't have time for any of this. I told you, I have a business to run."

T. J. slouched back farther in his chair, waiting a few beats before he answered. Finally, he said, "Dolla wants you to make sure the restaurant's back door is open tonight. He said he's got a shipment he wanna bring here. It's one he's gotta move quickly."

Ricky shook his head. "No! Hell, no! He knows I don't want any of that shit in my restaurant. If he has some stuff he's trying to move, he can bring it to Club Majesty like he usually does. Not here! He can't—"

"Nigga," T. J. said, suddenly leaning forward, "you and I both know Dolla can do whatever the fuck he wants. He says the club might be too hot now, that maybe the cops are starting to catch on to what's going down, so he wants to find another place to put his shit."

"But why does that place have to be *my* restaurant?"

"Because he fuckin' said so!" T. J. shot to his feet, yanking up his sagging jeans as he did it. "Man, just keep the door open like he told you to. Don't be stupid, get buck, and get your shit fucked up! You feel me?"

Ricky fought back his fury, stuffing it into the pit of his stomach as T. J. walked toward his office door and opened it.

"Hey," T. J. said, pausing in the doorway, "y'all do carry-out? I think I want some of the catfish but I'm gonna have to get that shit to go. Dolla got a few more peeps he wants me to pay a visit to tonight."

Ricky didn't answer him. He continued to glare at him openly though, making T. J. laugh.

"Guess not," T. J. said before walking out of Ricky's office and into the hall.

Chapter 3

Jamal

Jamal held his tight smile in place and nodded at the man speaking next to him, not paying attention to a word he was saying. Jamal could barely hear him anyway; he was surrounded by a swarm of people—partygoers in suits and other business attire who drank wine and sampled canapés on Krueger, McKenzie, and Sutton Law Office's dime. He was starting to get a headache thanks to the wall of sound that echoed from the museum gallery's high ceilings. The bright lights weren't helping either.

Jamal nonchalantly glanced at his wristwatch to check the time. When he saw what time it was, he cursed under his breath. Even if he left the cocktail party now, he was still going to be late meeting Derrick and Ricky for drinks. He could envision them talking shit about him over beers and glasses of whiskey in the small rundown dive bar they had been going to for years, even before they could legally drink.

"That motherfucka' ain't never on time," Ricky would say with a laugh.

"Told him he'd be late to his own funeral," Derrick would concur.

And Jamal hadn't wanted to make them wait for him, especially considering what he had to say to them tonight.

He stared over the lip of his wineglass at his girlfriend, Bridget, trying his best to make eye contact with her and signal that it was time to go, but she was completely oblivious to him and his growing desperation. He shouldn't be surprised; Bridget was in her element. She loved parties like these, where power and prestige hung heavy in the air like a cheap perfume and she could hobnob with D.C.'s elite. She loved to gossip about what was happening on Capitol Hill and relished dropping the names of friends and old classmates who were on staff at the White House.

Bridget always kept her business cards and cell phone handy, ready to make new contacts and set up a lunch date or a business call. Normally, Jamal admired her hustle and grind. He was even awed by it. Who knew a pampered princess from a WASP family in Connecticut could be so driven? But today he just wished she'd give that shit a rest.

He watched as she tossed her red hair over her shoulder and laughed at something one of her lobbyist colleagues said, some guy whose name Jamal had forgotten already.

"We'd love to go the Hamptons, Mike," she said, looping her arm through Jamal's and drawing close to his side, "but unfortunately we won't be taking any vacations anytime soon now that Sinclair here has been named the district's newest deputy mayor!"

Who the hell is Sinclair? Jamal thought and then realized, *Oh, yeah. That's me.*

He was going by his middle name now. "J. Sinclair Lighty" was on all his new business cards.

Bridget had said the name change would be a smart move.

"I love your name, Jamal. Really I do, but it just sounds so . . . so urban . . . even a little Middle Eastern," she'd said in bed one night a few months ago while scrunching up her nose, like she smelled something stinky. "But if you ever want a bigger future in politics, you should think of changing it."

"It doesn't sound any more Middle Eastern than Barack *Hussein* Obama," Jamal had argued. "Barack became president with his name."

"And the Republicans repeated it every chance they got! They know how a name like that sounds to 'mom and pop, small town' America. It scares the hell out of them! And besides," she'd said with a shrug before sinking beneath the covers, "Obama isn't saddled with a juvenile record."

"It's not like I'm a hardened criminal though, Bridge. It was breaking and entering and a vandalism charge when I was twelve years old. I broke open an old lock to an apartment building and tagged an exterior wall. The only reason I got such a stiff penalty is because that racist old judge wanted to teach me a lesson. It was a stupid, childish mistake. I never did it again!"

"But people won't know the difference, sweetheart. They won't care! Trust me. A new name is just the change you need. It'll make it easier to put that part of your past behind you."

"So you're deputy mayor, huh?" her colleague now asked, turning to Jamal.

His wrinkled face suddenly brightened with interest where before it had only held polite detachment whenever he glanced at Jamal. It was the same look you gave a waiter who offered you a drink. Jamal wondered if every time the man's eyes had landed on him—a short, unassuming, light-skinned black man in a dark suit and tie—he had just assumed Jamal was one of the waiters circulating around the room.

"Deputy mayor of what department, may I ask?" the old man continued.

"Planning and economic development," Jamal replied, finishing the last of his white wine.

"*Really?* I know a fellow at the mayor's office who I went to law school with many, many years ago. He's a good guy. You might know him. He's—"

"Probably not. It's pretty big place over there," Jamal said, cutting him off. He then turned to Bridget. "Honey, it's starting to get little late and I've got an early start tomorrow morning. Do you mind if we head out?"

Her freckled cheeks flushed bright red and her brows knitted together. He'd pissed her off. The tell-tale signs were there. But Bridget only allowed her mask of pleasantry to shift out of place for a few seconds. She immediately wiped away her angry expression and replaced it with a bland smile.

"No! Of course, I don't mind, sweetie. I've got an early start too. We can totally head home."

"It was a pleasure to meet you," Jamal said, extending his hand to her colleague.

He glanced down blankly at Jamal's hand then gave it a firm shake. "Y-yes, pleasure to . . . uh . . . meet you too, Sinclair."

"Could you have been any ruder?" Bridget snapped as they stepped out the museum's revolving doors onto the sidewalk.

Jamal instantly got a whiff of smog and the Chinese food wafting from the restaurant down the street. Several feet away a man played "In a Sentimental Mood" on a saxophone. A Big Gulp cup sat at his feet where pedestrians tossed in loose change and dollar bills.

"I wasn't being rude," Jamal said as they walked toward the musician. He dug into his pocket, retrieved a dollar, and tossed it into the man's cup. The man nodded in appreciation. Jamal then returned his attention to his girlfriend, glancing down at her stern face under the lamp light. "That guy had been rambling for a good ten minutes. I had no idea what he was talking about anyway, and he wasn't even interested in what I had to say until you told him I was the deputy mayor!"

"Damnit, he's one of the partners, Sinclair! I was trying to make a good impression. I brought you there to schmooze, to show off my successful boyfriend, and you *completely* ruined it."

"I wasn't trying to ruin it, honey. I just wanted to leave. That's all! There will be other cocktail parties. You guys have one at least once a month, don't you? Next time, I'll let the guy talk as long as he wants. It's just this time, I couldn't."

They walked under a stone archway and drew near escalators leading to the metro. They stepped aside for another couple heading in the opposite direction.

"You are *completely* missing the point." He watched as she dug into her purse, pushing aside compacts and lipstick. She pulled out her metro card as they stepped on the escalators and descended to the tunnel below. "You make the best impression at each event, at *every* moment, Sinclair, because you never know when the opportunity will come around again. Tonight was a missed opportunity."

He didn't respond, deciding to let the argument drop since he had to be on his way anyway. As they stepped off the escalator and reached the metal turnstiles, he kissed her on the cheek.

"I hear what you're saying. And like I said, I'm sorry. But I have to get going. I'll meet you at home."

She frowned again. "Going where? I thought you were heading home with me!"

He glanced up at the digital sign overhead that showed the next blue line train would be arriving in only four minutes. He needed to be on it if he wanted to make it to the bar by eleven o'clock.

"I told you that I have to meet Derrick and Ricky tonight, honey."

Her frown deepened. The flush in her cheeks was back. Even her neck erupted in streaks of red. "Are you really telling me you rushed me out of that cocktail party so you can meet your *homeboys* at a bar?"

"Don't say it like that. Don't call them 'homeboys.' It's so—"

"Well, that's what they are!" she cried. "They're your homeboys . . . your *homies*." She rolled her blue eyes toward the metro station's water-stained ceiling, whipping her hair over her shoulder. "I can't believe this! I don't even know why you keep them around considering you're supposed to be—"

"Look, I'm going there to do what you told me I should do, all right?" he said, leaning in close to her and dropping his voice down to a whisper. "You said I needed to move on, and I'm telling them that tonight. But I'm not going to do it over the phone. They've been my friends since we were twelve years old. The least I can do is say something like this to their faces."

Bridget's expression softened. "I see what you mean." She tucked her hair behind her ear. "Sorry, I chewed you out, sweetheart. I didn't know that's what you were going to do."

He shrugged and glanced up at the digital sign again. Another two minutes had passed. "It's fine," he mumbled.

She stood on the balls of her feet, looped her arms around his neck, and kissed him. The kiss reminded him of what lurked under Bridget's no-nonsense, sometimes ball-busting exterior. It reminded him why he'd hooked up with the little redheaded spitfire in the first place.

"I know it'll be hard but I bet they'll understand." She smoothed the lapel of his suit jacket and adjusted the knot in his tie. "They know where you're headed, and they don't want to hold you back."

"Yeah, I doubt they'll see it that way, but I don't have much of a choice." He glanced at the digital sign yet again as he unwound her arm from around her neck. "Look, I better get going. I've got like a minute to make my train."

He then turned back toward the turnstile and slapped his card over the reader. He rushed through the turnstile as the train doors opened.

"It'll be fine!" she shouted over the roar of the incoming train as he ran down the platform.

Jamal managed to hop on the train just before the doors closed.

Twenty-five minutes later, Jamal swung open the glass door to Ray's Bar and Lounge. The name made the establishment sound loftier than it actually was. It was really just a dilapidated bar filled with wood paneling, cracked glass tiles along the walls, pleather couches, and a small parquet dance floor that hadn't been used since 1992. The lounge's rickety laminate tables were covered with stains but you could barely tell, thanks to how dim Ray Willard, the owner and head bartender, kept the lighting in there.

Jamal, Derrick, and Ricky were some of the youngest patrons. The bar usually attracted the forty-and-older set—the players whose player days were behind them, or would be soon.

Jamal, Derrick, and Ricky had tried over the years to transition to more glamorous spots for their weekly meetups—tapas bars with crystal chandeliers and pretty waitresses, or cigar lounges with glass-enclosed fireplaces and velvet sofas. They had even tried Club Majesty once, though neither Jamal nor Derrick had enjoyed the experience despite the beautiful strippers. It was strange to watch their boy, Ricky, as a hyped-up strip club owner who slapped dancers on their asses, threw back shots like they were tap water, and did lines of coke and Molly in between. Every now and then Ricky would give Jamal and Derrick a knowing look or a wink to let them know he was just playing the role that was expected of him, that he was still the low-key, funny Ricky they knew. Jamal got an eerie feeling like he was watching a theater performance where the actor kept breaking the fourth wall. He hadn't wanted to go back to Club Majesty and was glad neither Derrick nor Ricky had suggested it.

After hopping from place to place, they would always end up back at Ray's. From the selection of nineties hip hop and hometown go-go music that seemed to play on an endless loop on the bar's sound system, to the cheap drinks and shit-talking bartenders, they couldn't let go of the old bar and lounge.

On some level Jamal suspected they felt a kinship to this place because it represented them as a group. They didn't have to code-switch here, lose their drawls, or watch their cuss words; they could just be themselves. Ray's represented their humble beginnings, their strong connection to the grimy, "chicken wings and mambo sauce," Rare Essence, "rep for your area code" part of D.C. that most people who frequented the tourist traps like the Smithsonian and White House never got to see. It was a part of them they could not, *would not,* let go.

But not anymore, Jamal thought forlornly as he nodded to Ray who stood behind the bar. The old man paused from wiping down the counter and nodded back in greeting.

"I'll bring your drink over in a minute," Ray called to him, making the cigarette at the corner of his mouth bob up and down as he spoke.

Though Jamal was reluctant to do it, he knew he had to move on from this place, from his neighborhood and the people in it. If he wanted to ascend the social and political ladder, it meant accepting that some people weren't going to climb that ladder with him. He couldn't allow them to drag him down either, and Ricky and Derrick would do just that—even if it wasn't their intention.

He spotted his two best friends at the same table they always sat at.

Derrick's back was facing him but he was gesticulating, as if he was telling some story, and Jamal watched as Ricky threw back his head and laughed.

He remembered when he first spotted them together at the Branch Avenue Boys Institute nearly two decades ago. They had been slumped against the brick wall, laughing and watching the other boys play basketball. Though they were all the same age, Derrick and Ricky had stood almost a foot taller than Jamal. He had liked the vibe they had about them, how they carried themselves among the other boys: slightly apart from the rest, but not bothered by the fact that they weren't connected to the cliques. Jamal had wanted to be friends with them. He had wanted their swagger, their air of "I don't give a fuck," since he was a boy who *always* cared what other people thought. He had been bullied for his slight build and small height, his "faggoty" middle name, and the North Carolina drawl he once had before he learned how to mask it. But Derrick and Ricky hadn't seemed weak like him. They weren't easy targets. Derrick had had a rep, even back then. So had Ricky. Meanwhile, no one knew or cared who Jamal was even though he tagged about a dozen buildings between Barry Farms and Hillcrest with his name in the hopes of gaining some notoriety. The only thing it had done was land him at the Institute where he had been at the mercy of bullies until Derrick and Ricky had rescued and protected him.

His friends had seemed to be impenetrable back then—but they weren't anymore. He could see the cracks in their armor now.

"We was wondering if your ass was gonna show up," Ricky said with a grin as Jamal grabbed one of the wooden chairs from an empty table and slid it across the floor to their booth.

"What's up, fellas?" Jamal said, tugging off his suit jacket and tossing it on the back of the chair. He leaned forward and gave them both a fist pound before sitting down.

"Look at him . . . trying to act all casual," Derrick said. "No, what's up with you? You the nigga with the busy schedule, Mr. Deputy Mayor."

Derrick was chiding him but Jamal heard nothing but pride in his friend's voice. One of the Branch Avenue boys had made good, and a man like Derrick would hold no ill will against him.

Jamal squinted at Derrick, leaning forward so he could see him better in the dim lighting. "No, what's up with you? You look like you owed someone some money and they took it out on your face!"

Ricky burst into laughter again, clapping his hands.

Derrick had always been ready to rumble in the old days. He had gotten Jamal out of more than one scrape at the Institute, but Jamal had assumed those fighting days were behind them.

Derrick loudly blew air out of his nose and raised his glass to his busted lip. He took a drink. "I had to break up a fight between a couple of boys today and got some collateral damage. That's all."

Jamal furrowed his brows, taking in all of Derrick's bruises and his swollen nose. "It looks like a lot more than 'collateral damage,' Dee. You look like—"

"Stop," Derrick said. "Stop, all right? You sound like Melissa. She was bitching me out about it. It turned into another argument about me working at the Institute." He shook his head and took another drink. "I'm so done with that shit. She keeps bringing it up!"

"Maybe she has a point though," Jamal said softly with a shrug. He watched as Ray sat a glass of whiskey on ice in front of him. He nodded in thanks to Ray as the old man walked off.

"What do you mean maybe she has a point?" Derrick asked. "You think I should quit?"

"I'm just sayin' maybe you should hear her out. You've got a bachelor's in elementary education and a master's in psychology. You're telling me you spent all that time in college just to get your ass whupped by delinquent thirteen-year-old boys? Maybe it's . . ." He shrugged again. "I don't know . . . Maybe it's time to move on, Dee."

Derrick wasn't pale like Bridget and, therefore, didn't flush a shade of red at that moment, but Jamal knew a pissed-off face when he saw one.

"Where is this shit coming from?" Derrick snapped.

Ricky lowered his bottle to the table top and held up his hands. "Hey! Hey, Dee, he didn't mean anything by it. Just chill, man!"

"No, he meant what he said. He said it's time to move on

from a job that I love, from a place that *made us* who we are today. How can you be cavalier about that shit, Jay?"

"It made us who we are, but it isn't *who* we are," Jamal corrected, taking a drink. "I'm a grown ass man, and I'm not gonna feel bad that I want to put that part of my past behind me."

Now even Ricky was eying him slyly. "Grown ass man, huh? But is this grown ass man speaking and thinking for himself—or letting his girl do it for him?"

Jamal clenched his jaw. "Man, fuck you, Ricky."

Ricky leaned back in the booth and tilted his head. "I'm just sayin', don't let yourself get brainwashed, bruh! No pussy is worth half the shit she makes you do. She's got you changing the clothes you wear and . . ."

"I wear suits now. *So what?* That's part of my job. I'm deputy mayor. You expect me to roll up to City Hall in baggy jeans and a doo-rag?"

"She got you to change your name too," Ricky continued, taking a swig from his bottle.

"Yeah, explain that shit, *Sinclair,*" Derrick chided with widened eyes, making Jamal even more irritated.

"I mean if you're gonna do all that, at least get a chick with a bomb body," Ricky insisted. "Those itty bitty titties your girl is working with can't be—"

"Ricky," Jamal began warningly.

"I'm just saying, I've got a thirty-six double-D redhead with freckles down at the club if you want me to introduce her to you since that's your thing. Just think of it as an upgrade."

"There is no 'upgrade' from Bridget. She's not a goddamn cellphone. I don't want to trade her in!"

Ricky raised his brows and took another sip from his bottle. "You sure about that, bruh?"

"Yeah, I'm sure," Jamal answered firmly, taking a guilty glance at Derrick over his whiskey glass.

The truth was, there was only one woman in the world who Jamal would consider pursuing if the opportunity ever came, who Jamal would "risk it all for," despite being in a relationship with Bridget—and that woman was engaged to Derrick.

Though Jamal had known the beautiful Melissa Stone just as long as Derrick—meeting her on the same day as he had nineteen years ago, Derrick had connected with her first. He'd often wondered, if he had been the one standing in the hall when she came in that day versus Derrick, would their lives have played out differently? Would *he* be the one engaged to Melissa, not his boy?

Over the years, though Derrick and Melissa had broken up and made up quite a few times, Melissa only seemed to have eyes for Derrick and never seemed to consider Jamal in that way. Jamal wasn't surprised. Derrick was taller, darker, and admittedly, better looking than him. It was hard to compete with that. He suspected Melissa would always see him as just her man's best friend—and he would always have to keep his unrequited feelings and desires to himself.

"You look like you're hesitating there, Jay," Ricky joked, as if reading Jamal's mind. He ran his thumb and forefinger over his beard. "Got a nice side piece in mind?"

Derrick burst into laughter.

"It's okay. You're in the circle of trust," Ricky continued, making Derrick laugh even harder. "I swear, we won't tell. Just blink once for 'yes' and twice for 'no.'"

That's when Jamal lost it. He had come here to tell them something important, not to be made fun of the whole night, which is what they usually did. It was always

Derrick and Ricky ganging up on him, making him the butt of some dumb ass joke.

"Oh, this shit is funny . . . real fuckin' funny," Jamal snarled. "Don't you get tired of being the jackass, Ricky? Or is that all part of this bullshit, 'Pretty Ricky' persona you've created?"

Derrick fell silent and Ricky looked taken aback.

"That's why I'm so tired of this shit—all of it! That's why I'm ready to move on," Jamal muttered sullenly before taking another drink.

"Why do you keep saying that?" Derrick asked, squinting again. "Move on from what?"

"From us," Ricky answered for him. His affable smile had disappeared. "That's what you mean right, Jay? You've been dancing around this shit the whole time. You're ready to move on from us. Just say it!"

"Man, that's not what he means. Don't exaggerate," Derrick insisted, waving him off and sucking his teeth. He turned back to Jamal. "That's not what you mean, right, Jay?"

Jamal hesitated. This was what he came here to say, wasn't it? But now he found it hard to utter the words. He dropped his eyes to his glass, staring at the brown liquid inside.

"I've . . . I've been promoted to deputy mayor now, and the mayor and other people at City Hall won't look kindly on me being close friends with someone who owns a strip club, who's in business with dudes like Dolla Dolla. Something like that could ruin my reputation and the career I've worked really hard to build and . . . and I've gotta be smart." He finally raised his eyes from his glass and looked at his friends. Derrick looked stricken. Ricky looked furious. "I know I can't tell you what to do with your lives, but I can't let that dictate my life either. For that reason, I . . . I've gotta break ties. I'm sorry."

The table fell silent. Only the music playing on the overhead speakers filled the void. Finally, Ricky let out a cold laugh and shook his head.

"This is some bitch ass shit, man," he said. "That's cold blooded as fuck! I'm a liability now? Funny, I wasn't a fuckin' liability when you were asking to borrow money to pay your rent when you were a broke law student. We weren't fuckin' liabilities when we were keepin' niggas in the neighborhood from beatin' yo skinny ass!"

"You think I wanna do this?" Jamal asked, leaning forward. "I don't. You guys are like brothers to me. I don't wanna do it, but I *have* to, Ricky. Don't you get that?"

"Man, you ain't gotta do shit! No one's forcing your hand but that bitch you live with," Ricky said, slamming his beer bottle back to the table.

"Leave Bridget out of this."

"No, I'm not leavin' that bitch out of this! You started acting stuck up as soon as you started fuckin' her—you punk pussy ass! She's tryin' to turn you into the next Clarence Thomas and you're too stupid to figure it out!"

"Look, Ricky," Jamal said, pointing his finger at him menacingly, "you can call me whatever names you want, but keep Bridget's name out your mouth, okay?"

"Or what, nigga?" Ricky shouted, rising to his feet, drawing attention from other patrons in the bar and lounge. He spread out his arms. "What you trying to do about it?"

Jamal started to rise to his feet too. He wasn't a fighter, but his days of being bullied were over.

"Y'all stop!" Derrick said. "You're not gonna fight. Just sit and calm the fuck down. All right?"

Jamal and Ricky continued to glare at each other before they finally sat back in their chairs.

"Look, Jay, we understand that you're doing big things

now," Derrick began. "You're on the come up. We get it. We're proud of you, man. But that doesn't explain—"

"It doesn't explain why the fuck you're cuttin' off Dee, too!" Ricky interrupted, pounding his fist on the table. "He doesn't have a strip club and he ain't in business with Dolla! What's your weak ass excuse for cuttin' him off, you ruthless motherfucka?"

Jamal pursed his lips. "I don't want to cut him off, but I know if I told you we weren't boys anymore, Derrick would say then forget his number too. Am I right, Dee?"

Derrick hesitated, then nodded.

"Yeah, because Derrick understands what *loyalty* means, unlike some other bitch ass niggas up in here," he said, rising to his feet again. He opened his wallet and slapped a few bills on the table. "Well, you delivered your message. We heard that shit loud and clear—and now I'm out of here. Here's the money for my drinks."

"Come on, Ricky," Derrick lamented, closing his eyes. "Don't leave like this. We can—"

"No, I'm good." He stepped out of the booth. "I got somethin' to do back at the restaurant anyway. It'll be a better use of my time." He glowered down at Jamal. "Nice knowing you, *Sinclair.*" He then walked across the bar room to the glass door, mumbling to himself. "You punk ass . . . bitch ass . . ."

"How could you do this shit?" Derrick asked, making Jamal turn back around to face him. "Don't you realize how messed up this is?"

"I told you why I did it. I can't—"

"But that doesn't make it any less fucked up! We've been boys since we were kids, Jay . . . or Sinclair . . . or whatever the fuck you call yourself nowadays. Ricky's grandmother passed and you remember what happened to his sister, Desiree. We're all he's got, and you're just going to toss him aside like this? Like his friendship . . . like *our* friendship, don't mean shit to you?"

"Dee, we're all grownups. We've gotta make choices and—"

"Yeah, I get it," Derrick snapped, scooting out the booth and slapping a twenty-dollar bill on the table. "And I guess you've made yours. Now I'm making mine. When you get tired of being in the sunken place, hit a brother up, all right? Until then . . . peace out."

Jamal then watched, dejected, as his boy stalked off.

Chapter 4

Derrick

Derrick walked down the stone path, bordered on both sides by a yard crammed full of garden gnomes, ceramic toads, and clay pots overflowing with ferns and colorful daises. He climbed the concrete steps leading up to the brownstone, ducking slightly to avoid a brass wind chime. He glanced around the brownstone's front porch. It was just as cluttered as the yard, with more flowers, a hammock, a metal dinette table, and two chairs. There was barely space for the welcome mat that urged visitors to "Wipe Your Paws!"

He hesitated before he pressed the doorbell, contemplating instead going back down the steps and to his car, which was parallel parked along the curb on the quiet, residential street.

Maybe this is a bad idea, Derrick thought, wiping his hand over his face.

If Melissa found out he had come here, there'd be hell to pay. But still, he felt like he needed to do this. There were so many things that seemed to be going awry at the

Institute and now, his personal life. He had to get some advice, some insight, on how to handle all of it. The only real place where he could get that advice would be here.

He rang the doorbell and waited a beat. A few seconds later, he heard barking and saw a tall figure walk past the front door's stained glass window. The door swung open revealing a skinny dark-skinned man wearing a T-shirt and jeans covered with splatters of paint. A chocolate-colored Labrador was at his knee, barking and trying its best to push its way through the door.

"Hey, Dee! I wasn't expecting ya'! What are you doin' here?" Mr. Theo called out, wiping his hands on a wash cloth. "Back! Get back in there I said!" Mr. Theo shouted to the dog, nudging it aside.

Now standing before his mentor and Melissa's father, Dee shoved his hands into his jean pockets anxiously. "Just decided to stop by. Did I . . . uh . . . did I come at a bad time?"

Mr. Theo shook his graying head. "Hell, no! I was just painting an old piece of furniture and making a damn mess of it. Besides, I can always make time for you, son!" He waved him forward. "Come on in!"

Derrick nodded and stepped over the threshold. He immediately bumped into a two-foot-tall stack of newspapers sitting by the entryway, sending them tumbling onto the welcome mat.

"Oh, damn, sorry about that!" Derrick exclaimed.

Mr. Theo rolled his eyes heavenward and sighed before leaning down and reassembling the haphazard stack. "Don't apologize. I blame Lucas for having this shit everywhere." He gestured to the pile and gave a rueful laugh. "As you can see from our front yard and porch, he's the biggest damn pack rat. I complain about it all the time, but it don't seem to make a bit of difference!"

"I heard you scandalizing my name, Theo Stone! I am *not* a pack rat," Lucas called out from farther down the hall.

He leaned out through the archway leading to their kitchen, and the dog trotted toward him. He was about the same age as Mr. Theo, though he wore glasses, was several shades lighter, and slightly heavier in build. He smiled and waved in greeting.

"Morning, Derrick! How's it going?" Lucas asked, leaning down to rub the dog's head.

Derrick cleared his throat. "Uh, good. I'm good," he mumbled.

"Well, you're just in time for my little experiment." Lucas stepped into the hallway. "I was just making a frittata I saw on the Cooking Channel the other day, and it should be ready in fifteen minutes or so if you wanna be my guinea pig and try some with me and Theo."

Derrick quickly shook his head. "Nah, uh . . . I'm good. Thanks though."

"You sure?" Lucas inclined his head. "I made it with fresh basil and tomatoes we grew in our backyard. And the eggs were—"

"Lucas, honey," Mr. Theo murmured, "the boy said he doesn't want any frittata. Okay? Leave him be."

Honey . . .

Derrick tried not to visibly wince when he heard the word come from Mr. Theo's mouth.

He knew Mr. Theo was gay, but he'd managed to ignore that fact most of the time. But being around Lucas, Mr. Theo's boyfriend, and seeing them together, hearing them use words like "honey," or "baby," was a jarring reminder that the Mr. Theo he knew today was not the same Mr. Theo he'd thought he'd always known.

The man he'd admired for years—the one who had taught him discipline and courage, strength and sacrifice—had obviously been leading some secret life during that time. He had locked away a piece of himself from everyone: the boys at the Institute, Derrick, Melissa, and even his wife.

Derrick now watched as Lucas shrugged. "All right. I'll take the hint. But you're missing out on a five-star breakfast, Derrick. I promise you!"

"He'll survive," Mr. Theo said. "Maybe you can wrap some up for him and he can take it with him."

"Yeah, maybe," Lucas answered absently before heading back to the kitchen.

Mr. Theo tilted his head towards an adjoining hall. "Come on, son. Let's head on down to the basement. If you came this early in the day and didn't call first, you must have somethin' on your mind."

Derrick nodded. "Yeah, I do."

"Well, you can talk while I paint."

"So what you got to tell me?" Mr. Theo asked a few minutes later as he leaned over an old coffee table, with a paintbrush in his hand and a small can of antique white at his feet.

The room they sat in was damp and smelled of wet newspapers. It likely used to be an old cellar, based on aged brick walls, concrete floor, and solitary awning window. But now Mr. Theo and Lucas used it as a storage room.

Derrick shrugged and exhaled loudly from his perch on a nearby stool, filling his lungs with the smell of paint and turpentine. "A little bit of this. A little bit of that. There's a lot of shit going on right now at the Institute and—"

"There always shit going on at the Institute," Mr. Theo said with a chuckle as he began to paint one of the coffee table legs. "That place has hardly any funding, little resources, an overworked staff, and more children that need help than you could possibly help in one lifetime."

"Yeah, well, I got word earlier this week that the city might not renew our grant. That's a fifteen-percent cut to our budget."

Mr. Theo raised his gray brows. "Why aren't they renewing it?"

"Don't know. The mayor and his folks are supposedly rethinking his funding priorities. He's *re-assessing*," Derrick said, using air quotes. "They said maybe the city wants to look at other worthy causes."

"'Other worthy causes,' my ass!" Mr. Theo shook his head as he continued to paint. "I swear that motherfucka' is trying to push all of us black folks out of this city. First, we had a corrupt mayor. Now we've got a tight-assed Uncle Tom! He just wants to make it as rich and white as possible. Of course, he doesn't want to give money to the Institute when it's full of poor black kids." Mr. Theo paused. "You talk to Jay about it? I bet he can help out. He got that promotion over at the mayor's office, didn't he? Ain't it his division? Maybe he can make them give you the money."

"I didn't get a chance to talk to him about it. I don't think he would listen anyway."

"*Why not?* I thought y'all always had each other's back . . . that you, Jay, and Ricky, were like brothers. You have been since you were kids."

"Yeah, I thought so too, but Jay is moving on up in the world," Derrick said while gazing down at his clasped hands. "He's even going by his middle name, Sinclair, now. He said he's ready to move on from his old neighborhood . . . his old friendships . . . his old *life*. He said he thinks we'd hold him back."

Mr. Theo rolled his eyes and grumbled. "You know, even when Jay was a young boy I could see that need in him to be so big and grand. Remember how he told everybody that he came from money?"

"Yeah, I remember. He said he had some rich daddy down in North Carolina." Derrick snickered. "Not with those raggedy ass Converse kicks he used to wear. Ricky and I knew he was full of shit, even if we didn't tell him that we knew."

"He wanted y'all to look up to him, Dee. In some ways, he still does. He wants to prove himself. He just keeps going about it the wrong way."

Derrick pursed his lips. Maybe Mr. Theo was right, but it still pissed him off that Jamal could treat friends that he'd known for almost twenty years like a basic chick who he was trying to shake off the morning after a one-night stand.

"I don't know. I guess," Derrick reluctantly conceded.

"Trust me, son. He's still trying to find himself." He squinted as he leaned down to examine a spot he'd just painted on the table.

"He's thirty damn years old. Shouldn't he know who he is by now?"

"Hell no! I sure as hell didn't at thirty. The man I was then wouldn't recognize the one I am today. I was confused as hell back then."

Derrick fell silent.

He felt like he was wandering into delicate territory with Mr. Theo. He had come here to unburden himself, not to have Mr. Theo to do the same. But he had questions, so many questions, that he was afraid to ask and wondered if Mr. Theo would even be willing to answer them.

How the hell can he be gay? How does that even happen?

Derrick had been asking himself this since Melissa revealed three years ago that her mother and father were separating. Six months later, her father had moved in with Lucas.

"That's the reason why they separated. He's been fucking some other dude on the low this whole time!" she'd shouted. "My own father! Can you believe that shit?"

She'd cut off all contact with Mr. Theo thereafter, and spoke about him only when she had to. Essentially, Theo Stone was dead to her.

Derrick hadn't cut off all contact with Mr. Theo, though Melissa assumed he had. Whenever he went to see her father, he felt like he was lying to her, like he was cheating on her. He just couldn't see what Mr. Theo did in as black-and-white terms as she did.

But he hated seeing her in pain. She and her father had been close—very close. He knew how much it hurt her to no longer have a relationship with him. He wondered if Mr. Theo felt the same way.

"So you were confused back then," Derrick began tentatively. "You aren't . . . confused anymore?"

Mr. Theo glanced at Derrick as he continued to paint. "What do you mean?"

"I mean . . . the way things are now . . . the life you have now feels right?"

Mr. Theo stopped mid-brushstroke then turned so that he could level Derrick with an unwavering eye. "Do you mean, 'Am I OK with huggin' and kissin' up on men?' Is that what you're asking, Dee?"

Derrick grimaced.

"Look, it may be hard for a fella like you to wrap your head around this, but let me drop some knowledge on you. Some of the roughest, toughest dudes you see out there standing on street corners," Mr. Theo said, pointing to the awning window with his paintbrush, "have been known to slip, slide, and dip with other men. They just aren't open about that shit. They don't wanna lose face, at best—or end up beaten to death, at worst. It ain't easy being a gay black man—even harder to be a gay black man in the ghetto."

"Yeah, well, it's not easy being the *daughter* of a gay black man either," Derrick ventured, meeting him stare for stare. "Things may be hard for you, but have you ever thought about what Melissa is going through?"

"Of course, I have."

"Well, I don't see how you're okay with all of this then. I don't get how you can just . . . just walk away from everything. Your wife, your daughter, your—"

"Hold up!" Mr. Theo said, dropping his paintbrush into the paint can and taking a step toward Derrick. "I didn't walk away from them. I love my baby girl with all my heart. I love my ex-wife too."

Derrick rolled his eyes in exasperation.

"You can roll your eyes all you want, but it's the truth. Love just wasn't enough for me to keep living a lie. The man they knew wasn't a whole man, Dee. I told them that. I told them everything . . . about how I really felt all these years, about the stuff I had been hiding from them. I didn't expect them to be happy about it. I knew it would be hard to hear it after I had been lying for so damn long. But I'd hoped they'd hear me out . . . that they'd try to understand." He tilted his head. "And you know what happened? My wife told me to pack all my shit and get the hell out of her house. I went to go live in a raggedy motel off of Route 4 for two damn months. And my daughter told me to lose her number and never speak to her again. That was their choice, Dee, not mine."

Derrick slowly shook his head in denial.

"*What?* What you got to say now?" Mr. Theo challenged, sitting on his stool. "Just spit it out!"

"Look, Mr. Theo," Derrick held up his hands, "none of this is my business."

"No, it ain't—but we've already started down this road so we may as well keep going. Go ahead and say whatever you got to say."

"Well, Melissa and I have been arguing more lately and frankly, I . . . I think a lot of that shit has to do with you."

"What the hell do I gotta do with it?"

"She doesn't like me working at the Institute because it reminds her of *you* working at the Institute and how it kept you away from her. She keeps questioning my commitment to her . . . to our relationship because *you* cheated on her mom."

Mr. Theo raised his gray brows again in surprise. "Who said I cheated on Sandy?"

Melissa, Derrick thought, but didn't say it aloud.

"I didn't cheat on my wife, Dee. I'd thought about it—many times. I even came close to it in my younger days, but I never did it. Me and Lucas didn't get together until Sandy and I were separated. We knew each other socially, but that's about it. I wouldn't do something like that to my wife."

Derrick squinted. This isn't at all the story he'd been told. He wondered how Melissa had gotten the facts so wrong. Had her mother told a different story—or was his mentor lying to his face?

"I didn't want to sacrifice my family to finally live the life I wanted . . . the life I *needed* to live, but I knew it may come to that. I just couldn't be a hypocrite anymore. I had been teaching young men for *years* about . . . about being honest with themselves, about knowing who they are in here," he said, pointing at his chest. "You remember the day when I pulled you aside, when you were about fourteen years old, when I asked you, 'What do you really want to do with your life, Dee? Because the decision is yours—no one else's. Who are you now, and who do you want to be?' Well, I had to answer that question myself."

"And this is it? This is what you wanted?"

"No, it's not what I wanted, but it's what I had to accept. I had to make sacrifices to be who I am, son." He went somber. "Every man has to do it at some point in his life. Sounds like Jamal already has, based on what he told you and Ricky. Maybe you will too someday. I just hope your price isn't as steep as mine."

The storage room went silent. They could hear the dog barking upstairs and the thud of Lucas's footsteps on the floor above.

Making sacrifices . . .

Derrick's thoughts went back to Melissa. She had been pressuring him to leave the Institute for months now, and he wondered if one day she would give him an ultimatum. If she said he had to make the choice between her or his job, which would he choose?

"Thanks for talking to me, Mr. Theo," Derrick said, rising to his feet.

"No problem, Dee. You're always welcome here. You know that."

"I'll let you get back to your painting and show myself out," he said, walking toward the opened doorway, but he paused just before he stepped into the downstairs hall. "And I'll work on Lissa. I'll see if I can get you two talking again."

"I don't know about that. But if you can work a miracle, I'm ready. I'm ready whenever she is."

Derrick nodded. "See you, Mr. Theo."

Mr. Theo waved before bending over to retrieve his paintbrush. "See you, son."

Chapter 5

Ricky

"Ricky? Hey, Ricky!"

Ricky turned away from the stage, eying the hulking Club Majesty bouncer who stood at his side.

"What?" he snapped, not even bothering to mask his irritation.

"The cute dyke is back."

"*Huh?* What the hell are you talking about?"

Ricky was distracted. He still felt the sting from earlier that night when he'd met Derrick for drinks at Ray's. Seeing the empty spot in their booth where Jamal usually sat, Ricky and Derrick both had to face the sinking realization that it was official: that bitch ass nigga Jamal was done with them. Though both men had tried to pretend they didn't care or notice the difference, Ricky knew they had. Jamal's absence was as pronounced as his presence—maybe more so.

Ricky still couldn't wrap his head around his former buddy's reasoning for breaking up with his friends. Who the hell breaks up with their boys? They had known each other for almost two decades. Ricky had thought they would be tight for decades more, until they were old, gray, and senile. How could Jamal pull a move like this?

Ricky knew in his gut that Bridget was likely behind it; he'd put good money on it. But if Jamal insisted on following her lead, there wasn't much they could do about it.

Maybe we're better off without his bitch ass anyway, he mused.

And now Ricky was getting pissed off all over again watching one of his dancers make a fool of herself on center stage.

Before his bouncer walked up, he had been staring at Shana, a buxom Halle Berry lookalike. He could tell even under the hazy blue spotlight that she was either drunk or high as a kite based on the glassy look in her eyes and her wobbly strut in her platform stilettoes. Ricky didn't play that shit.

He certainly was no saint when it came to alcohol and drugs. He was basically running two businesses, and a line of blow could keep him awake and alert better than any cup of coffee, but he didn't let it interfere with his work. He expected the same of everyone else—from the bartenders, to the DJ, to the dancers who worked at the club.

Shana's set would be over in the next five minutes, and once she made it to the stairs, he was pulling her aside and telling her if she ever did anything like this again, she'd have to pack her locker and not set another foot in this club.

"I said the cute dyke is back," the bouncer repeated louder, trying to be heard over the heavy base of the stage music. His dark eyes shifted to a spot across the room, about twenty feet away from the mezzanine, where Ricky's table sat. "You told me to keep an eye out for her. She walked in about fifteen minutes ago."

Ricky tore his gaze away from Shana and now looked where the bouncer's gaze was focused. "Thanks, Ty. You did good."

Ty nodded then walked down the short flight of stairs leading to the ground level where most of the club patrons sat. Ricky finished the last of his drink, rose to his feet, and soon followed him.

He had noticed her in the club about a month ago. She was hard to ignore, one of the few women at Club Majesty who wasn't working a pole or waiting a table. He also noticed she always sat alone. She had one of those old Rihanna razor-cut bobs that looked almost masculine, but she softened it with her delicate features and heart-shaped face. She had a nice build too—sinewy arms and round thighs and ass. Ricky had watched more than one guy at the club try to chat her up and buy her a drink, but she gave them all the cold shoulder. She only seemed to have eyes for the dancers, asking the girls for a private lap dance in the champagne room. This is how she earned the nickname "the cute dyke" among the Club Majesty staff and dancers.

Ricky couldn't care less if the mystery woman was a lesbian. As long as her money was green and she didn't cause any trouble, it made no difference to him. He only started to be wary of her when a couple of the dancers mentioned that during their lap dances, she asked questions and not the usual, "So where are you from?" or "You got a man at home?"

She wanted to know if any of the girls who were working at Club Majesty were underage, if any of the girls turned tricks on the side. She had even shown one of the girls a cellphone picture of young woman who looked to be around sixteen, and asked if they had ever seen her in the club.

That's when Ricky started to suspect the woman was a

cop—and worse, a *nosy* one. There were too many illegal things going on at Club Majesty to have the police sniffing around here. Ricky had finally gotten Dolla Dolla to agree once again that Reynaud's was off limits. If he got wind of something like this, he'd panic and shift his operations wholesale from Club Majesty to the restaurant. Ricky couldn't have that. He had to get this cop out of here, but he had to do it carefully.

He strolled across the room, forgetting about that punk ass Jamal and trying his best to ignore Shana, who he could still see in his periphery. He had bigger worries at the moment.

As he approached the mystery woman and stood less than a foot away from her table, he noted that she didn't look up at him. Instead, she kept her eyes focused on the stage and downed whatever had been in her martini glass. He also noted that she smelled nice; it was a musk mixed with some flowery fragrance and vanilla.

"I can get that refilled for you," he said to her, pasting on a charming smile. He looked her up and down. She was wearing a white tank top knotted at the waist and white skin-tight jeans tonight, giving her an almost neon glow in the darkened club. "What were you having?"

"I don't want a refill," she answered in a monotone, lowering her glass back to the marble tabletop. Her eyes didn't shift from the stage.

"Well, okay." He chuckled. "Just trying to be hospitable. We want our customers to be happy. You see, sweetheart, I'm the owner of—"

"I *know* who you are. You're Ricky Reynaud. Thank you for your concern about your customers, Mr. Reynaud, but I have everything I need, and I'd appreciate it if you'd just let me do my thing. Okay?"

He cocked an eyebrow. *Is this chick brushing me off?*

At that, his fake smile disappeared. "Well, if you know

who I am, then you also know I can kick you out of this joint at any second, so I'd be a lot nicer if I were you, sis."

He expected her to flinch then, or at least finally make eye contact, but she didn't. Instead, she drummed her nails on the table. They were neat, short, and clear—unlike the acrylic bedazzled talons many of the dancers at Club Majesty liked to wear. "*Are* you kicking me out, Mr. Reynaud?"

"No—not yet anyway. I'm still considering it. I want to have a conversation first."

And that's when she looked up at him. He could see all her delicate features up close—the doe-like brown eyes, pert button nose, and full glossy lips. "*A conversation?* A conversation about what?"

He grabbed the back of the chair and leaned forward, drawing close to her face. He could smell chocolate on her breath. She must have been drinking one of their chocolate martinis. "A conversation about why you're here and what you've been asking my dancers. Come with me."

He turned and started to walk away from her table. She didn't budge from her chair though, making him turn back to her.

"You can come with me, or you can leave right now. It's your choice, honey."

A few seconds later, she rose to her feet, though she seemed to do it with great reluctance. She grabbed her purse from the table. "Lead the way," she said, gesturing to him.

He took her to his office at the back of the club. As they walked, they passed dancers in gradual stages of undress. They all stared at him and the woman quizzically.

When he opened the door to his office and she stepped inside, brushing past him as she did it, he looked her up and down again. In addition to having a nice little body on her, he finally noticed now under brighter lighting that her nutmeg skin glowed like she had slathered it with body oil.

She was also wearing open-toed, snake-skinned stilettoes that showed off her ruby red toenails. Ricky had always been a sucker for red toenails.

Just as his thoughts started to turn carnal, he caught himself.

This chick might be a cop, he thought. It didn't matter how fine she was or what color her toes were, she posed a real risk for him and Club Majesty. He had to know what she was all about.

"Have a seat," he said, gesturing to one of the chairs facing his desk.

He watched as she sat down on the white leather cushion and crossed her legs. Though she was trying to give the illusion of being casual, he could tell she was tense being in here. Her body practically radiated the message.

"You sure you don't want another drink?" he asked, as he walked to a wet bar near his desk. "I'd be happy to make you one, Miss . . ."

"It's Simone and no, I don't want another drink. I told you that already, Mr. Reynaud."

"Everybody calls me Ricky." He grabbed one of the decanters and poured himself a glass of bourbon. He turned to her. "And yes, you told me you don't want another drink, but what you haven't told me is why you've been coming to my club."

"I like to see beautiful women dance topless." She shrugged. "It's pretty simple."

"Yeah, see, I'm not buying that. You've been asking them some very interesting questions, which makes me believe that you're here for more than watching a bunch of girls pop and drop it low on stage." He sat on the edge of his desk and stared down at her. "Why have you been coming to my club, Simone?" he repeated. This time there was a harder edge to his voice.

She didn't answer him but stared right back at him defiantly. Part of him wanted to smile at her reaction. She wasn't easily intimidated. He liked that, but he couldn't let on that he did.

"Are you doing an investigation?" he continued. "If you are, honey, it was a shitty one. You've already blown your cover."

"I'm *not* undercover," she said between clenched teeth.

"But you're a cop. Right?" He took a sip from his glass.

Again, she didn't answer.

"I'll just take your silence as a yes. So look," he said, setting down his glass beside him, "I card all the girls who work here myself, and all of them are of legal age to strip. *No one* turns tricks in this building—or they'll get fired. Whatever shit these girls choose to do on their own time is up to them, but they know not to do it here. Club Majesty isn't that kinda place."

She let out a snort of contempt, making him incline his head.

"What's so funny? You know something I don't, sweetheart?"

"I know this club isn't the perfectly legal place that you make it out to be. Everyone knows who you're in business with."

"If you're referring to my business partner, Mr. Stanley Hughes," he said, using Dolla Dolla's government name, "I can promise you that he wouldn't be involved with prostitution or sex trafficking. It's not his thing."

She crossed her arms over her chest and raised her chin into the air, irritating him. "I wouldn't be so sure of that if I were you."

"Simone, I answered your questions. I showed you that your worries about my club are unnecessary. So at this point, I expect you to not ask any more questions of my dancers and continue to be a happy customer, or you can no longer bring your ass up in here. *Understood?* So you can tell whatever captain or lieutenant or whoever the fuck you report to—"

"I'm not reporting to anybody!" she burst out, catching him by surprise. "I'm just a patrol cop and I came here on my own time. I'm looking for my little sister."

Ricky fell silent.

"Skylar disappeared three months ago and according to her girlfriends, she hooked up with an older guy who told her she was cute. That she could be a model or a dancer in videos. He said he could help her make money, that he could get her work. The guy put her in touch with Dolla Dolla." She uncrossed her legs and leaned forward in her chair. She reached for her purse and pulled out her cell phone. Ricky watched as she tapped a few buttons on the screen. She then turned the phone toward him to show the smiling image of a girl. "She's only seventeen. She's young and naïve . . . *way* too trusting, so I could see how she could get sucked into something like this. My mom and I tracked down Dolla and I asked him, point blank, if he's seen her, but he laughed in my face. He told me he's never heard of her. But that motherfucka knows where my little sister is! I can *feel* it! I thought she might be here. Have you seen Skylar?"

Ricky stared at the cell phone image.

The girl looked like a younger version of Simone with long curly hair. She was wearing a Catholic school uniform and posing with a Scottish Terrier in her lap. She was smiling at the camera and waving when the shot was taken. She *was* a pretty girl and very well could be a model if she wanted to be.

Ricky shook his head.

"I've never seen her in here and I've never seen her with

Dolla either." He reached for his glass again. "Besides, if she's seventeen, she's of age, ain't she? She can do whatever the hell she wants. Maybe she just ran away."

"She didn't just run away! Skylar wouldn't do that. She was—"

"Whatever!" he said tiredly, waving his hand dismissively. "It makes no difference either way. I'm sorry about your sister, honey, but you're barking up the wrong tree. Okay?"

He watched as she exhaled and angrily shoved her phone back into her purse. "I should've known better."

"What's that supposed to mean?"

"It means you're just another low life like he is. You'd protect him no matter what! I thought you might understand considering what happened to your sister, but I guess not."

Ricky paused mid-sip at the mention of his sister. His eyes narrowed into slits. "What the fuck did you just say to me?"

She shot to her feet. "You heard me! I said considering what happened to your sister, Desiree, I thought you might help me. That's the only reason why I agreed to come back here and talk to you. I saw the crime report, Ricky. She was only fifteen when her pimp killed her. He used her up, tricked her out, then beat her to death. I don't want that same shit to happen to my sister! I need your help!"

Simone's words sliced through him, flayed him open.

Ricky tried not to think about Desiree or what she'd gone through, but the memories haunted him anyway. He had wanted better for his kind little sister. He had tried to save her more than once, to keep her off the streets, but by then she was already in her boyfriend's clutches and solidly addicted to crack. He'd known she walked the track at night, hopping into strangers' cars, giving hand jobs and blow jobs for as little as twenty dollars.

The last time he'd seen her before she was murdered, she barely resembled the girl Ricky had remembered. Her face was covered with scars and bruises, her once bright hazel eyes were dull, and she wore a lopsided wig that was matted to her head. He'd taken her to McDonald's and bought her a Big Mac and fries since she'd said she was hungry and hadn't eaten a real meal in days. He'd told her that he could get her cleaned up, that she could move in with him. She had given him some elusive response and he had given her his cell phone number, making her promise to call him if she needed him. The next day, she was dead.

He now glowered at Simone. "Get out," he said in a strained whisper. "Get the fuck out or I'll throw you out, and don't ever come back to my club again. You hear me?"

"Oh, I hear you. And I hope you and Dolla rot in jail someday, you son of a bitch," she said over her shoulder as she stomped toward his office door and slammed it behind her.

Ricky finally took a sip of his drink, lowered his glass from his lips, and realized that his hand was shaking.

Chapter 6

Jamal

"Hey, Mr. Lighty! Mr. Lighty, can I ask you just one more question, sir?"

Jamal glanced over his shoulder at the pudgy white man wearing glasses and an ill-fitting gray suit who was jogging toward him. A camera bounced around the man's neck. A digital recorder was in his hand. The rubber soles of his shoes squeaked on the linoleum tile as he ran to catch up with Jamal.

"You've been asking me 'one more question' for the past fifteen minutes, Phil." Jamal loosened the knot in the tie around his neck and continued toward the recreation center's glass doors. "I really need to get out of here."

"I know. I know! But I swear it really is one more this time—and it's a quick one!"

Phil was a reporter for the *Washington Recorder* and was as dogged as he was annoying. He held his digital recorder toward Jamal's face, only inches away from his mouth.

Fatigued and hungry enough to eat his own briefcase, it

took all of Jamal's will power not to shove the recorder away in frustration.

"So," Phil began, "you said during tonight's meeting that the mayor plans to—"

"Look, I'd be happy to answer more questions, just not right now. The meeting ran a lot longer than expected, and I'm pretty damn tired." He yawned for illustration.

The public meeting about the new small business incubator was supposed to end at nine, but had dragged on to almost eleven o'clock. Mayor Johnson had snuck out of the packed room more than an hour ago, leaving Jamal to field the rest of the questions from D.C. residents who wanted to know every detail about the program. They wanted to argue the pros and cons until Jamal had exhausted all possible responses and finally, just politely nodded at each person who stepped up to the microphone to praise or rail at him. He was tired of talking and tired of standing. He just wanted to go home, grab a quick bite, climb into bed next to Bridget, and fall asleep.

"I understand, sir," Phil said. "But I—"

"How about this?" Jamal pushed open one of the glass doors and stepped into the cool September night. "How about you give me a call in the morning and I'd be happy to answer whatever questions you want. But for now, I'm going to have to say, no more questions. All right?"

Phil opened his mouth as if to argue with him, but Jamal gave him a congenial slap on the shoulder, waved, and sauntered down the concrete steps before he had the chance. "Goodnight, Phil," he called over his shoulder as he walked toward his car.

"Uh, good . . . goodnight, Mr. Lighty," Phil called halfheartedly after him.

As Jamal sauntered across the deserted parking lot, his phone buzzed. He reached into his pocket, prepared to find a text message from Bridget, asking if he was headed home soon, but he saw instead it was an alert from one of his phone apps. It showed the final score from tonight's Wizards versus Mavericks game. He cursed under his breath.

"Are you kidding me? They got fuckin' slaughtered."

He shook his head in exasperation and began to type a text to Ricky as he walked. The only sounds he could hear were his footsteps on the cracked cement and a police siren wailing in the distance.

"Did U see your boys got stomped by the Mavericks tonite?" he typed. "U gonna . . ."

His thumb abruptly halted.

He couldn't text Ricky about the Wizards game.

"*You're not talking to Ricky, remember?*" a voice in his head mocked. "*He's criminally adjacent. He's a liability.*"

"You're better off without them, honey. Trust me," Bridget had assured him when he told her that he finally severed ties with his old friends.

But he hadn't realized how much his boys had been interwoven into the fabric of his daily existence: how he was used to texting them about random bullshit during the day, how he mentally catalogued funny stories to tell them about over drinks, and how he could go to them when he just needed to escape from Bridget or his job or the world, in general.

He knew severing ties with Ricky and Derrick had to be done for the sake of his career and his aspirations. Someone who wanted to move up the ladder at city hall couldn't have underworld ties. But walking away from them was starting to feel like a divorce—like a *painful*, contentious divorce. He wondered how long this feeling would linger.

Jamal tapped the delete button until the draft of the text message to Ricky disappeared. He looked up from his phone screen and gazed around him, puzzled.

He didn't remember the parking lot being this poorly

lit. He wondered why he had decided to park so far away from any of the street lamps and in some murky corner of the lot. You could get robbed, or worse, walking alone in the dark in a neighborhood like this. He had grown up in enough bad neighborhoods to know that. How could he have been so dumb? But then he remembered that when he'd arrived at the recreation center, the parking lot had been filled to capacity. It still had been light outside.

Jamal tucked his phone back into his pocket. He pulled out his keys and walked swiftly to his Audi. He pressed the remote button to open his car door, but paused when he heard the squeak of tires and the heavy bass of a car sound system behind him.

Jamal turned and spotted another car pulling into the parking lot—a black Lincoln Navigator with glistening rims. It came to a screeching halt about fifty feet away, next to a Mercedes.

Jamal didn't recognize the Navigator, but he certainly recognized the silver Mercedes Benz; it was the mayor's.

That's weird, Jamal thought. He'd assumed the mayor had gone home already.

Jamal climbed inside his Audi, shut the door, and observed as the Navigator sat idle for another minute or so. Finally, one of the passenger doors flew open and two men hopped out. One was Mayor Johnson; the other was a big dude with a build of a linebacker, wearing a brightly colored Versace shirt. The big dude's back was facing Jamal but he could clearly see him hovering over the mayor, almost bearing down on him like he was trying to intimidate him. Even from this distance, Jamal could see the look of fright on the mayor's face. His eyes were wide. His mouth was tense. He looked like he wanted out of whatever conversation they were having.

The big dude jabbed Mayor Johnson in the chest with his forefinger, shoving him against the side of the Navigator.

The mayor nodded, said something, and the man finally turned slightly so that Jamal could see his face in profile under the parking lot lamp. When he did, Jamal's mouth fell open in shock.

It was Dolla Dolla.

Jamal had only seen the drug kingpin a few times in his life, always with Ricky around, but he had seen him enough times that he could clearly recognize his dark hulking mug.

"What the hell?" Jamal whispered aloud.

Dolla Dolla gave the mayor another hard shove that sent the older man careening back against his own Mercedes. Dolla Dolla then climbed into the Navigator's backseat and slammed the door closed. The SUV pulled off with tires squealing again, sending up pebbles and dust in its wake.

The mayor looked badly shaken by the encounter. Jamal watched as the older man wiped the front of his pants and adjusted his tie and his jacket. He took a wary glance around him.

Jamal sank low in his seat so that the mayor couldn't spot him. His head almost grazed the arm rest. The gesture probably wasn't necessary. It was so dark where he was parked he doubted anyone could see him at all. He raised his head a little, so that he could see just over the top of the steering wheel. He watched as the mayor then opened his Mercedes, climbed onto the driver's seat, and pulled off a few seconds later.

"Are you okay?" Bridget asked, dabbing her wet face with a hand towel as they both stood in front of their double sinks. Her skin was bare and pale, making her blue eyes stand out like two bright marbles under the bathroom's halogen lights. "You're so quiet this morning.

You're usually such a chatterbox that I have to tell you to shut up."

Jamal spit the frothy mint of his toothpaste into the sink then stared at Bridget's reflection in the bathroom mirror. He rinsed off his toothbrush.

He had been up most of the night, tossing and turning in bed, thinking about what he'd seen at the parking lot of the recreation center. Why had Mayor Johnson been with Dolla Dolla, of all people? What could their conversation possibly be about?

Nothing good, Jamal surmised, judging from both of their body languages last night.

Jamal wondered how Mayor Johnson's constituents would feel about him climbing out a Navigator and having a heated conversation with such a notorious person in the criminal underworld. And this was just eight years after former-mayor Clemmons's wife had been caught flushing hundred dollar bills down the toilet when their house was raided by the FBI. The former mayor and his wife had been sentenced to nearly a decade in prison for corruption and money laundering along with several of Mayor Clemmons's associates.

Johnson had run on an anti-corruption platform. He had promised his constituents sweeping changes at all levels of his administration. Hell, "A Clean Slate," had even been his campaign slogan. And now Jamal had stumbled upon this . . .

If the press got wind of it, it could easily draw Johnson's credibility into question. It could even end his political career. If Johnson was meeting in secret with Dolla Dolla, what else had he been doing on the low? People had been muttering for years that Johnson was just as corrupt, if not more, than Clemmons. He just hid it better. But Jamal had given no credence to the rumors. He'd dismissed it as gossip from bitter adversaries. Now he was starting to wonder if maybe the rumors were true.

"Jesus, sweetie, just tell me already!" Bridget exclaimed with a laugh. She began to apply her makeup, grabbing a few brushes from her spot on the counter, and swiping on concealer. "Whatever it is, it can't be *that* bad!"

Jamal pushed himself away from the granite countertop and turned slightly to face her. "I . . . I saw something last night after the meeting I went to in Ward 8."

"Okay," Bridget said examining her reflection. She swiped more concealer with her brush on the bridge of her nose. She looked like she was wearing peach tribal war paint. "Well, what did you see?"

"I saw Mayor Johnson in the parking lot. It was late and he was . . . he was talking to this guy, a known criminal who goes by the name Dolla Dolla."

Bridget's hand stilled. She lowered her brush and stared at Jamal, now frowning. "How do you know it was him? Couldn't it have been someone else?"

Jamal shook his head. "It was him. I've seen him enough times to recognize him. He's Ricky's business partner at the strip club."

At that, her frown deepened. "Did you hear what they were talking about?"

Jamal shook his head again. "No, but it looked pretty intense. He was even shoving the mayor around. They acted like . . . like this wasn't first time they'd talked. The whole thing looked shady as hell!"

She shrugged and raised her brush back to her cheek, smoothing out the lines so that now her entire face was covered. "You're inferring a lot from a conversation you couldn't hear, Sinclair. Frankly, I don't see what the big deal is. The mayor is allowed to talk to people. Just because he had a conversation with a criminal doesn't mean it was 'shady.' "

"Bridge, there was nobody else around but me. That wasn't a coincidence. They also did it in a deserted parking lot at eleven o'clock at night. They did that shit on purpose. The mayor didn't want anybody to see him talking to Dolla Dolla."

"You're acting like *he's* the criminal, not this Dollar Dollar guy," she said dryly, purposely mispronouncing his name.

Jamal shrugged. "I don't know. Maybe he is."

Bridget stilled again. She tossed her brush back onto the counter with a clatter and leaned against the granite surface. "Do you like your job, Sinclair? Are you happy that you were appointed deputy mayor?"

"Of course, I am. What does that have to do with anything?"

"I'm just saying maybe you should focus on that. Focus on the fact that you've accomplished all that you have by the mere age of thirty. Focus on what you need to do to execute your job well, and maybe one day, you can become mayor yourself." She slowly linked her arms around his neck and smiled seductively. "I can see it in you: you've got the drive . . . the capability. What you could achieve could be limitless, sweetheart."

"But what about—"

"You've got a full plate now," she said, softening her interruption with a kiss. "You're always juggling meetings, hearings, and events. Don't get distracted by things that have nothing to do with you."

"*Nothing to do with me?*" Jamal eyed her. "So . . . what? You're saying pretend like I didn't see what happened last night? Pretend like it didn't happen at all?"

"I'm saying don't lose focus, sweetie," she whispered hotly against his lips, removing her arms from around his neck. She lowered her hands to the waistband of his pajama pants and dug inside, wrapping her hand around his manhood and giving it a gentle tug that made him immediately forget about the mayor and Dolla Dolla, that made him groan. "I'm saying enjoy the moment. You've *earned* this. And it's only going to get better."

He then watched as she yanked down his pants. His legs and ass lit up with goosebumps in the cold bathroom air. She then dropped to her knees and blew him right against the bathroom sink.

Chapter 7

Derrick

Derrick gave an anxious glance at his wall clock, zeroing in on the second hand as it wound its way back to twelve. His 2:15 appointment was now officially thirty minutes late. He had scheduled the interview with the potential carpentry instructor, hoping to quickly replace the one who had abruptly quit. But it looked like the dude was going to be a "no show."

Too bad, he thought, pushing his chair back from his desk and rising to his feet.

The man's resume had shown lots of potential; Derrick had thought it would be an easy hire. And he was hoping to check this one task off the long list of things he'd wanted to accomplish this week, but he guessed that wasn't going to happen.

At least, not today.

Derrick just couldn't wait any longer. He'd planned to leave the Institute early to beat Melissa home. When she arrived at their apartment after a long day of battling it out with fourth graders, he wanted her to find rose petals leading to a warm bubble bath surrounded by candles. A medley of her favorite neo soul artists would be playing on their stereo and a platter of chocolate and fresh fruit would be waiting for her on their bedspread, along with massage oil on her night table. Where things went from there was totally up to Melissa, but he hoped it would be a memorable night—memorable enough for her to forget the argument they'd had a couple weeks ago.

Derrick reached for his satchel and tossed the strap over his neck and shoulder. He walked across his office, gave one last glance at his desk to see if he'd left anything, and turned off the overhead lights. He stepped into the hall, shut the door behind him, and began to lock it just as he heard the rapid thump of footsteps behind him. He turned slightly and saw a woman jogging down the hall.

"I'm here! I'm here!" she shouted.

Derrick frowned as his eyes scanned over her.

The woman was tall and lean with the athletic build of a track star or basketball player. She was wearing a pair of skin-tight jeans and a white T-shirt. Her curly hair bounced around her shoulders as she ran. When she skidded to a halt in front of him, she pushed a lock of hair out of her eyes, revealing jade green irises and long lashes.

"I'm so sorry I'm late, Mr. Miller," she said breathlessly. Her cheeks were flushed pink. A light dew of sweat was on her brow. "I took the metro to get here, and it was a big mistake. One of the trains broke down. I tried callin' to tell you I'd be late, but couldn't get reception in the subway tunnels and well . . ." She adjusted her purse on her shoulder and flapped her arms helplessly. She gave a sheepish grin. "Anyway, I'm here now!" She extended a hand to him for a shake.

"I'm sorry but . . . who are you?" he asked, squinting down at her hand.

She blinked and barked out a laugh. "Umm, I'm Morgan.

Morgan Owens! We had an interview scheduled at 2:15." She paused. "You *are* Mr. Miller, right?"

He stared at her, genuinely surprised. When he saw the name Morgan on her resume, he had assumed that she was . . . well . . . that "she" was a "he." Morgan supposedly had been crafting furniture for years out of a private cooperative studio in Bethesda, and had a degree from the Rhode Island School of Design in furniture design. Based on her resume, he had expected a big hulking dude in overalls and work boots with weathered hands and strong arms. Instead, he saw the lithe, feminine specimen in front of him.

"Yes, I'm Mr. Miller, but you can call me Derrick," he said, finally shaking her hand, which had a few callouses, but was far from weathered. "And we did have an appointment thirty-five minutes ago, but I'm afraid I have to go now."

"Oh," she said, looking crestfallen.

"But we can always reschedule . . . uh, maybe sometime next week?"

Her smile returned and she eagerly nodded. "I can do that. Sure, next week would be good!"

"Okay, I'll shoot you an email to set up another time."

"And I'll make sure I'll drive next time and not take the metro," she replied, making them both laugh.

"See you, Morgan."

"See ya' next week," she said with a wave.

He began to walk down the hall in the opposite direction than she came, but paused to turn back around to face her.

"Umm, you know the Boys' Institute isn't a regular school, right? It's all boys, like the name says, but a lot of them have criminal records . . . some for serious offenses."

"Yeah," she said, nodding, "I looked you guys up online before I applied. I saw you do a good job rehabilitating them though. Only a thirteen percent recidivism rate."

"Well, most of them are good kids," he continued, hoping that she was getting exactly what he was trying to say. "But we *do* have a few bad apples in the bunch, and I can't vouch that you won't run into—"

"Derrick," she said, holding up her hands, "why are you telling me this?"

"What do you mean?"

"I mean . . . do you *not* want me to work here?"

"I didn't say that."

"No, you didn't say it, but you're not selling the job well either! It's like you're trying to . . . I don't know . . . trying to scare me off."

"I just want to make you aware of what you're really getting into if I offer you the job and you accept. That's all."

"I'm aware of what I'm getting into. I wouldn't have applied if I wasn't."

"I'd just hate for you to feel like you were in over your head."

"Why would I feel that way?" She paused, dropping her hands to her hips. "Wait. Are you saying all of this because I'm a woman? You think I wouldn't be able to handle myself with all those big, bad boys? Is that it?"

"No, we have female instructors who work here already, but . . ."

She inclined her head. "But . . . what?"

None as pretty and as young as you, he wanted to say, but didn't.

Derrick didn't want to offend her, but he could easily anticipate how some of the older boys would react to having Morgan in their classroom. And even though they may be sixteen and seventeen years old, they had the height and builds of grown men. Some of them could get very aggressive. He didn't want to put her in harm's way.

"Listen to you!" a voice in his head chided. *"You were defending those same boys to Melissa more than a week ago, and now you're acting like Morgan needs to be protected from them?"*

Okay, I'm a hypocrite, he conceded, but all the same, he didn't know if he wanted a problem like that on his hands.

"Hey, I don't have a clean rap sheet either, if that makes you feel any better," Morgan argued. "I did my dirt back in the day too—a long time ago. I could tell you some stories. Don't let the green eyes fool you!"

He pursed his lips, still hesitant.

"Look, the truth is, Derrick . . . I *really* need this job. The studio I work out of is closing and needless to say, there aren't too many companies clamoring to hire a twenty-nine-year-old black woman who makes furniture for a living. Let's just do the interview. If you want to hire me after that, we can try me out on a trial basis. And if I can't hack it, then I'm out. No problem, right?"

After a few seconds, he nodded. "Okay, we'll do the interview. I'll see you next week."

"See you!"

"Dee, are you home?" Derrick heard Melissa call out. He then heard the sound of her keys landing in the ceramic bowl they kept on their hallway console and the sound of the front door slamming shut.

He hurriedly lit the last candle, swiped his hand over the bedspread to fan out the rose petals some more, and stood back, surveying their bedroom. The scene looked pretty damn romantic, if he did say so himself. The space had a soft, orange glow to it thanks to the dozen candles perched strategically around the bedroom on the dresser and night tables. The smell of vanilla wafted in the air.

"Why are all the lights turned off?" he heard her mumble. She sucked her teeth as she made her way down the hall. "Are you in bed, Dee? You're not sick are you, baby? I can make you some—"

Her words trailed off when she shoved open the door and entered the bedroom. Her big brown eyes widened.

He pressed the button on the remote to cue their stereo. D'Angelo's croons suddenly filled his ears.

"What is this?" Melissa exclaimed, dropping her purse to the floor. He walked around the bed and wrapped his arms around her waist.

"What does it look like?" he asked, leaning down to kiss her earlobe then her neck.

"Did you total your car?" she joked. "Forget to pay the rent this month?"

"No, nothing like that. I just wanted to show you that you're special. I wanted to let you know how much you mean to me," he said, drawing her close and tugging her shirttail out of the back of her pencil skirt. He lowered his mouth to hers just as she cocked an eyebrow and leaned back to gaze up at him, keeping her plump lips out of reach.

"That's sweet, Dee, but why does you showing me how special I am require me to spread my legs?"

"It doesn't, baby! It can if you want it to, but I'm cool with you just taking a bath, giving you a massage, and letting you chill for the evening. I swear . . . it's all about you."

"Well . . ." Melissa rubbed her hands up and down his arms. "I'll be honest. After seeing how you went all out to surprise me, and with you looking as fine and sexy as you do, I wouldn't mind if a little leg spreading was involved in between that bath and massage," she whispered, making him laugh.

"That's my girl!" He dropped both hands from her waist to her behind and grabbed her bottom. He lowered his mouth to hers again.

This time she didn't pull back when he kissed her. Her tongue danced with his. She let out a soft whimper and he tugged the rest of her shirt out of her skirt and began to unbutton it. He pushed the shirt off her shoulders and lowered the zipper at her back, shimmying her skirt down her hips.

"Nu-uh," she murmured against his lips, "I was promised a bubble bath. And that's what I'm gonna get."

He watched as she stepped back and walked across their bedroom, pushing her skirt down the rest of the way so that it pooled at her feet. She then removed her bra and tossed it to the floor before continuing to the bedroom door wearing only a lace thong and a broad smile.

Brownie trotted over to the pile of clothes and sniffed them.

"You coming?" Melissa called over her shoulder, hooking her finger.

Derrick began to walk toward the bedroom door, taking off his clothes as he did it. He tripped over Brownie along the way, who was also following Melissa to the bathroom.

"Oh, hell no!" he said, tugging off his shirt and nudging Brownie aside before he stepped through the bathroom doorway. "She was talking to me, not you."

He then shut the bathroom door behind him. He heard their cat mewl his displeasure on the other side, but Derrick didn't care. He watched as Melissa tossed aside her black thong and climbed into their bathtub. She sank beneath the cloud of bubbles and saucily stuck out her tongue. She flapped her hands, making the water lap dangerously close to the edge, almost spilling onto the tiled floor.

"You better get in here before the water gets cold!"

She didn't have to tell him twice.

Derrick let his pants fall to his ankles and did a little

hop and a kick to send them sailing across the bathroom and smack against their walk-in shower glass, making her snort and laugh at his enthusiasm. He then tugged down his boxer briefs.

"I'm ready," he said, stepping into the warm water.

She glanced at his burgeoning arousal; he was already almost fully erect. Her laughter tapered off as she licked her lips. "I can see that! Come over here, baby," she said, reaching for him. Within seconds of sloshing into the water, she was on top of him.

Ricky had once asked him how he could stand having sex with the same woman day after day, year after year.

"Don't you get bored, man?" Ricky had asked with a puckered face, like he had been sucking on a sour lemon.

Derrick had explained that there could be some monotony that came with sex with the same woman. But he and Melissa always tried to switch things up—and that didn't have to mean using lots of toys or twisting themselves into crazy sexual positions. It meant just making an effort, enjoying sex in a slightly different way each time. And it wasn't like predictability was always a bad thing. Hell, this was the same woman who had lost her virginity to him when she was fifteen years old. He knew her body almost as well as he knew his own—every beauty mark, scar, and dimple. He knew what to do to make her moan and what tricks made her yell. He knew the sharp breaths and yips she let out when she was close, and the face she made when she came. Ricky might not understand it, but in many ways, Derrick took comfort in those things, in the predictability of being with someone he knew so well.

Right now, she was moaning as he licked the bubbles off her right nipple then her left. She was straddling him in the water as he did it. Her hands were braced on his broad shoulders and his hand was in between her legs. He moved his fingers fast then slow, doing it in the way he knew she liked. She started panting. She started to squirm. He felt her shift against his fingers, urging him to keep going not with her mouth, but with her body.

He took her nipple into his mouth again and began to suck it, tease it with his teeth. All the while, his fingers continued to move. The sharp bursts of breath were coming now. He heard a yip, then another. She started to rock her hips, making the water lap dangerously close to the tub's edge again. The yips turned into yells. She dug her nails painfully into his shoulders and threw back her head, begging him to stop then keep going. She cried out before falling against him. A few seconds later, she raised her head from his shoulder and gave him a dimpled grin.

"That was a good one, baby," he murmured against her ear.

"That was a *big* one. Now your turn," she whispered before bringing her mouth to his.

They kissed languidly, sucking on each other's tongues, nibbling on one another's lips. In one fluid move, she held his dick, adjusted her legs to center him in between her thighs, and lowered her hips. He slid smoothly inside her and shuddered at the sensation. They both began to move in the water. The tempo was slow at first, but gradually it increased to a frenzied pace that did make water spill over the edge of tub and onto the tiled floor. It made them groan and scream. Melissa shifted her hands from his shoulders to the tile wall. She grabbed the soap dish to steady them, to keep them from rising out of the tub and falling to the floor themselves. They didn't come simultaneously, but it was close enough.

When Derrick did, he closed his eyes and swore he saw stars. He cursed, cried out her name, and jerked liked he'd been tased. He fell back into the water, overcome with a sensation of pure ecstasy.

* * *

An hour later, Melissa rolled onto her back and smiled up at him.

After they had left the bathtub, they'd shifted the festivities to their bedroom. As it turned out, she was the one who ended up giving him the massage, but that had only lasted fifteen minutes before he grabbed her hand and tugged her back on top of him. Within seconds, the moaning and groaning started up again.

Now exhausted but deliriously happy, Derrick gazed down at the woman he'd been in love with for almost two decades. He knew he wanted to be with her for two decades more, and two more decades after that. Hell, he wanted to spend his life with her.

"Let's get married," he said, gazing into her eyes.

"We are getting married," she said with a giggle, holding up her hand, showing her engagement ring. The emerald cut diamond caught the dying light from the candles and sparkled in the dark.

"No, I mean, let's just get married, Lissa. Let's just do that shit! Elope at the courthouse. Do it in front of a judge. We can do it by the end of the week."

She lowered her hand. "*What?* Are you serious?"

"Hell yeah, I'm serious!" he shouted, making her laugh again. "We don't need a big wedding. We've been saving up for one for more than a year. Keep that money in the bank, baby. All we need is just our family and friends there." He kissed her, feeling buoyant with excitement. "We can invite my mom. She can be a witness. We'll have your mom there and your dad and—"

"We're not inviting my dad, Dee." Her face had changed. The giddy smile disappeared. "That's out of the question."

"Come on. He's your dad. You can't get married without him. It wouldn't be—"

"I said no! After what he did to Mama, there is no way . . . *no way* in hell I would disrespect her *again* on my wedding day by making her stand next to that man, let alone make her play nicey-nicey with him."

That man? She was talking about her father like he was a total stranger.

Derrick had felt like he was floating on a wave of euphoria only seconds ago. Now he felt like he he'd gotten a hard smack back down to earth thanks to Melissa's blunt words.

"Baby, your dad didn't *do* anything to your mom. He told her the truth about how he felt, about how he'd been feeling all those years they were together. He didn't—"

"What the hell do you mean, he told her the truth? He cheated on her with another dude, Dee!" Melissa yelled, pushing herself up to her elbows. "He humiliated her and lied to her!"

"No, he didn't. Mr. Theo said he didn't hook up with Lucas until after he and your mom separated. He never cheated on your mom, Lissa. He never would have done something like that to her." He held her hand. "Look, I know it was a shock to find out your dad is gay. It would be for anybody, but—"

"Wait a minute! Back the hell up! You . . . you talked to my dad about this?" she asked, narrowing her eyes.

Derrick fell silent. *Shit*, he thought as Melissa pushed herself upright completely, yanking her hand out of his grasp. She climbed off the bed and glared down at him in all of her naked glory.

"Did you talk to my dad about this, Dee?" she repeated louder, slowly enunciating her words. "Did you talk to him about my parents' fucking marriage? About him cheating on my mom?"

"Yes, I . . . I talked to him."

He watched as Melissa balled her fists at her sides. As she sucked in a breath and pushed back her shoulders, making her breast rise then fall.

"Look, I wasn't trying to start anything, baby. I just told him that you were hurt . . . that what happened between him and your mom really affected you, and he explained where he was coming fro—"

"That wasn't your job, Dee! You shouldn't be talking to him about me . . . about my mom . . . about any of it. None of this shit has anything to do with you!"

"Yes, it does. What affects you, affects me. You know that!"

"And *you* know that I don't talk to my dad anymore, and you deliberately went behind my back and did it anyway!"

"I didn't . . . I didn't go behind your back. I just—"

"No, that's exactly what you did." She reached for her robe at the end of the bed and began to shove her arms into the sleeves. She tied the belt around her waist.

"Lissa," he said, rising from the bed, "come on, baby. Let's just—"

"Dee, if you know what's good for you, you won't say another fuckin' thing to me!" she shouted over her shoulder before striding into the hall.

Derrick fell back onto the bed, closed his eyes, and let out a long, loud groan.

Well, that hadn't gone the way he'd expected.

Chapter 8

Ricky

The echoing crack of billiard balls knocking together filled the hall along with male laughter and the faint smell of wood, beer, and pot smoke. Ricky squinted at the table as he held his pool cue between his forefinger and index finger, lining up his shot.

"You about to lose some money tonight, bruh," he declared to Derrick who stood on the opposite side of the pool table, partially hidden in shadow in the darkened pool hall.

Derrick chuckled and raised his beer bottle to his lips. "Nigga, stop talking shit and just take the shot."

They had been playing pool for the past hour, deciding to try a different spot than Ray's tonight. Derrick had asked him to meet up. He'd said the past few weeks had been filled with more drama than he could handle and he needed to de-stress. Ricky had been happy to oblige him, leaving the restaurant a little before closing to meet his friend.

"Right corner pocket," Ricky called out. He took the shot, like Derrick ordered, and they both watched as the cue ball sailed over the felt—a purple cannonball against a green background. It clacked against another ball and sent it careening into the right corner pocket.

"Damn it," Derrick muttered.

Ricky stood upright and grinned. He cackled in triumph. "I'm one lucky nigga, ain't I?"

"Nah, I'm just unlucky."

Ricky lowered his pool cue to the floor, leaned against the table, and raised his brows. "Why you say that?"

"Because it just seems that way. I told you, I had a rough week. Nothing seems to be going right. Even me and Melissa had a big blow up last night."

"Again?"

Derrick nodded.

"Damn, y'all have been going at it a lot lately. Why'd you argue this time?"

Derrick sighed gruffly. "She found out I've been talking to her dad."

"Shiiiiiit," Ricky exhaled, shaking his head sadly. "I told you that shit might come back to bite you in the ass! Didn't I tell you?"

"Yeah, you told me. But I can't cut him off just because she's not talking to him. It's Mr. Theo, man! He's like a father to me!"

"But he's not your father, Dee. He's *her* father and she's *your* woman. I'm not even hooked up with a chick, and I'd know where my loyalties would lie. *She's* who you have to share a bed with every night, not Mr. Theo!" Ricky's eyes drifted back to the table as Derrick began to line up his shot. His upper lip curled into a sneer. "Besides, if I was her, I probably wouldn't have anything to do with him either. What girl wants a daddy who sucks more dick than she does?"

Derrick paused mid-shot. He slowly raised his eyes to glower at Ricky. "First of all, you don't even know who the fuck your daddy is. Let's just put that shit out there. Secondly, don't talk about Mr. Theo like that. Okay?"

"But it's the truth!"

"No, it ain't true! Besides, there are worse things in the world than suckin' a dick."

Ricky snickered. "You speaking from experience?"

"Nigga, grow the hell up!"

"Okay. Okay! You're right," Ricky conceded, nodding thoughtfully. "I'm bein' small minded. There are worse things than suckin' another man's dick." He took a drink of his beer. "It's still not as bad as eatin' some dude's hairy ass."

"Fuck you, Ricky," Derrick murmured in exasperation just as he finally took his shot and missed, making Ricky burst into laughter again. But Ricky's laughs abruptly tapered off when he heard his phone buzz. He pulled his cell from his pocket and squinted down at the text message on screen.

"Gonna have to cut this short," he said, lowering his pool cue and beer bottle to the pool table's edge, making Derrick frown.

"*Why?* What's up?"

"Just got a text from Big D. I gotta jet over to his place on Wisconsin Avenue. He says he's got something for me," Ricky said, tucking his cell into his back jean pocket. "Shit, and I didn't have to go to the club tonight. I've got one of the managers covering for me. I thought tonight would be my night off."

Derrick didn't say anything in response but gave him a look—a look that Ricky had seen many times before. It was the same look he'd given him when they were nineteen and Ricky had gotten so drunk, he threw up in the back of the cab and on himself. It was the same look he'd given Ricky when he saw him snort his first line of blow.

It was the look of a big brother's disappointment.

"What the hell do you want me to do, Dee?" he asked, chafing at his friend's silent judgement. "I have to go! He's a dude that doesn't like to wait."

"I just don't understand why you get mixed up in that shit," he said, making Ricky frown. "You don't need someone like that in your life!"

"Oh, so you're turning into Jay now? You gonna lecture me about my life choices?"

"No, I'm not turning into Jay! I wouldn't do that to you. But none of this is new; I've said it before! We both know who Big D is and what he does. I can't ignore that shit."

"Hey," Ricky said, holding up his hands, "I ain't got nothing to do with any of that stuff. That's his business—not mine."

"That's a damn lie, man! Your restaurant and Club Majesty are funded through all his shady shit. Even if you aren't doing it directly, you're making your bread off of the proceeds."

"So you're saying I'm just like him?" he asked, feeling his hackles rise.

He could take the joke about not knowing his father, because he didn't. He could even take Derrick chastising him for his homophobia. But for some reason, he couldn't let this one slide. Maybe it was because he got a flashback to the last time someone had castigated him about his relationship with Dolla Dolla. He remembered Police Officer Simone standing in his office back in Club Majesty a couple of weeks ago and the expression of utter contempt on her face. Derrick didn't look remotely like Simone, but Ricky could swear the woman's face was superimposed over his friend's right now.

He had been thinking about her off and on since that night, at random moments. He didn't know why she lingered in his memory. He wasn't responsible for her little sister and he doubted Dolla Dolla had anything to do with the girl's disappearance but still, he couldn't let go of what she'd said to him.

". . . you're just another low life like he is! You'd protect him no matter what!"

Is that what Derrick thought about him too?

Derrick loudly exhaled. "No, I'm not saying you're just like him, bruh—but I'm worried someday you could be. You keep working with him, he's going to rope you in eventually. You can keep tiptoeing around shit, but it's only so long before you end up with some on your shoes."

"Wow, that's deep," Ricky replied dryly.

"I'm serious! Back away from him and do it fast. Stop being stupid about this!"

"Yeah, well, I appreciate your concern, but I'm still gonna jet." He angrily turned away from the pool table and strolled across the room, but he paused when he was only a few feet away. He turned back around to face his friend. "Considerin' how many folks—your girl, included—look down on you and judge you for working at the Institute, I expected more from you, Dee. I've never lectured you about how you make your paper and pay your bills. As far as I'm concerned, that's your business—not mine. So don't lecture me."

He watched as Derrick's face fell before he turned back around again, and headed out of the pool hall.

Less than hour later, Ricky stepped through elevator doors onto the top floor of an apartment building. He walked to the end of the corridor, listening to the thump of his footsteps in the floor rug. When he approached the door, he rang the bell and was greeted by a familiar face—a large man in a black T-shirt and slacks. His broad shoulders were about the width of the doorway.

"What's up, Ricky?" Dolla Dolla's bodyguard, Melvin, said, nodding his bald head.

"What's up, Mel? I'm here to see Dolla."

"Yeah, he's waiting for you in the living room," Melvin said, gesturing over his shoulder.

Ricky nodded again and walked into the apartment as Melvin shut the door behind him. His eyes went straight to the ceiling, where an oversized, multicolored chandelier hung. It looked like an exploded octopus. Ricky knew that Dolla Dolla had to have dropped more than ten grand on the custom piece, though the drug kingpin wasn't exactly a collector of avant-garde art. Dolla Dolla just had a lot of money to spend, but didn't quite know what to do with it; hence, the monstrosity over Ricky's head.

Further evidence of Dolla Dolla's willingness to blow his money on just about anything could be found in his living room where a six-foot tall, eight-foot long fish tank sat. Inside were more than a dozen exotic fish swimming around a miniature replica of the Las Vegas Strip. The furniture in the room was just as disjointed. It was a hodgepodge of expensive pieces in all styles and mediums: etched glass and Italian leather, chrome and Cherrywood, chinchilla and plush velvet. It hurt Ricky's eyes just to look at it all; it was like stepping into a high-end fun house. He felt like he was buggin' out on a bad high, and this was without sampling the lines of coke Dolla Dolla had set up on the coffee table.

Ricky descended the three steps that led to the living room's seating area. He watched as Dolla Dolla snorted one of the lines through a rolled up hundred-dollar bill, pinched the bridge of his nose, then slowly raised his blood-shot eyes to stare at Ricky.

Dolla Dolla was an imposing figure, a Rick Ross lookalike but with more muscle mass than blubber. Rumor had it that he had been dealing since he was ten years old, getting in the crack game in the early days. Supposedly, he had killed a man by the age of twelve. Though he didn't hustle on street corners or whip out a pistol as quick as he had decades ago, Dolla Dolla still didn't mind getting his hands dirty every now and then. He cast a long shadow in the streets of D.C., from the hustlers to the pimps to the gangsters. The few who had tried to challenge him didn't last long. He either ran them out of town—or had them taken out.

Despite Derrick's warning, Ricky knew it was smart to stay on Dolla Dolla's good side. The drug kingpin was good to those who were good to him—he always had been.

"Hey, Pretty Ricky," Dolla Dolla said with a lazy grin as he sat upright, grabbed the glass sitting in front of him, and leaned back against the sofa cushions. "What you doin' here?"

Ricky narrowed his eyes. "You texted me and told me to come. Remember?"

"Oh, yeah!" Dolla Dolla took a drink from his glass. He then waved him forward. "Come over here. Have a seat."

Ricky walked toward the hulking man and took the arm chair facing him.

"Have some of this good shit, bruh! Came in just last week."

He held out the rolled up bill to Ricky. Ricky took the bill from Dolla Dolla, leaned over the line of coke, and took a quick hit, feeling the sharp burn of the powder in his nostrils and the taste of it in the back of his throat. He blinked and licked his lips, before slouching back into the arm chair, waiting for the coke to shoot through his system like nitrous oxide through a car engine.

"You been doin' a good job with Club Majesty, Ricky."

Ricky nodded and handed him back the rolled up bill. "Thanks, Dolla. I appreciate that."

"A damn good job." Dolla leaned down and did another line himself. He sat up again. "Money's good. Customers are happy. That makes me happy, Ricky. So I got a proposition for you."

He wasn't sure if it was the coke, but Ricky suddenly felt his stomach tighten and his heartbeat pick up its pace at those words. The last time Dolla had offered him a "proposition," he had saddled him with co-ownership of a strip club he'd never wanted that was a front for a criminal enterprise that he wanted nothing to do with.

What the hell does he want me to do this time?

"I'm thinking about starting a new business in real estate. Buying up and building properties and shit."

"Real estate?"

"Yeah, I know it ain't shit that I usually do, but I got partners that say they can handle most the regular business stuff. And I figure white folks been making money building in the city. I need to get in on that shit, too."

Ricky stared at Dolla Dolla, confused about the direction the conversation was going.

"Well, anyway," Dolla Dolla continued, "I need someone to be the face for my company . . . to head that shit up and watch out for my interests. My partners had a few dudes in mind, but I told them I only trust niggas I already work with. I ain't about to trust my money to nobody I ain't never heard of before! So I told them about you." He slapped Ricky on the knee and grinned. "I told them what you've done for me so far, that you've got that magic touch, man!"

Ricky gave an anxious smile in response. It was a challenge. The coke has been as good as Dolla had advertised; it was starting to make his face go numb.

"So what you say, Pretty Ricky?" Dolla asked. "You ready for the come up? Ready to go big time, my nigga? Cuz I'll be honest . . . you the only nigga in these streets that I'd trust with somethin' like this."

"Well," Ricky said, rubbing his hands together, "I'm . . . I'm happy that you've got that much faith in me, Dolla. I really am, but . . . uh . . ."

Dolla's grin faded. His heavy brow lowered, making him look like a bull dog at that moment. "But *what*, nigga?"

"But I've already got a full plate with Club Majesty and the restaurant. I barely sleep as it is, running between two businesses on the opposite sides of town and—"

"So then hand off that shit!" Dolla Dolla leaned forward again to take another hit of coke. "The restaurant and the club are doin' good. You gotta learn how to . . . what they call it? Delegate! Let some other niggas manage them for you. This company would make you a helluva lot more money than any restaurant or strip club anyway."

Ricky's jaw tightened.

He'd be willing to walk away from Club Majesty. Bossing around women in thongs and keeping an eye out for rowdy patrons who he'd have to toss out of the club wasn't exactly his life's dream. But the restaurant was a very different story.

Reynaud's was an ode to his deceased grandmother. Mama Kay Reynaud—who had practically raised him and his sister, Desiree—had loved cooking as much as she'd loved the Lord. Half of the dishes on the menu were either straight copies or inspired by some of her favorite recipes. There was no way in hell he would leave Reynaud's in someone else's hands. It would be like walking away from Mama Kay's memory. He'd rather die than give up his restaurant.

"Look, Dolla," he began, "like I said, I'm happy that

you've got so much faith in me. No doubt. But I don't want to—"

"What the fuck are you doing out here?" Dolla Dolla barked, making Ricky jump in his chair and stop midsentence. He seemed to be shouting at someone standing behind them. "Didn't I tell your ass to stay in the bedroom when I'm doin' business?"

Ricky turned slightly to look over his shoulder. A half-naked young woman stood at the hallway entrance, between the living room and the apartment kitchen. She wore an open pink kimono, showing that she wasn't wearing much else underneath besides a black lace thong and a belly ring. Her eyelids were heavy. Her long curly hair hung limply into her face. She held onto the wall to keep her balance. She looked high and out of it.

"I'm hungry," she slurred in reply. "I just . . . I just wanted to get somethin' to eat. That's all."

She pushed the hair out of her eyes, and Ricky did a double take.

The woman looked a lot like the girl Ricky remembered seeing on Police Officer Simone's cell phone. She looked a lot like Simone's little sister, Skylar.

"This look like a damn cafeteria?" Dolla Dolla roared, rising to his feet. "Just take your stupid ass back to bed! Go back in there!"

"B-but . . . but," she stuttered, now trembling, "I just want some crackers or some—"

"*You deaf?* Take your ass back to the room, or I'll knock you back! You heard me!"

Ricky watched as the girl turned and staggered back down the hall with her head down. She disappeared into one of the rooms and shut the door quietly behind her.

Dolla Dolla grumbled before lowering himself back onto the sofa and glancing at Ricky. "Bitches," he muttered. "They more trouble than they worth."

Ricky nodded limply, still stunned. "Yeah, I-I feel you," he stuttered.

"So what were you saying before that dumb bitch walked in? I hope you weren't about to tell me no again, Ricky. Cuz I don't like hearing no."

"Not a no, but . . ." Ricky glanced back at the hallway, at the closed bedroom door that the young woman had just walked through. "Let me think it over and see how I can work it out."

Dolla Dolla nodded. He was smiling again. "That's what I like to hear."

Chapter 9

Jamal

He shouldn't have done it; he knew it as soon as he opened the files on his desktop computer. Once he started, he felt compelled to keep going, to keep looking. Jamal opened one document, then another, two online news stories, then three more—going farther and farther down the proverbial rabbit hole. He started to ask questions around the office. Light ones that he blended into casual conversation, but the answers fit in the holes to the puzzle he was completing. The more pieces he added, the more his blood went cold.

Bridget had warned him not to do it. She'd told him to leave it alone and mind his own damn business.

"Focus on the fact that you've accomplished all that you have by the age of thirty. Focus on what you need to do to execute your job well, and maybe one day you can become mayor yourself," she'd said that morning in their bathroom.

She'd even given him a blow job to make sure he stayed in line—something she usually did only once a month, or on his birthday—but it hadn't worked. Jamal couldn't resist digging deeper, wanting to know more about Mayor Johnson and his relationship with Dolla Dolla.

Once Jamal started researching, it was easy to pick up the trail of the mayor's questionable business dealings. They included contracts awarded to companies that were subsidiaries of subsidiaries of subsidiaries. All of them had an endless line of parent companies that made it obvious that the true owners were trying to hide their identities. These companies had been hired to build homeless shelters or rehab facilities across the city, receiving millions in payments. They'd always begin design or construction, and then let the projects stall for years. Some of those shelters and facilities still hadn't been completed. The companies had taken the money and run, and Jamal wondered if the mayor had gotten his cut before the companies disappeared for good.

Then, about two years ago, Mayor Johnson started getting a big boost in campaign contributions from hundreds of private donors who all donated five hundred dollars here, a thousand dollars there. An intrepid reporter followed up with the people who donated and saw that they were all living in tiny apartments in the rough part of town or in Section 8 housing. With their limited incomes, they couldn't possibly have afforded the contributions on their own. The reporter had asked them where they got the money, but they either came up with vague answers or didn't answer his inquires at all.

Someone had given them the money, but who? Jamal suspected he now knew the answer: it was Dolla Dolla. The drug kingpin had given money to all those poor people and paid them, in turn, to donate the money to the mayor. Secretly donating what totaled to hundreds of thousands of dollars to the mayor's re-election campaign would certainly enamor Dolla Dolla to Johnson. It could also earn him quite a few favors.

Jamal considered what to do with this information for more than a week. Should he confront the mayor with it, or take the info straight to the press? Should he pretend like he never saw any of it?

He didn't feel equipped to answer these questions by himself, and he didn't trust any of his colleagues with this type of information. He couldn't talk to Bridget about it either; she'd told him to stay the hell out of it.

So who could he turn to?

There was only one man Jamal knew who would "keep it real" with him about what to do, who had the type of moral compass and level of honesty to give him the best advice. It was Derrick. But he and Derrick weren't talking anymore. They hadn't spoken in weeks—and yet, he couldn't imagine his old friend turning him away if he approached him with something this important.

To test the waters, he tried sending Derrick a friendly innocuous text:

You catch the Redskins game last night?

Derrick never responded.

He tried calling him, but the phone just rang. Jamal hung up when he heard Derrick's voicemail message.

That weekend Jamal drove to Derrick's neighborhood. When he parallel parked along the busy tree-lined street and gazed at the seven-story apartment building where Derrick lived, he only hesitated for a few seconds before he climbed out of his Audi. He rode the elevator to the fifth floor, walked down the hall, and knocked on the door 522.

When Derrick opened the door, he looked surprised to find Jamal standing there in his hallway. But his shocked expression quickly morphed into anger.

"What are you doing here, man?" Derrick asked. His

body language conveyed anything but friendliness at that moment.

"Well, I . . . I hadn't seen in you in a hot minute," he said awkwardly, feeling his mouth go dry as he gazed up at his childhood buddy. "I wanted to—"

"You haven't seen me in a hot minute because you didn't wanna see me," Derrick interrupted loudly. "Remember that weak ass speech you gave us at Ray's? You basically told me and Ricky to lose your number."

Jamal looked down at his feet. He hadn't expected Derrick to greet him with open arms, but he'd hoped he wouldn't make him have to work this hard just to start a conversation.

"Look, I told you why I did it, Dee. I didn't want to do that to you guys, but—"

"But you did. So why are you here now?"

"I just . . . I just had to ask you . . . well, I needed to—"

"Jay, just say whatever you gotta say, man. All right? I don't got all damn day."

Derrick looked five seconds away from slamming the door in his face.

"I came because I needed to talk to you, Dee. I . . . I need your advice. It's important."

Derrick's glare and stony expression disappeared. He looked genuinely interested now. "Advice about what?"

"It's some heavy shit and . . . and I need your opinion on what to do about it. You're the only person I would trust to give good advice about something like this. It would have to stay between us though. You couldn't tell anyone else—including Ricky."

Derrick stepped aside. He waved him forward, gesturing Jamal into his apartment.

When Jamal stepped inside, he saw their cat, Brownie, staring at him curiously from the end of the hall. Jamal looked around him. It was Derrick's place but Jamal was always vaguely aware that Melissa also lived here. He could see her fuchsia raincoat hanging on a nearby coatrack, still damp from the rain shower earlier that day. A vase filled with fresh peonies and hydrangea sat at a small desk in front of the hallway mirror. A whiff of her perfume draped itself lazily in the air.

"Is Lissa home?" Jamal asked hopefully.

"Nah, she went to go get her nails done. She said she'd be back in a bit though. Why?"

Jamal stopped looking around him and met Derrick's gaze. He didn't want to admit to Derrick that part of him was hoping he'd see Melissa today. He hadn't seen her in a while.

"No reason. Just wondered if she was here too."

"Let's go in the living room," Derrick said while strolling down the hall.

Again, Jamal saw traces of Melissa in here, too—in the furniture choice and the artwork on the walls. He tried his best to ignore it and focus on the subject at hand.

"So what did you have to tell me?" Derrick asked, reclining back on his suede sectional.

Jamal sat on the cushion facing him. He stared down at the carpet beneath his feet, unsure of where to start.

"It better be somethin' real deep if you're hemming and hawing this much, bruh," Derrick joked, cracking his first grin since Jamal had arrived.

Jamal took a deep breath. "Fuck it," he said, then unloaded. He started from the beginning, telling Derrick about what he'd seen in the community center parking lot more than a week ago. He told him about his research since then, and all that he'd dug up on Mayor Johnson. When he finished talking, he felt like a boulder had been lifted from his shoulders. He stared at Derrick expectantly.

"So what do you think?" he asked.

"What do you mean, what I think?"

"I mean . . . now that I know all this, what the hell do I do with it, Dee?"

He watched as Derrick pursed his lips then shrugged. "Well, as I see it, you've got two options. You either quietly hand in your resignation now that you know what type of dirty motherfucka you're working for, and let Johnson stay dirty—or you put all that info in a big envelope, anonymously send it off to a reporter at the *Washington Post* or somethin', then resign."

Jamal squinted. "Why in both scenarios you have me resigning? I'm not the dirty one. Why should I have to quit?"

"Because I doubt the mayor did that shit all by his lonesome, Jay. There are other people in city hall covering up for him, working deals just like he is. That's the only way it could work. The whole damn system is corrupt. Open your eyes!"

Jamal exhaled and slumped back onto the sofa. "Come on, man, you don't know that. He could've done all of this shit on his own. It doesn't mean everybody in the mayor's office has to be rollin' in the dirt too."

"*Why the hell not?* Besides, even if, by some extreme chance, he did do all that shit alone, how long do you think it'll take for him to be pushed out of office? He's not gonna step down. Not Johnson! This is how he makes his money; he's got too much to lose. You saw what happened with Clemmons. They investigated that dude for *years* before they finally charged him with anything! An investigation of Johnson could last for years and years, too. Meanwhile, you'll still be working for a corrupt boss!"

Jamal clenched his jaw in frustration. "I can't just quit, Dee! I've worked too hard and paid too many dues just to walk away."

"Oh, so you're willing to walk away from a friend of

twenty years because he's associated with Dolla Dolla, but you won't walk away from your job as deputy mayor you've had for less than six months even though the mayor is associated with Dolla Dolla too? Is that what you're telling me?"

"It's not that simple! I've got a career. Rent and bills to pay. I can't just come home and tell Bridget—"

"Nah, man, it *is* that simple. It's as simple as you being a hypocrite or not being a hypocrite. It's as simple as you saying what you mean, and meaning what you say."

"Yeah, well, sorry I'm not fucking perfect like you. Sue me!"

"Don't give me that shit! This has nothing to do with being perfect. If you know the mayor is dirty and you continue to work for his ass, as far as I'm concerned," Derrick said, pointing at him, "you're as dirty as he is."

"That's some bullshit!"

"No, it's not bullshit! It's the truth, nigga!"

"Whoa!" Melissa cried as she strolled into the living room, holding up her hands.

Neither man had heard her come into the apartment and shut the door behind her, because they both had been shouting at one another. Even Brownie had slinked off to find solace in the quiet of Derrick and Melissa's bedroom.

Melissa looked back and forth between the two men. When Jamal saw the bewildered look on her face, he clammed up and went sheepish.

"Why are you guys coming at each other like that?" she asked, removing her purse from her shoulder and dropping it to the carpeted floor. "You sound like you're about to fight."

"I'm sorry," Jamal mumbled, rising to his feet. "I shouldn't have come here."

"No, you shouldn't have," Derrick agreed, glowering up at him.

"I'm out," Jamal said before excusing his way past Melissa. "Sorry I wasted your time, Dee."

"Wait! What the hell is going on with you two? Wait, Jay, come back!" Melissa shouted after him, but he didn't stop. He continued to walk to the front door and swung it open. He strode down the hall, but stopped when he neared the elevators and felt a hand drop to his shoulder.

He angrily whipped around, expecting to see Derrick. It was on the tip of his tongue to unload all his frustrations, to rail at his former friend for condemning him for something he hadn't done wrong, but he saw Melissa instead. Kind, beautiful Melissa. When he realized it was her—not Derrick, his anger immediately dissipated.

"What's going on, Jay?" she asked softly. "Why were you two arguing?"

He unclenched his fists and took a deep breath. "We just had a . . . a disagreement. That's all."

"Then sort it out! Don't just storm out like this! Come on, y'all are friends, right? You can work through it."

Jamal looked at her in shock. Derrick must not have told her about the conversation they'd had at Ray's weeks ago. He shook his head. "No, we're not friends, Lissa. Not anymore."

"Huh?"

"Dee and I are just too different." He turned back around and pressed the down elevator button. "We may have been tight years ago, but we've obviously grown apart. I can't . . . I can't live up to his standards. Deep down I admire who he is . . . how he thinks, but I . . . I'm not him. I'm not all self-sacrifice and honesty. I'm not some saint. I may want to be, but I'm not."

"I get it," Melissa whispered. "Dee can be pretty judgmental sometimes. But believe me, he's no saint, Jay. You shouldn't let this drive you guys apart. Come back. Talk it over."

The elevator bell dinged. The metal doors opened and Jamal shook his head again.

"I'm sorry, but I can't. This way is best. Dee knows it, too," he said before stepping into the elevator compartment and pressing the button for the first floor. He watched her until the elevator doors closed.

Chapter 10

Derrick

"What the hell was that?" Melissa asked as she charged back into their apartment and closed the door behind her.

Derrick shook his head and waved her off. "It was nothing, baby. Don't worry about it."

He walked back across their living room to their stereo shelf where he had been sorting through vintage albums before Jamal had knocked on the door and rudely interrupted his day. He dropped to his knees and returned to the stack that he'd compiled on the floor.

"How can I not worry about it?" Melissa persisted. "Your best friend of almost twenty years just stormed out of here, and you didn't even bother to try to talk him into staying. You're acting like you don't give a fuck one way or the other!"

"Because I don't!" he barked over his shoulder, making her jump.

He dropped his head as she gaped at him. He hadn't meant to yell at her, but the whole situation was beyond frustrating. He didn't need yet another reason to have a fight with Melissa.

He certainly didn't want to waste his breath arguing over Jamal.

When he saw his old friend standing in his apartment hallway, he'd thought Jamal had come to apologize, to say that he'd made a mistake. He'd realized how tight their trio was and wanted to make amends.

"Y'all my brothas. Always will be," he'd thought Jamal was going to say.

Instead, Jamal had come asking for something, like the callous user that he was and always would be. And when Derrick had given him what he asked for—the advice he'd sorely needed, Jamal had gotten defensive.

I don't need that shit, Derrick now thought. *Fuck him!*

"Look, baby, Jay and I are done with each other as far as I'm concerned, but it's what he wanted—not me. He said he was ready to move on from me and Ricky. He said we were holding him back. So let him do his thing, and I'll do mine."

Melissa squinted, looking confused. "That doesn't sound like Jay. Why would he say you were holding him back?"

"Well, not me specifically. He really meant Ricky. He said it wouldn't look good to be friends with someone who works with known criminals. I wasn't cool with that shit, so he dropped me too."

"But it doesn't look good, Dee! Jay has a point. He's a city official. He has a reputation to uphold. You might choose to keep Ricky around despite the shady shit he does, but that doesn't mean everyone has to do it."

Derrick stared at his fiancée, now dumbfounded. "Why the hell are you defending him? Why are you defending his bullshit?"

"Because he's right! He made a smart decision that needed to be made. Maybe if you made that decision too,

Ricky would wise up and finally get his act together. He doesn't need friends who enable him, Dee. He needs friends who can intervene and call him on his shit!"

"Are you serious? You're really fucking serious right now?"

"Yes, I'm serious! You keep making allowances for all these other people . . . Ricky . . . my father . . . but the folks whom you should have their backs, you completely ignore. It's like our feelings don't matter."

"Our?" Derrick slowly rose to his feet. "Please don't tell me you think what happened between me and you over your father is remotely close to the shit that went down with me and Jay?"

"Why wouldn't I? What's the difference?"

"*What's the difference?* What's the difference?" he yelled. "You honestly going to compare my relationship with you . . . the woman I love, the woman who I got down on bended knee and asked to *marry me*, to my relationship with J. Sinclair Lighty—a nigga who's so fake and out of touch with himself he won't even go by his own fuckin' first name anymore? Are you kidding me right now, Lissa?"

"How do I know you're not going to throw me under the bus like you're throwing Jay?"

He stared at her, utterly horrified. "Lissa, how can you even ask me that? Let's understand something. You matter to me. You will *always* matter to me. There is nothing—"

"Actions speak louder than words."

"What the hell is that supposed to mean?"

"It means lately I've been seeing a lot of talking and not a lot of action on your part. You say you love me. You say you have my back, but I'm not seeing it!"

He took one step toward her then another, wondering if he was hearing exactly what he was hearing. It had to be a mistake, some malfunction in his ear canal, because there was no way possible Melissa could be accusing him of such a thing.

"You think . . . you think I don't have your back? You think I betrayed you?"

She didn't answer him. Instead, she obstinately crossed her arms over her chest. Her silence was golden and it resonated louder with him than if she had yelled at him.

"I . . . I just . . ." He shook his head in bewilderment and held up his hands. "Look . . . umm . . . I'm gonna leave now, before I say some shit I can't take back. All right?"

She shrugged and pursed her lips. "You do what you gotta do."

He gritted his teeth, turned, and walked out of the living room and down the hall, slamming their bedroom door behind him.

"And here we have the teachers' lounge area," Derrick said over his shoulder as he strolled down the hall. He gestured into the opened doorway. "We've got a sofa and some tables. A lot of the instructors like to hang out in here and grade papers, read, or just unwind for a bit. It's not a library, but we try to keep the volume down in case anyone is trying to get some work done."

Morgan nodded. "Good. That sofa looks the perfect size to sleep on. I'd hate for anyone to interrupt my nap."

He paused in the middle of sipping his coffee and narrowed his eyes at her.

"Joking," she said shamefacedly.

"Right," Derrick muttered, continuing down the hall. "Let's keep going." He excused his way past a group of boys who were headed in the opposite direction.

He was giving the newly minted instructor a tour of the Institute. It was her first day and her carpentry class was scheduled for later that morning. Derrick still had his misgivings about whether Morgan Owens was the best fit for this job and whether the boys would respect or even connect with her—but based on her credentials and her stellar interview, he was at least willing to give her a try. She seemed eager to prove that she was the right woman for the job. She had asked him plenty of questions during the course of their fifteen-minute tour of the facility. Unfortunately, his responses weren't anywhere near as thoughtful or insightful as her questions. Derrick was just too preoccupied.

He kept replaying his fight with Melissa this weekend and the silence between them all last night and this morning. None of it sat well with him. For the past few weeks he had been constantly asking himself, "What can I do to make it up to her, to prove how much I love her," but now he was starting to wonder, "Will anything I do ever be good enough?" It seemed like he was doing all the giving, offering all the understanding—and not getting any back in return.

He and Melissa had known each other for decades and he had loved her just as long. She should know his heart by now. She shouldn't be questioning him like this.

"So I guess you guys eat lunch in here?" Morgan said, leaning into another doorway.

"Uh, yeah . . . yeah, we do," Derrick replied, snapping his thoughts away from Melissa and back to the present. "This is our rec room and cafeteria." He pointed into another room, stepping aside so that Morgan could have a look around. "Everyone at the facility can use this area—instructors, janitorial staff, and security. The only exception is the students. We've got a few vending machines, a coffee maker, and a water cooler. We have a small fridge, too, where you can store your lunch if you want."

Morgan peered around the room, squinting under the

glare of the track lights. "Oh, wow! You guys got a TV and everything." She turned to him and grinned. "I can catch up on my soaps."

He stared at her, making her laugh anxiously.

"Uh, that was . . . that was another joke," she mumbled.

"I figured."

"Hey, sorry, Mr. Miller." She shoved her hands into the pockets of her jeans and glanced at the empty room, and then the boys who ran past them. "When I'm nervous, I say goofy shi—I mean, stuff. Don't pay it any mind. It's my first day and I'm . . . well, I'm really nervous. Hell, I'm so nervous, I'm sweating." She pulled at the collar of her T-shirt and fanned her neck.

Derrick lowered his coffee cup and smiled for the first time that morning. "I told you to call me Derrick. And you don't have to be nervous. You'll do fine. I know you will."

"You *do?*" she asked, looking doubtful.

"Of course, I do! I wouldn't have hired you if I didn't."

"Well, that's good to know. I wasn't sure if maybe you were just desperate or somethin'. Maybe I was the only person who responded to your job ad."

He blinked in surprise. His smile disappeared. "Why would you think that?"

" 'Cuz the first time I showed up for the job interview you seemed to be trying your damnedest to convince me to not take the job. Then you offered it to me and as soon as I said yes . . . well, it's probably dumb to admit this, but instead of being excited, I started second guessing myself. I thought, 'Maybe I *am* being naïve. Maybe I will be in over my head with these kids.' I'm pissed that I started to doubt myself, but now it's there and I can't get rid of it. It's like a damn rash."

"Morgan, first off, I'm sorry I made you doubt yourself. I just wanted to give you the full scope of what working here would be like. I wasn't trying to scare you off."

"*And,*" she continued, "today you seemed kind of . . . I don't know . . . standoffish, I guess. I wasn't sure if I'm talking too much. Joking too much. Again, when I get nervous, I—"

He held up his hand and she instantly fell quiet. "You aren't talking or joking too much. And I'm sorry if I seem standoffish. It's not you or anything you did, and if I gave you that impression, I apologize. I just had a rough weekend and I'm . . . well . . . I'm not masking it very well."

She nodded as they began walking down the hall again. "Was your weekend as bad as mine? The first time in a week I decide not take the metro and drive instead, and some dude sideswipes my car, takes my rearview mirror with him, and drives off. Then when I got home, I see that my landlord had the nerve to give me notice he's raising my rent. An increase of one hundred fifty bucks starting next month."

"Damn."

"I know! And my ex moved out just a few weeks ago. We shared the rent. I was already stressin' because I can barely afford it on my own, so when I got that notice for the rent increase, I damn near lost it! I should send my ex a bill for the extra $150 since he left me high and dry," she murmured, sucking her teeth. She glanced up at Derrick. "So can you top that? Did you have a worse weekend than me?"

"If you look at them side by side, probably not." He shrugged. "It wasn't that bad, I guess. I'm just taking it harder than I should."

"Well, what was it?" she exclaimed then laughed when he looked taken aback. "Hey, I'm not trying to get all up in your business." She paused. "Okay, maybe I am *a little,* but I'm a busy body! Have been as long as I can remember. And I can usually feed my habit because folks like to talk to me. My mama likes to call me the light-skinned Oprah," she said, making him chuckle.

"That's a skill that should be useful with the kids . . . but I feel kind of weird talking to you about personal stuff." He held up his hand. "No offense."

"None taken!" she said cheerily. They then fell into an awkward silence.

They finished the tour fifteen minutes later, ending it at Morgan's new workroom, which was in the basement of the building. He watched as she walked across the room that was filled with sanders and saw tables. Sawdust and random bolts and nuts littered the floor.

Even though he knew she was a carpenter, she still looked out of place in the space—this tall, slender woman with the chin-length curls and the big green eyes. Even as she tugged on her suede work gloves, she looked like she was playing a game of dress up or engaged in some role-play fetish.

Hot Chicks with Power Tools, he bet would be the soft porn title, then blinked in surprise.

He already had her starring in a porn movie?

Better slow your roll.

He was not only her boss now, but he was also engaged. This line of thinking was far from appropriate.

"I'll let you get situated before your class starts," he called to her.

"Thanks, Derrick. And thanks for the tour—and the pep talk. I needed it."

"You'll be fine."

She smiled. "You're right. I will. I know that now."

"And you know where to find me if you need me, right?"

"Upstairs, second to last door on the left," she replied as she placed a pair of protective goggles onto her head.

He nodded and waved before turning toward the door.

"And I hope your week gets better," she called to him, making him halt in his steps. "If you ever feel comfortable talking about it, you know where to find me, too."

He nodded again, watching her as she arranged a stack of two-by-fours on one of the tables. He then strolled back into the hall, but not before taking one last glance at her over his shoulder.

Chapter 11

Ricky

Ricky sat in the driver's seat of his Mercedes, tiredly rubbing his eyes and staring out the tented window at the entrance of the doughnut shop across the street. The establishment was one block down from the police station. He'd heard that the local cops, in typical cop fashion, liked to eat doughnuts and drink coffee there and decided it was a safer and less conspicuous way to run into Patrol Officer Simone Fuller than go strolling into the police station and asking for her at the front desk.

Besides, police stations gave him the hives.

After what he'd seen at Dolla Dolla's place, he knew he had to talk to her—even though a voice in his head kept yelling at him to stay the hell out of it. He worked for Dolla Dolla. He didn't owe this woman a damn thing and yet, here he was waiting for her. He didn't know if it was guilt or the woman herself, but he couldn't resist the urge.

It had been a lot easier than he'd thought to find out her full name and the station where she worked. One of the bouncers at the club was friends with a D.C. cop. He'd looked her up for Ricky as a favor. Unfortunately, it wasn't as easy to run into her. He'd been sitting in his car for hours—since about six a.m.—and still hadn't seen her at the doughnut shop or along the block, for that matter. He wondered if he was wasting his time.

Finally, at around 8:55, he spotted her. She was strolling toward the shop with another officer: a tall, fat guy with a paunch and a graying handlebar mustache. She was talking and nodding.

Goddamn, he thought as he watched her. Had she looked this good the last time he'd seen her?

She'd been in plain clothes, not a police uniform back then. He had to admit reluctantly that she looked damn sexy in her cop gear, like one of the strippers at Club Majesty when they wore their themed costumes for Halloween. Except Simone's uniform didn't rip away to reveal glitter pasties and a G-string underneath.

Or maybe it does, he thought wickedly, watching her as she walked and talked.

She emerged from the shop fifteen minutes later, with a coffee cup and a small pastry bag in her hand. Ricky put on his sunglasses and tugged the brim of his baseball cap low. He reached for the stack of books in the passenger seat, opened his car door, and stepped out. He jogged across the street, pausing to let a Volkswagen pass. He walked toward her, looking down at his cellphone, pretending to be engrossed by what was on the screen. When they drew close, he bumped her shoulder, sending her Styrofoam coffee cup and paper bag flying and his books tumbling to the sidewalk.

"Hey! Watch where you're goin'!" she shouted, glaring at him and reaching for her spilled coffee cup. "I barely got to drink any of that."

"Sorry, officer," he murmured with a smile, bending down to slowly gather his books. "I should've looked where I was going. My bad."

She squinted at him. When she realized who he was, her pretty face settled into scowl. "Wait. Ricky, is that—"

"Don't make it obvious," he said barely above a whisper, still staring down at the books he was now stacking in his hands. "If I went through all the trouble to do this, don't fuck it up."

"All the trouble to do this?" She looked around her, furrowing her brows. "You mean you ran into me on purpose? Why are you even pretending to—"

"Because I think I found her. I think I found Skylar," he whispered grimly, then reached for her pastry bag. "Let me get that for you," he said in a louder, peppy voice.

"*You found her?*" she shouted and he gave her another censuring look. She dropped her voice to a whisper as they both rose from their knees and stood up. "You better not be fucking with me, because if you are, I swear to God, I—"

"I wouldn't do that. I wouldn't waste your time. I think I saw her and I wanted to tell you."

"*Where?*" she cried desperately. "Where did you see her? Did she look okay? Is she—"

"Not here," he said, shaking his head and peering up and down the busy block. "I'm not doing that shit here—not in the middle of the street where half of D.C. can see us."

Not with fifty cops eating doughnuts a block away, he thought.

"Okay, then tell me inside the station," she said, gesturing down the street. "I've got a cubicle where—"

"Are you crazy? Dolla has eyes *everywhere*," he whispered, still looking around him cagily. "Believe it or not, he may even have eyes inside your little police station."

This is taking too long, Ricky thought.

He had planned to bump into her, give her the info for the meeting spot, and move on. It was supposed to be a quick pass—an interaction that lasted less than a minute—

but it wasn't turning out that way. He should've known she'd have five million questions. She was a cop; of course, she'd screw this up.

"Look, I gotta go. I'm sorry I ran into you, officer. I'll pay better atten—"

"Wait! You can't just leave. Take my number," she said, reaching into the breast pocket below her name tag. "It has my extension and my cell number is written on the back of the card. You can call me whenever and—"

He quickly shook his head. "You're not going to have my number in your phone records. If this shit goes left, I don't want any of this traced back to me."

"*What?* But how do I—"

"And I want a promise that this stays on the low. No prosecutor better be subpoenaing my ass in court later."

"Fine," she asked tightly. "But if I can't call you and you won't talk to me here, then how the hell should we do this? You plan to tell me with the sheer power of your mind?"

He tilted his head. "No, sweetheart." He handed her back the pastry bag. Tucked into the folded top of the bag was a receipt where he'd written an address and the meeting time on the back. "Enjoy your doughnut."

It took her a few seconds to notice the receipt. When she did, she quickly read it, crumpled it up in her palm, like it was trash, then nodded.

She finally got it.

It took you long enough, he thought with exasperation.

"And make sure you don't wear your uniform next time." He casually turned away from her and began to walk back to his car. "It's sexy as hell, but it ain't the least bit inconspicuous."

He glanced back at her just as he crossed the street, and laughed when he found her scowling again.

* * *

As it turned out, she arrived ten minutes early, at around 10:20. Ricky had anticipated this, knowing the type of woman Simone was, so he'd shown up at 10:15 to beat her.

The dim sum restaurant where they were meeting was constructed in a banquet-style with two stories, and rows upon rows of long tables and high ceilings painted a garish green and orange. More than a hundred diners were in the restaurant, filling it with a cacophony that made it hard to hear what someone was saying even if they were sitting right next to you. The crowds and seating style also made it hard to spot two people sitting together who didn't want to be seen with each other publicly.

Ricky gave a small smile when he saw her walk in. Again, he questioned her definition of inconspicuous. She'd done as he requested and skipped wearing her uniform; tonight, she wore a purple halter dress that was cut low in the front and back, pairing it with gold, strappy heels. Yes, she looked like she was going out on a date and not investigating a missing person, but she certainly didn't blend into the room. It was like a spotlight followed her around.

He watched as she walked from table to table and then finally took a seat at one of the banquet tables on the first level, toward the back of the restaurant next to what looked to be a trickling water fountain with a smiling Buddha at the center. A waitress sauntered toward her and leaned down with notepad in hand to take her order. Simone said something he couldn't hear. The waitress nodded then walked off and Simone glanced down at her watch. She gazed around her again, on the lookout for him.

He grabbed his drink and rose from his table, descending the stairs and taking a path that let him approach her from behind so that she couldn't see him coming.

"You're early," he said when he stood a foot behind her chair.

She whipped around and stared up at him. "So are you."

He pulled out the free chair next to her and sat down.

"There isn't much privacy in here," she said, leaning toward his ear to be heard. She glanced at the couple sitting beside them.

He felt her warm breath on his beard as she spoke, and it caused a twitch in his groin.

"I didn't promise you privacy. I said to be inconspicuous, and that's what we are. No one will notice us in a place like this."

"I guess you're right," she said, leaning back.

The air in the restaurant was chilly, making goosebumps sprout on her bare arms and she started to shiver a little. If it were a date, he would offer her his suit jacket, but this wasn't a date, and he didn't want it to be mistaken as such, so she would just have to bear the cold.

Ricky wondered if the cold air was also the reason why her nipples were hard. They looked like two little pointy erasers, jutting through the silk fabric of her halter top, begging for his attention. He felt another pesky twitch in his groin. Maybe he *should* offer her his jacket.

He raised his drink to his lips, trying his best to mask his reaction. This shit was starting to be a pain in the ass. He took a drink.

"That was a smart move you pulled today by the doughnut shop by the way . . . that whole 'bumping into me' thing on the sidewalk," she said. "Where'd you learn to do that?"

"Where do you think I learned to do it?" he answered flatly, wondering where she was going with this.

"Well, considering you've probably never been a secret

agent, I'm guessing a move like that was from your criminal days. Maybe a drug handoff?"

He didn't respond.

"But those days are behind you. Right, Ricky?"

He exhaled impatiently. "I thought we were here to talk about your sister. Not me."

"Oh, we are. But I just want to make sure I know who I'm working with . . . who's helping me. Because if you're not on the up and up, if you are engaged in *any* criminal activity—"

"Come on, Officer Fuller. Beggars can't be choosers."

"—and if I get wind of it," she continued, ignoring him, "then I'm obligated to put you in handcuffs. Okay?"

He smirked. "Don't tempt me, honey."

"*Excuse me?*"

"You putting me in handcuffs might not be such a bad thing. I might even like it." He shrugged and took another drink. "Who knows?"

At that, her face changed. Her mouth fell open. He enjoyed watching her shocked reaction. She seemed like a woman who liked to stay in control. Seeing her break her restrained façade was amusing. But she was back in control at lightning speed. He watched as she pushed back her shoulders and stubbornly raised her chin.

"I'm serious, Ricky."

"I know you are—and I've been forewarned. If Ricky is a bad boy, Simone takes him to jail," he said dryly. "Got it. Now are you ready to talk about what we actually came here to talk about, or what?"

She nodded. "Of course. So where did you see Skylar?"

"I think I saw her at his place on Wisconsin Avenue."

"By 'his place,' you mean Dol—"

"Yes," he answered tersely, annoyed that she was actually going to blurt out Dolla Dolla's name after all the subterfuge they were going through. "I can't say for sure, but

I think it was her. She kind of looked like the girl you showed me."

"Was she okay? Was she hurt?"

For the second time that night, he saw her reserve break a little. She sounded less like a no-nonsense police officer and more like a worried big sister. He hesitated, unsure how to put this part into words without alarming her. He remembered the young woman who strolled down the hall into Dolla's kitchen with heavy-lidded eyes and a silk robe that barely covered her. After waffling for a few seconds, Ricky decided to just spit it out.

"She didn't look good. She was kind of out of it, like she was high on something. I don't know what. I think she's one of his girls now."

Simone cringed. She turned away from him to blink back her tears. It took a few seconds. Again, he saw the control break a little. When she pulled herself back together, she faced him again with stoic resolve that looked forced. "And . . . and you're sure it was her?"

"No, I'm not. I told you I only *think* it was her. I can't say for sure."

"Then one of us has to confirm it. You either need to ask her point blank—or I need to get in there to see her myself."

"That would be a no and a hell no! I'm not confirming shit with her, and I'm definitely not sneaking you into his goddamn apartment."

He felt bad for her, but he didn't feel *that* bad.

"Better than me going in there with guns blazing. Right?"

He chuckled. "I don't know you that well, Simone, but I'm guessin' you wouldn't be that reckless."

"No, you don't know me, so don't assume what I would do."

He was taken aback by the hard edge in her voice and

the glint in her eyes, but slowly, her face softened. She inclined her head.

"Look, I'll . . . I'll be honest with you, Ricky. The longer my sister stays missing, the more desperate I get. It's taken a toll on me . . . on my mom. She doesn't eat. She doesn't sleep anymore. It's hard to watch her be like this. I just want this to *end*, and every day is a battle not to go charging to that man's place, bang on the damn door, and scream Skylar's name. But I don't do it, because I *know* it's stupid. I know it's dangerous. I'm trying to keep from following that impulse, but it's a struggle. That's why I'm turning to you. I thought you would know a better way to go about it. I thought you came here to help me."

"I did. I told you everything I saw, everything I know."

"Which is frankly jack shit! You *think* you saw a girl who looked like my sister at his place, but you don't know for sure. What the hell am I supposed to do with that information? How does that help me?"

"Look, sweetheart," he said, leaning forward and glowering at her, "I'm risking my business and *my life* to tell you this stuff. If that was your sister and he found out I was talking to you about her, that I snitched on him—it could be my ass! I don't assume that just because he and I have been tight for fifteen years that he wouldn't hesitate to put me six-feet under, so don't try to act like what I'm doing right now is nothin'."

He expected her to argue with him, to give him a good excuse to stand from the table and storm out. Instead, she slowly nodded. "You're right; I was wrong. I'm sorry."

Ricky didn't respond. He took another drink from his glass instead.

"I told you. My sister being gone has . . . affected me and my family. But I shouldn't take it out on other people. I shouldn't take it out on you. I appreciate you doing this. Really I do," she said, reaching out and grabbing the free hand he rested on the tabletop. She squeezed it and now the twitch in his groin was turning into a full stirring. He kept reminding himself that she was a cop. He *hated* cops. But the reminder wasn't working. Mercifully, she let go and returned her hands to her lap. "I know you're risking a lot. I'm just scared for Skylar. So scared. I feel responsible for her. I'm . . . I'm her big sister. I should've listened to her. I should've seen the warning signs. This never should've happened!"

"Don't do that," he said, making her frown.

"Don't do what?"

"Don't start blaming yourself. It's not gonna help anything. Trust me. I've been down that road and it doesn't change a goddamn thing. You'll just wallow in 'shouldabeens.'"

"You felt guilty too?" she asked quietly. "You felt guilty about . . . about her."

She didn't say his baby sister's name which was a good thing, because he *definitely* would've gotten up and left if she had.

"Yeah, I felt guilty. I still do. Who wouldn't? I was her big brother and I was supposed to protect her. I didn't do that and now she's dead."

"I'm sorry."

He shrugged and once again tried to shut out memories of Desiree, of her singing in her Barbie nightgown in front of the television when she was eight years old, of her smiling in her sequined junior prom gown on the front stoop of their old apartment building. He hadn't thought about that stuff in *years*. The only thing more frustrating than his attraction to Simone, was getting swarmed by those memories.

"I don't want the same thing that happened to your sister to happen to Skylar," Simone now said.

"I know you don't."

"So *help* me, Ricky," she begged, leaning toward him again, gazing beseechingly into his eyes. "Please! You said yourself that she's seventeen. Skylar is of legal age. My own police department won't take on the case. They said she's just a runaway. I have to prove to them she's being held against her will."

"But I don't know if she's being held against her will!"

"If she was high and out of it like you said, I can't see how she would be able to leave!"

"I'm not a detective, Simone."

"And neither am I. I'm just a low-level cop who handles car break-ins and house burglaries most of the time, but I have to save Skylar. I *have* to. And I can't . . . I *cannot* do this without you. You know that. You're the only one in Dolla's crew that I trust."

Their faces were only inches apart now and she was dangerously close to getting kissed. He raised his glass to his lips again, forcing her to lean back. He took another drink, draining the last of his glass.

"I don't know what else you expect me to do. I told you I can't—"

"Get a picture of her. A *good* picture and let me see it. That way I can know for sure if it's her. Then . . . then we go from there."

"*Go from there?* What the hell does that mean? And how am I supposed to get a picture of her? I don't think I was even supposed to see her! You really think he's going to let me roll up in there and snap some pics of her with my cellphone?"

For the first time, Simone smiled. "You're a smart guy. You're cunning. You wouldn't have made it as far as you have if that wasn't the case. I know you can figure out a way, Ricky. If anyone could, it would be you."

"Look at you pouring on the charm! You really think

that just because you flattered me, I'm gonna do this shit? You've got a lot of confidence in yourself, honey."

He watched as she rose from her chair. She then leaned down inches from his face, giving him a full view of the breasts peeking over the top of her halter top. She had nice breasts. They looked soft, like they would be a perfect handful. This time he couldn't help himself. He did lick his lips.

"No," she whispered into his ear, "I have a lot of confidence in *you*."

She then reached into her purse, pulled out a business card, and handed to him. "When you do get her picture, call me. I know how you feel about leaving phone records, but the other cops will start to wonder who's the guy I keep meeting outside of the doughnut shop in our neighborhood."

He tore his eyes away from her breasts and gazed at her business card. He grudgingly took it from her.

She stood upright and playfully pointed a finger down at him. "I'll be waiting for your call, Ricky," she said over her shoulder before she walked off.

He watched her, staring at her ass as she strolled across the restaurant, then cursed under his breath.

Chapter 12

Jamal

"Do you see them?" Bridget asked, standing on the balls of her feet, craning her neck.

She had to shout to be heard over the noise of the several hundred people making their way through Union Station. The train arrival and departure announcements blaring over the PA system also made it a challenge to be heard.

Jamal gazed at the passengers streaming through the opened glass doors, all dragging rolling luggage behind them and carrying duffel bags on their shoulders. He looked for two familiar faces among the crowd, but didn't see either. He shook his head. "No, not yet."

He and Bridget had come to Union Station to pick up her parents. Susan and Martin Yates had ridden the 4:45 Acela Express from New Haven to D.C., and would stay overnight at a hotel before they headed to a wedding near Charlottesville, Virginia, tomorrow. Bridget was driving the trio to the wedding. She had asked Jamal if he wanted to come along, but he'd begged off and said he had too much work to do back at city hall; he'd have dinner with them all instead.

But the truth was—considering how his dilemma with Mayor Johnson still kept him up at night—he didn't know if he had the fortitude or energy to deal with Bridget's family. He couldn't stand being confined in a car for more than two hours with them and then sitting through a wedding.

They were upper-class New Englanders who thought J. Crew was inexpensive and made constant references to the Ivy League schools they went to, their garden and golfing clubs, and Humane Society fundraisers. He noticed that whenever her mom, Susan, was around him, Susan would turn him into a walking, talking encyclopedia on all things black—asking him about everything from Beyoncé to Black Lives Matter. They weren't bad folks necessarily, but he never felt like he could relax in their presence. He was as careful of what he did and said in front Bridget's parents as he was at any major political event. Frankly, being around them was emotionally and intellectually exhausting.

"There they are!" Bridget said, pointing in the distance. "Mom! Dad!"

Jamal looked in the direction where she'd pointed. He finally spotted them among the tide of people. Bridget's mom looked very similar to Bridget though her graying red hair barely swept her shoulders and she was about twenty pounds heavier. Jamal wondered if Susan looked how Bridget would look in twenty-five years. In contrast, Bridget's father, Martin, was a tall, slender man who wore glasses and stiffly carried himself with an air of importance. Though her mother was smiling, Bridget's father had the same pained expression on his face that he always had—like he was annoyed with world around him.

"Mom . . . Dad, over here! Over here!" Bridget shouted, cupping her hands around her mouth like a megaphone. She then waved frantically.

Her parents finally spotted them. Her mother waved in return and her father nodded, but rather than walk toward where Bridget and Jamal stood, they lingered near the sliding doors, looking over their shoulders. That's when Jamal noticed the slim blond man coming up behind them.

"Shit," Jamal spat, resisting the urge to roll his eyes.

"*What?*" Bridget asked as she squinted at the throng.

"Did you know he was coming?"

"Who was . . . Oh!" she exclaimed when she finally recognized the man, too. "My parents mentioned that Blake might be coming along. I guess he made it!"

"Yeah, I guess he did," Jamal said flatly.

Blake Hobbes was Bridget's ex. Bridget and Blake had grown up together, dated in prep school and in college before going their separate ways when Bridget was twenty-three. Jamal didn't mind Bridget staying in touch with her ex, or seeing him occasionally at lobster bakes and Fourth of July celebrations that her or his parents held. He didn't even mind that Blake was still so close to Bridget's family. No, what annoyed the hell out of him about Blake, was that he felt the constant need to remind Jamal and everyone who would listen, that he had been Bridget's first love, her first boyfriend.

"I was her first in many, *many* ways," he had once drunkenly boasted to Jamal with a suggestive wiggle of the eyebrows last year. "No guy will ever top that."

Jamal had wanted to punch him in the face that night, but had fought down the urge. Now, seeing that pompous asshole stroll toward him along with Bridget's parents, he again felt the overwhelming desire to punch him.

"Just try to be nice. OK, sweetie?" Bridget whispered,

knowing how he felt about her ex. "Blake really is a good guy if you get to know him."

Jamal didn't respond.

"It's so good to see you guys!" Bridget gushed, rushing toward her mother and father. She embraced them both in a wide-armed hug. When they were done, Bridget's mom gave Jamal a hug as well, though it was admittedly more awkward. Her father shook his hand.

"Jamal," the older man said with a nod.

"Martin," Jamal replied with equal stiffness.

While the Yates family continued their greeting, Jamal and Blake stared at one another. Blake extended his hand first for a shake.

"Hey, what's up, bro?"

That was the other annoying thing about Blake, how he constantly called him "bro."

"I'm good. How are you?" Jamal answered. He attempted to shake Blake's hand but the other man grabbed it and dragged him into a hug. Blake's palm was even softer than Bridget's, illustrating that Blake probably hadn't done a hard day's work in his entire life.

"I'm good too! Taking a long weekend so that I can go to this wedding. I had to rearrange some things at the firm to make the trip but I'll be honest, I'm going to enjoy the wine country in Virginia while I'm out there. I've scheduled a tour for all of us at a few vineyards. It'll be like a mini-vacation."

"I didn't know you were headed to the wedding, too."

"Yeah, I'm friends with the groom. We used to play lacrosse together in prep school."

Of course, you did, Jamal thought dryly. He swore all these people knew each other.

"Marty and Sue mentioned that they were driving there with Bridge and asked if I wanted to come along on their little road trip."

"Oh. That was . . . nice of them," Jamal said while glancing at Bridget's parents who were still talking to Bridget.

"You don't mind me going along, do you, bro? All of us hanging out?"

"No." Jamal's eyes snapped back to Blake. "Why would I mind?"

"I wasn't sure if you were okay with me being Bridge's plus one?"

"You're not my 'plus one,'" Bridget quickly clarified, looping her arm through Jamal's. "And of course Sinclair doesn't mind you going. He has absolutely nothing to worry about." She kissed Jamal's cheek.

"Who's Sinclair?" Blake asked, frowning.

Jamal opened his mouth to answer but Bridget beat him to it.

"Jay's going by his middle name, Sinclair, now," Bridget said proudly. "Doesn't it sound so sophisticated? I told him he should've done it sooner."

"It does sound rather nice," Susan said with a nod. "Doesn't it, Marty? Very stately."

Martin grunted in reply and looked longingly at the corridor leading out of the train station.

"Changed your name, huh, bro? Trying to evade the IRS?" Blake asked, nudging his shoulder.

"That'd be hard to do as deputy mayor of the nation's capital," Jamal replied with a tight smile.

He wasn't one to boast about his job, but sometimes you had to let a dude know. You had to put him back in his place when he got out of pocket, and Blake was getting dangerously close to getting out of pocket.

"So are we heading to dinner now?" Martin asked, grimacing. "It was a long train ride and I'm famished."

"We made reservations for four at a restaurant a few blocks from here," Bridget piped.

"But what about Blake? We can't leave him to fend for himself for dinner!" Susan cried.

"I'm sure if we add one more to our reservation, it won't matter," Martin said. "Just let the restaurant know we have another person."

"Dad, we had to make our reservation three weeks in advance just to get our table. We can't just show up with a fifth person."

Jamal glanced at Blake, waiting for him to interject and say that he was fine eating dinner alone. After all, getting reservations at a four-star restaurant in D.C. for five people with little to no notice was almost impossible. Some had waitlists going out a couple months. But instead, Blake continued to smile foolishly, like he was enjoying watching them argue over him. The man who usually could not shut up had gone conspicuously silent.

"Don't you have a friend who owns a restaurant, Jamal . . . I mean, Sinclair," Susan asked, turning to him. "I believe you mentioned it once. A Creole restaurant."

Jamal's face went blank. She was talking about Reynaud's—Ricky's restaurant. He hadn't spoken to Ricky in more than a month, not since the last time he'd seen him and Derrick at Ray's. There was no possible way he was going to just roll up at Ricky's establishment with a party of five and expect to get seated. He'd be lucky if Ricky didn't cuss him out as soon as he stepped through the door.

"Mom, you don't want to go there," Bridget said with a nervous laugh, darting her eyes up at Jamal. He wondered if the desperation showed on his face. "You wouldn't like the food there anyway."

"*Why not?* I bet the food would be lovely," her mother gushed. "I'm in the mood for something hearty and African American! You people make such soulful, filling food, Sinclair. I'd love to eat there! Wouldn't you, Marty?"

"It's fine," Martin mumbled. "Frankly, I don't care at this point. I'd just like to eat *some*where."

"I'm okay with some soul food, bro," Blake said with a shrug. "Bring on the fried chicken!"

Jamal's jaw tightened as he narrowed his eyes at Blake.

"I don't even think the restaurant is open today," Bridget said, laughing nervously.

"What's the name of the restaurant?" Blake suddenly whipped out his cell phone.

"Why?" Bridget asked.

"So I can see if it's open. The hours should be listed online, right?"

Bridget hesitated. "It's . . . it's Reynaud's."

Blake furiously typed on the glass screen, waited a beat, then nodded. "Yep, it's open. Open from five p.m. to eleven p.m."

"There you go!" Susan exclaimed. "Let's head there now!"

Bridget gave Jamal a panicked look, silently asking him what they should do next. Jamal felt just as panicked.

"Look, Sinclair, if it's an issue getting us all in there tonight, I can work my contacts to try to get us a table somewhere else." He gave a broad smile, infuriating Jamal even more. "Being deputy mayor and all, I would think you'd have no problem, but I guess that isn't the case in a town filled with politicians. I know a few guys who—"

"I can get us in," Jamal said firmly, cutting off Blake. "I hope you guys don't mind squeezing in the back of my SUV. It might get a little tight back there. Let me take your bag, Susan," he said, reaching for her rolling suitcase.

"Why thank you, Sinclair! What a gentleman you are!" Her mother patted him on the shoulder.

He began to walk swiftly toward the exit, fury propelling him forward. Bridget raced to catch up with him.

"What are you doing?" she hissed in his ear. "Why would you agree to go to Ricky's restaurant?"

The real answer was that he couldn't stand Blake's smugness for another second, and he was pissed to be put in this situation in the first place because Blake decided to tag along for dinner. But he couldn't admit that, so he forced a smile and gave Bridget a wink instead.

"Don't worry. I've got it covered."

Bridget pursed her lips. "I hope you do. I'd hate to be embarrassed in front of my parents!"

He'd hate to be embarrassed too, but he knew he ran a good chance of that happening.

They arrived at the restaurant thirty minutes later and saw the line of patrons waiting inside for seating already stretched to the door. They could barely fit in the confined waiting area.

"It smells divine," Susan said, looking around. "It's decorated quite nicely, too!"

"Wow!" Blake exclaimed. "This place is packed, bro! You sure you can get us a table?"

"Just wait here," Jamal said before he walked toward the reservation desk, feeling his throat go dry. He hoped to God that Ricky wasn't working tonight; that one of the assistant managers was on duty instead. He had no desire to be called a "bitch ass nigga" in front of Bridget's parents.

He approached the pretty young woman who stood at the marble-topped desk.

"Hello, welcome to Reynaud's," she said, brightening her comely face with a smile.

"H-hi, uh, I have a party of five and wondered if you could seat us."

"Do you have a reservation, sir?"

Jamal shook his head. "No, I don't. But how long would the wait be to get a table?"

"Right now the wait time is about two and half hours, unfortunately, sir."

"Two and half hours?"

She nodded.

He leaned toward her. "Do you have specially reserved tables for . . . well . . . for local celebrities?" he whispered.

The young woman raised a finely arched eyebrow. Her polite smile disappeared. "I'm sorry, sir. What do you mean by 'local celebrities?' "

"I mean D.C. dignitaries. You see . . . I'm . . . I'm deputy mayor for economic development."

She continued to stare at him blankly.

"I'm with *mayor's office* . . . I work for Mayor Johnson."

It pained him to have to drop the name of a man whose integrity he now questioned. And this would be the second time Jamal had done it tonight. It felt sad and desperate, but the truth was that he *was* sad and desperate at that moment. He would do just about anything to avoid humiliating himself in front of Bridget's parents, to avoid looking like a fool in front of Blake.

The young woman tilted her head, sending her long hair swinging. "I'm sorry, sir, but we don't keep special tables like that, even for 'local celebrities.' "

Jamal's shoulders sank. "I see."

"Would you like me to add you to the waiting list anyway?"

He shook his head again. "No . . . no, that's okay. I'll just try somewhere else. Thank you." He turned away from the reservation desk. He began to walk back toward Bridget and her family who stared at him expectantly. He was prepared to make some half-hearted excuse for why they couldn't be seated at Reynaud's tonight.

"Jay?" a familiar voice boomed.

Jamal stopped in his tracks when he heard Ricky's voice behind him. He turned slightly and saw his childhood buddy strolling toward him, looking standoffish and imposing in his dark suit and blood-red shirt.

"What the hell are you doing here, man?" Ricky asked, glaring at him, leaning his elbow against the edge of the reservation desk.

Jamal opened his mouth to answer, but no words would come out. He closed his mouth, cleared his throat, and tried again.

"I . . . I came here for dinner," he answered weakly.

Ricky's glare didn't soften. "There's plenty of damn places in this city to eat dinner. Why'd you come here? I'd think my place would be beneath a dude like you, since you're so elevated and shit now."

Jamal lowered his eyes. He had wanted to avoid this, but he should've known he wouldn't be that lucky. "I know you're pissed at me. It was a mistake coming here."

"Yeah, you right about that."

"It's not like I can get a damn table anyway. You don't have to kick me out. I was just about to leave." He then turned on his heel again. "See you, Ricky."

He walked back toward the restaurant's doors, wondering if Bridget's parents had witnessed their whole exchange.

"Hey, Jay!" Ricky shouted again. "Jay, come back, man!"

Jamal paused. He turned around again to face his former friend, only to find Ricky rolling his eyes and waving him back toward the reservation desk.

"Bring your ass back over here. How big is your party?" Ricky asked.

Jamal stared at him, unsure if he had heard him correctly.

"How big is your party, Jay?" Ricky repeated, slower this time.

"Uh . . . it's . . . it's five of us."

"*Five?*" Ricky grumbled. "Okay, I'll get y'all seated in a

bit. Give me fifteen or twenty minutes. One of our larger tables should come open by then."

Jamal gaped. This wasn't at all what he'd expected. "Th-thanks, Ricky."

Ricky waved him off before whispering something into the young woman's ear. She nodded as she tapped a few buttons on the screen in front of her.

They were seated twenty minutes later, like Ricky had promised. The food was as good as expected—even better. Susan had raved about the jumbo crawfish cakes. Martin grunted contentedly at the end, rubbing his full belly. Blake looked mildly annoyed the entire meal, which frankly made all the drama surrounding their dinner reservations worth it for Jamal.

When Jamal asked the waitress for their bill, she told him he didn't have to pay.

"Mr. Reynaud said your meals are on the house, sir."

Jamal stopped midway, tugging his credit card out of his wallet. He was left speechless again.

After he left a sizeable tip for the waitress, Jamal removed the napkin from his lap, pushed back his chair, and rose to his feet.

"I'll be right back," he said, leaning down to whisper the words into Bridget's ear.

She nodded. "Okay, we'll wait for you at the door."

He walked past the tables, excusing his way through a maze of restaurant goers and pausing to let a waiter pass who was carrying a tray of food. Jamal glanced around him—at the high-end décor with its aged wood and brocade booths, at the happy patrons who were drinking wine and almost licking the last of the meal from their plates.

Ricky had done this. He had done it all on his own, without a college or culinary degree. Yeah, he'd had to borrow money from Dolla Dolla to get here, but Jamal couldn't deny that Reynaud's was a huge success. Just looking around made him incredibly proud of his childhood friend.

The childhood friend who I dropped, Jamal thought forlornly.

He started walking again and headed to a corridor near the kitchen.

"I'm sorry, sir," one of the spikey-haired waiters said, striding toward him and pointing in the opposite direction. "The bathrooms are that way. Customers aren't allowed back here."

"It's okay. Umm . . . I'm a friend of Ricky's. I just wanted to go to his office and tell him thanks for comping my dinner. That's all."

The waiter slowly looked him up and down. Finally, the young man shrugged.

"Okay, whatever. He's three doors that way," the waiter said, nodding toward the corridor then walking off.

"I know," Jamal replied to the waiter's retreating back. He then continued on his way. When he reached the door to Ricky's office, he found it closed. He knocked and waited. He knocked again.

"Yeah? What is it?" Ricky finally answered.

Jamal slowly pushed open the door and found Ricky sitting at his massive oak desk. He was peering down at a stack of papers. When the door opened, he looked up and raised his brows in surprise. Ricky leaned back in his leather chair. "What's up?"

"Look . . . uh . . . I just wanted to say thanks for giving us that table . . . for taking care of our meal. You didn't have to do that. I mean . . . I appreciate you doing that for me."

Ricky laughed. "Nigga, you ain't special. I've been doing a lot of shit I haven't had to do lately. Guess I'm in a generous mood."

"Either way, I know how you feel about Bridget . . . about me. I . . . I wanted to say thanks."

Ricky didn't respond.

Jamal lingered in the doorway, wanting to say more. He wanted to confess to Ricky that he missed him and Derrick. Jamal missed their monthly meetups at Ray's, and stupid text chain messages they would send to each other throughout the week that would have him cracking up at his office desk. He didn't have to be on guard when he was around them. He never had. He could always just be himself with his boys.

He wanted to tell Ricky that he'd made a mistake—a big one. He had been wrong for putting him down; he was actually amazed at all that Ricky had accomplished on his own.

He wanted to say he was one sorry motherfucka, and he hoped they could all just hug this shit out and start all over again.

But he didn't say any of that. It felt wrong. It felt weak. So instead, he nodded and grabbed the door handle. "I'll let you get back to your work. Peace out, man."

"Peace out," Ricky called to him just as Jamal shut the office door. He walked back down the hall, and to the restaurant's glass doors where Bridget and her family were waiting for him.

Chapter 13

Derrick

Derrick was sitting at his office desk, finishing his second cup of coffee, when he heard a break in the crackle of static on the walkie-talkie sitting on top of his file cabinet. Up until that point, it had been the background music of his morning as he worked.

"Hey!" he heard Morgan shout. He then heard banging and the clamor of male voices. "Hey, uh . . . I need some help here in room 342! Rodney! Somebody! *Anybody!* Shit!" she yelled then the line filled with static again.

Derrick dropped his coffee cup to the table top, almost spilling its contents onto the numerous documents splayed on his desk. He then shoved back his chair and leapt to his feet, charging to the opened door and into the hall, barely pausing to excuse himself as he bumped into one of the other instructors on his way to the stairs.

He knew this would happen.

Sure, the first few weeks had gone smoothly in Morgan's carpentry class. He hadn't heard any complaints from her about the students, and all the boys generally seemed to like her. At the end of each day, Derrick had tried to pepper her with questions to make sure that everything was as tranquil as it seemed.

"You don't have to worry," she had assured him. "I'm settling in and so are the kids. The boys seem to really like the class. They're having a ball. I am too."

A ball?

It had seemed like she was laying it on a bit thick, but he hadn't questioned her about it. Maybe he should have though because now it sounded like the honeymoon period was officially over based on the ruckus he had heard over his walkie-talkie.

He thundered down the metal stairs to the basement level and shoved the steel door open. When he did, the shouts became even louder. He could hear Morgan screaming, "Tory, put it down! Put it down now!"

Derrick rounded the corner and saw Morgan standing with her back facing the entrance of the shop room and her hands extended outward, like she was being held at gunpoint. The rest of the students were on their feet, standing near the work tables and overturned stools, all staring in the same direction. Even Rodney—Otis's replacement and the new head of security at the Institute—was in the room, and had his hand on his holster.

"Drop it! Drop it right now, or I will light your ass up, boy!" Rodney yelled.

Rodney didn't carry a gun so Derrick supposed the security guard was referring either to his Taser or the pepper spray he only used in the case of emergencies. If he was planning to use either one of those today, whatever was going down inside that room had to be bad—*very* bad.

As Derrick stepped through the doorway, he saw what everyone was staring at. One of the boys—Cole, the new student whose mom had begged Derrick let him into the Institute—was leaning back over one of the tables. His lip was bloody and his clothes were disheveled. Defiance was on his face and in his dark eyes.

The other student—Tory, who had been to Derrick's office more than once in the past year for behavioral issues—had the front of the Cole's T-shirt fisted in his hand and was holding a nail gun only inches away from Cole's temple. Tory had not only a bloody lip, but also a bloody nose and torn collar.

Derrick stared at the nail gun warily. It wasn't a real gun but it could still do quite a bit of damage if Tory fired it.

Derrick walked toward Morgan and lightly touched her on the shoulder, making her jump in surprise. She whipped around to face him. "Oh, shit! Derrick, thank God you're . . ."

She instantly quieted when he held his finger to his lips and slowly shook his head. He then turned to look at the two boys and crept toward them. He wondered what he should do to defuse the situation.

What the hell would Mr. Theo say right now?

He knew that his mentor would be calm, but self-assured. He would speak with authority. Derrick swallowed, took a deep breath, and pressed forward.

"Tory," he began softly, "what are you doing?"

"What the fuck does it look like I'm doing?" Tory barked in reply, seeming almost wild-eyed. "I ain't lettin' this nigga disrespect me. I don't care who the fuck he is, or who he fuck with! *Nobody* disrespects me!"

"He disrespected you so much that it's worth going to jail twenty to thirty years for it?" Derrick continued. "Come on, Tory! Think about what you're doing! Put down the gun."

Tory seemed to hesitate. His eyes shifted from Cole to Derrick and back again.

"It's not worth it, son. You know it's not," Derrick said taking another tentative step toward the boys.

"I ain't no punk!" Tory yelled. His hand was shaking

now. Cole leaned back even farther, keeping a watchful eye on the nail gun.

Derrick nodded. "We know you're not."

"I ain't no bitch! A nigga' step to me, he gets dealt with!"

"*We'll* deal with it, Tory. I promise you." He then reached out his hand, gesturing to the nail gun. "Just give it to me. Give it to me and we'll chop all this shit up in my office. But we can't do that if you don't put that thing down."

Tory glanced again at the nail gun. Finally, ever so slowly, he lowered it from Cole's temple, and Derrick breathed a sigh of relief. Derrick took another step and took the nail gun, ripping out the cord attachment as he did it. As soon as he did, Rodney leapt forward, grabbed Tory's shoulders, and shoved him to the floor.

"Oww! Damn!" Tory screamed, as Rodney planted his knee into his back and wrenched his arms behind him, placing his wrists in plastic cuffs.

"Shut up!" Rodney bellowed. "You lucky this is all I'm doin!"

"You okay?" Derrick asked, tearing his eyes away from Rodney and Tory and glancing at Cole.

The young man nodded.

Derrick then looked back at Morgan, who looked shaken but relieved. "You okay, too?"

"Yeah, I'm . . . I'm fine."

Derrick glanced around the room at the boys who were all staring at Tory now. The boy was still kicking and screaming his outrage on the cement floor.

"Okay, y'all. Let's let Mr. Rodney do his thing. I think Miss Owens will be okay with ending the class for today. Right, Miss Owens?"

Morgan quickly nodded. "Uh, yeah. We're done for the day, guys."

Derrick clapped his hands. "All right, everybody clear out this room! Either head to your next class or go to the rec area until your class starts. You hear me?"

The boys began to shuffle to the doorway, letting Rodney and Tory go first. Tory was still yelling at the top of his lungs, screaming threats over his shoulder at Cole and anyone else who would listen.

Cole gradually stood upright and began to walk toward the doorway too, until Derrick dropped a hand on his shoulder, stopping him. "Oh, no! You come with me. We need to talk."

"I ain't do nothin' though!" Cole shouted, wiping away the blood at the corner of his mouth with the back of his hand.

"Tory's face says differently. He didn't get those bruises from the wind, Cole. You had to have hit him, and you know that's not allowed here. We're going to have to have a serious talk about how you conduct yourself while—"

"He was defending me," Morgan rushed out. "He was defending me, Derrick. That's . . . that's why he hit Tory."

Derrick squinted. "Defending you from what?"

Cole began to open his mouth to answer but Morgan shouted, "Nothing! It was nothing . . . nothing big."

"Well, if it was nothing big then how did it turn into a fight? How did it end with one boy holding a nail gun to the other's head?"

"He grabbed her ass!" Cole interjected. "Tory grabbed her ass when she was walking by. He always be saying shit on the sly to her, Mr. Miller. It ain't right! When he touched her I told him don't do her like that. He shoved me and told me to shut the hell up. I shoved him back. That's . . . that's how the fight started."

Derrick looked at Morgan again. She wouldn't meet his eyes. A flush of mortification was on her cheeks.

"Okay," he murmured. "We can talk more about this later. Let's get you cleaned up first, Cole."

After Derrick had talked with Cole and checked in with Tory and Rodney to get more details of exactly what had happened in the workshop that day, he tracked down Morgan in the teachers' recreational lounge. The room was mostly deserted. She sat alone, eating a bag of potato chips and reading a magazine with her elbow resting on the tabletop. When she saw Derrick walk into the room, she stopped mid-chew and lowered her chip bag to the table. She pushed a lock of hair behind her ear and sat upright.

"I know what you're going to say, but I swear, it wasn't that big of a deal," she argued before he even had a chance to utter a word.

"You should've told me what was going on, Morgan."

"But it really was nothing! I had it covered." She slapped closed her magazine. "Cole having my back like that was sweet—but it wasn't necessary. It escalated the situation *way* past the point it should have gone!"

Derrick pulled out the chair on the other side of the table facing her. He sat down. "Cole told me that Tory's been harassing you pretty much since the first day of class. It's *been* escalating, Morgan. What happened today was just a matter of time. You know that, right?"

"I've heard worse from dudes on the street when I walk past the corner store. I wasn't worried."

"But you should've been. He should've been called out and reprimanded long before now."

"I know. I know!" She balled up her empty bag. "But I didn't want to tell you because . . ."

"Because *what?*"

"Because I thought I had it covered. I thought he was just talking shit. That's what kids do! And you kept asking me if I was up to working at a place like this . . . if I could handle being around all these boys. I thought if I told you what he was doing, you'd basically decide that you were right all along. You'd decide that I shouldn't work here."

It was true. As he listened to Cole's recount of what happened, he'd started thinking that he had made a mistake by hiring Morgan; his first instinct had been the right one. But now, seeing the defeated look on her face, he was second guessing himself again.

"I really need this job, Derrick."

"I know. You told me that in the beginning, and I wouldn't fire you over something like this. But if you needed help, you really should've—"

"And I did . . . I *did* ask for help when I really needed it! I called for Rodney as soon as the situation went left, but again, until today, I thought I had it covered. I know better now though. When stuff starts looking shaky . . . before I lose control of the situation, I'll let you know right away."

He slowly exhaled, still feeling slight unease at everything that had happened today, but knowing there wasn't much more he could do at this point. Tory would no longer be an issue for her since his latest violation left Derrick with no choice but to transfer him from the Institute to the local juvenile detention center. And other teachers besides Morgan had experienced problems with their students, even seen fights break out in their classrooms, but for some reason he was warier when it came to Morgan. He couldn't help worrying about her. He didn't know where all these protective impulses came from.

"And I'm going to say it now," she began, "if you start dropping by my workroom every few hours just to check up on me, I'm gonna lose it! I don't need you babysitting me. I told you, I've got this now. Lesson learned."

He laughed.

"*What?* What's so funny?"

"You sound like my girlfriend. She's accused me of taking over too much, of thinking I know what's best. I guess I've developed a bad habit. Maybe that's why we argue so damn much."

"You have a girlfriend?"

"Yeah, she's my fiancée actually."

She raised her brows. Her eyes widened. "*Really? You're* engaged?"

He laughed again and nodded. "Why do you sound so surprised? A guy like me wouldn't be engaged?"

"No, I just didn't know. No one else mentioned it." She considered him, letting her eyes scan over him. "But now that I think about it, you definitely seem like type of dude that would be engaged. You've got 'taken' written all over you."

"Wait. Was that a compliment or are you coming for me?"

"No, it was a compliment. Trust me! Brothas like you never stay on the market long." She leaned back in her metal chair. "I never get the nice guys, to be honest. The most I could hope to be is their side chick."

He stared at her in shock and she winced.

"That was inappropriate, wasn't it?"

He laughed again. He noticed that he laughed a lot around her. "Just a lil' bit."

"Hey, but it's the truth! You got any single friends you can introduce me to?"

"I've got one single friend but I doubt you'd be interested. He's a bit of a player."

"See what I mean?" She threw up her hands. "The good ones are never single . . . hence, me being the side chick."

"I feel you . . . but you're too good to be anybody's side chick, Morgan. A woman like you deserves better."

This time she seemed caught off guard. Her easy smile disappeared as he pushed himself back from the table.

"Look, I better head back to my office. I hope your afternoon goes better than your morning."

She nodded. "You too," she whispered.

He then turned and walked out the rec room, feeling her eyes upon him as he stepped into the hall.

Chapter 14

Ricky

Let's just get this shit over with, Ricky thought as he strode through the French doors.

He'd heard the music and the shouts from the driveway when he'd handed off his keys to the valet, but the din inside the house was almost deafening. If it were any other home, Ricky would be worried that someone would call the cops, considering all the noise they were making in here. But Dolla Dolla's house was surrounded by an acre of grassland on each side, and frankly, if his neighbors could hear the noise, none of them were crazy enough to call the cops on the infamous Dolla Dolla.

Ricky walked down the short flight of stairs to the marble foyer that was bordered on both sides by a line of scantily clad women in high heels, holding trays of food and drinks. They were the only women in the room.

For these types of parties, Dolla Dolla liked to limit the guest list to almost entirely men. If you were dumb enough to bring a girl with you, don't be surprised if the host tried to make a move on her before the night was done. Those, like Ricky, who knew Dolla Dolla were well aware of this rule. The drug kingpin liked to play mind games with folks, to fuck with you. He had to act like the lion of the pride—all the lionesses were his for the taking. And if you didn't abide by Dolla Dolla's rules at his parties, there was hell to pay. In fact, Ricky recalled one dude who had brought his wife with him to a fight night party two years ago. He'd ended up pistol-whipped and carried out by Dolla Dolla's bodyguards when he tried to step to Dolla Dolla after seeing him grope his wife's ass. Disgusted by the brutality, Ricky had left the party early and watched the rest of the fight at home.

He hoped he wouldn't get treated to yet another ruthless display tonight, that the only bloodshed he witnessed would be on one of Dolla Dolla's many big screen TVs. Ricky hadn't wanted to come to the party tonight anyway after the six late nights and early mornings he'd had overseeing the restaurant and Club Majesty, but Dolla Dolla had sent him a text that afternoon reminding him about the fight night party at his crib. Ricky knew from experience that the reminder was an implicit order to show up that night. It was not to be ignored.

He grabbed a champagne glass from the silver tray of a tall blond. He then looked around him, scanning the faces of the women, hopeful that one of them might be Simone's little sister, Skylar, but, of course, she wasn't there.

Stupid ass, he thought to himself, disappointed.

Dolla Dolla wouldn't very well have the girl standing out in the open. He doubted she'd be anywhere near here. She was probably locked up in a room back at Dolla Dolla's place in D.C.

Ricky walked through the foyer, pausing along the way a few times to greet the men that he knew. He could see the family room where several more men sat on the leather sofas, drinking and smoking. A few women were in there too, sitting on their laps or serving them drinks.

"Ehhhh, Pretty Ricky!" Dolla Dolla called out as Ricky stepped into the room. He'd cupped his beefy hands around his mouth so he could be heard over the noise. He then spread his arms. "What's up, nigga?"

Ricky smiled as he strolled toward him. The two men embraced and as they did, Ricky caught a strong whiff of weed and Hennessey. It seemed that their party's host was well on his way to getting the party started himself.

"Where you been?" Dolla Dolla asked with heavy-lidded eyes and a dopey smile, thumping Ricky on the back. "The fight started already."

"I got a little caught up, but I'm here now."

"That's right! My nigga Pretty Ricky is in the house, y'all!" he yelled to no one in particular. "Go and fix yourself something to eat. My people set up a buffet and everything. We got drinks too. Coke. Bitches. Anything you want!" He slapped Ricky's back. "Treat yourself, nigga!"

Ricky did a double take, lowering his champagne glass from his mouth. "You've got bitches, too?"

"That got your dick up, didn't it?" Dolla Dolla laughed drunkenly and drew closer to him. "They're upstairs," he whispered into his ear. "Don't tell nobody though. I'm just letting a few of these niggas have a taste, but I'm charging them next time. I'll let you have a little taste too." His smile widened. "Think of it as an early Christmas present. Santa left a little pussy for you under the Christmas tree."

Ricky casually took a sip, hoping he was adequately masking his anticipation at the prospect of finding Skylar tonight. "I appreciate it, Dolla."

"I bet you do!" Dolla Dolla said, slapping him on the back again. "Go and get you some pussy, nigga. Enjoy that shit!"

Ricky didn't go upstairs directly. He continued to drink and pretended to watch the fight, though his eyes kept drifting back to the foyer and the wooden staircase that led to the rooms upstairs. Finally, after about twenty minutes he made his way there. Two of Dolla Dolla's body guards stood at the bottom of the staircase, as if guarding the entrance.

"Dolla said it was cool for me to go up," he said to them.

One nodded before stepping aside to let Ricky pass.

He forced himself to keep his footsteps slow, to not look too eager. When he climbed the last stair and stepped onto the plush carpet, he heard the voices—the moans, groans, and laughter.

He stared at the line of six doors along the darkened hallway. Was Skylar in one of these rooms?

He tried the first door where he heard the loudest moans and yells. When he opened it, he saw a woman naked and bent on all fours. A man knelt behind her with his jeans around his ankles and the skin on his back slick with sweat. His hand was fisted in her hair, tugging at it like a horse rein. When the door opened the man stopped mid-stroke and turned to glare at Ricky.

"Damn, nigga! You mind?" he asked.

The woman glanced over her shoulder to look at Ricky, he could see that it wasn't Skylar.

"My bad," Ricky said, stepping back into the hall and closing the door behind him. Within seconds, the moans resumed.

Ricky took a deep breath and headed farther down the corridor.

"Door number two," he whispered to himself. He tried the handle but this one was locked. He raised his fist to knock but thought better of it. He continued on this path.

He tried the door knob for door number three. It wasn't locked. He pushed the door open, prepared to see another couple or maybe even threesome going at it. Instead he found a woman in a lace thong wearing one silver stiletto, splayed on her back on the red satin sheets like she was sleeping. When he stepped into the bedroom, she slowly pushed herself up to her elbows. She shoved her long hair out of her face and looked up at him.

It's her, he thought with surprise. *Well, I'll be god-damned.*

He'd found her again.

"Who are you?" she slurred, squinting at Ricky as he closed the door behind her. "Don't I know you?"

"I'm nobody," he said, reaching into his pocket and pulling out his cell phone. He pressed a few buttons on screen and pointed the camera at her, leaning in close. He saw the image of her looking back at him dazedly, those big brown eyes like her big sister's but rimmed with runny eyeshadow and smudged mascara. He snapped a few pictures.

"You're not nobody." She sneered. "You work for him. You *all* work for him! Just leave me alone, all right? I can't do it tonight. I'm . . . I'm sick. Can't you tell I'm sick?" She slung her legs over the end of the bed and held her stomach, sounding very much like the seventeen-year-old girl that she was. "I . . . I really don't feel well. I'm not faking it this time! I don't know if it's the flu or . . . or . . ."

Ricky lowered his cell phone.

"I keep telling y'all I wanna see a doctor. Can you tell him, please? I don't wanna be sick anymore. I keep . . . I keep throwing up!"

He had gotten the pictures like Simone had asked. He could leave now but something in Skylar's eyes drew him in, kept him from setting a foot back into the hallway. He flashed back to his baby sister, Desiree, sitting across from him at McDonald's the last day he saw her alive. She had the same tortured look in her eyes that Skylar had now.

Ricky tucked the phone back into his pocket.

"I just wanna see a doctor," she pleaded. "I promise I won't tell on him. I won't—"

He dropped to his knee in front of her. "Skylar. Skylar, that's your name right?"

At the sound of her name, she quieted.

"Skylar, do you want to get out of here?"

She was staring at him cagily now, like she wasn't sure if he was playing a trick on her. She glanced at the closed bedroom door.

"Do you want to get out of here? Is he not letting you go? Is that it?"

She raised the bedsheets to cover herself, as if suddenly aware of her nakedness. She slowly shook her head. "You're . . . you're trying to get me in trouble."

"I'm *not* trying to get you in trouble. I'm trying to help you. I can sneak you out of here, I think." He rose to his feet and walked to the bedroom window. He pulled back the curtains. "If this opens, maybe . . . maybe we can sneak you out that way."

She shook her head again, making her hair whip around her skinny shoulders. She gave another panicked glance at the door. Tears sprung to her eyes. "You're just trying to get me in trouble so I get beat up like Natasha! I saw what happened to her. I'm not dumb!"

He returned to her side. He reached out and touched her shoulder and she flinched. He dropped his hand. "I'm not trying to get you in trouble. I told you, I'm here to help! Your sis—"

"Get out!" she screeched, balling her hands into fists. "Get the fuck out!"

"Skylar, just listen to me."

"No! Leave me alone! All of you just leave me the fuck alone! Get out or I'll—"

She stopped when the bedroom door swung open.

Ricky turned to find one of the bodyguards and T. J. standing in the doorway. The bodyguard stared at him quizzically while T. J. glowered.

"What the hell is all this noise, man?" T. J. said in a harsh whisper. "Folks can here this bitch yelling all the way downstairs."

Ricky put his "Pretty Ricky" mask back on. He shrugged indifferently. "I don't know. Ask her! I came in here to fuck and she went off. She just started screaming for no damn reason."

T. J.'s glower shifted from Ricky to Skylar who was cowering on the bed with her head bowed. His lip curled as he charged toward her.

"What the fuck we tell you, bitch? What the fuck you think happens when you act up? Huh?"

Skylar began to whimper.

T. J. raised his hand, like he was about to slap her. "I'ma knock the shit outta—"

Ricky caught him mid-swing, grabbing T. J.'s wrist before the blow landed. "Don't do that."

T. J. stared up at him in amazement but the shock quickly coalesced into fury. "What, nigga?" he said, tugging his wrist out of Ricky's grasp.

"I said don't do that. Don't hit her. That shit ain't necessary."

T. J. seemed to be struck silent for a moment but he quickly regained his voice.

"Who the . . . who the *fuck* are you to tell me what's necessary and what ain't? Don't you ever touch me again in your fucking life, nigga, or I'll put you in a grave and have your mama cryin'!" He pulled up his shirt and revealing the Glock tucked in his boxer briefs. "You feel me?"

Ricky didn't respond. He was carrying tonight too, but having a shootout with T. J. wouldn't solve anything. He could get killed. Skylar could get killed. What was the point?

So instead, he glared right back at the younger man, not backing down. Finally, the standoff ended and T. J. turned away from him. He stalked back to the bed and out of childish spite, gave Skylar a hard shove that sent her sprawling across the mattress.

"You keep the noise down, bitch, and don't let me have to come back up here!"

"But . . . but I'm sick," she cried.

"You bitches always *sick!*" T. J. glanced over his shoulder at Ricky and waved him off. "Just get the fuck out of here. This bitch is useless as fuck. You ain't getting your dick sucked tonight!"

Ricky gazed at Skylar one last time then turned and walked out of the bedroom.

Chapter 15

Jamal

Jamal checked the contents of the manila envelope before sealing it, tucking it under his arm, and stepping out of his office into the waiting area.

"Heading to lunch?" his secretary chirped to him as he passed her desk.

Jamal nodded distractedly. "Uh, yeah. I . . . I should be back by one though," he replied before continuing into the hall.

"Enjoy!" she called after him.

He was finally going to do it. After debating with himself for weeks over what to do with the information he had gathered about Mayor Johnson, he had decided to hand it all over to the Phillip at the *Washington Recorder*.

Phil will know what to do, he reassured himself as he boarded the elevator that would take him to the lower level.

Jamal had decided to at least partially follow Derrick's advice: he would mail the contents anonymously. He would drive to a mailbox far away from the Wilson Building and, hopefully, make it almost impossible for anyone to trace it back to himself. He didn't know what the fallout would be once the story was published. Would Mayor Johnson get arrested? Would other people within his administration also face charges for corruption? Would everyone think Jamal was guilty by association? After all, he was working for the man and had been appointed by him.

These scenarios all seemed like strong possibilities, but despite what the blowback could be, he couldn't keep this on his conscience any longer. He had to be rid of it.

Jamal exited the elevator and stepped onto the lower level that overlooked the Wilson Building's gallery. He paused when he reached the top of the staircase.

He saw about thirty or so school children, all in identical yellow T-shirts with bobcats on the front. They milled about at the bottom of the steps, staring slack-jawed at city hall's high ceilings, at the way the light from the overhead windows played off of the stonework. Their young, jubilant voices rose up several floors, filling the gallery with their laughter and squeals.

Normally, he would have found their eager interest cute, even endearing. He'd get the same warm feeling he got when he watched Hallmark commercials—but Jamal wasn't in the squishy kind of mood today. He had a heavy task ahead of him, and he had to be on his way before he lost his nerve.

Jamal walked down the flight of stairs, pasting on a polite smile, and prepared to excuse his way through the crowd of children to reach the glass doors on the other side of the gallery. But he halted again when he saw a woman rushing across the marble tiles, holding the hands of two kids. Both children were running to keep up with the woman's long strides.

When Jamal saw her, his heavy mood instantly lightened and the manila envelope tucked beneath his arm was momentarily forgotten.

"All right!" Melissa shouted, swinging her head from right to left, surveying the space and the children in it. The movement made her long braids whip around her shoulders. "Everyone line up! Straight line, kids. Terrell, stop that, please!"

She then dropped the children's hands and said something to another woman standing near the staircase.

Watching Melissa, he felt a stirring in the pit of his belly that he always felt when he caught a glimpse of her.

"Lissa!" he called out and she snapped up her head and looked toward the staircase. Her dark eyes crinkled up at the sides as she grinned.

"Jay, hey!" she said, waving at him.

"Didn't expect to see you here today." He walked down the last of the stairs and stepped onto the tiled floor.

"It was a last-minute replacement field trip. We were going to take the kids to the old city hall, but found out that it's undergoing renovations so," she shrugged, "here we are." She looked at the children who surrounded her. "Boys and girls, I would like you to meet Jamal Lighty. He's the deputy mayor of the city. Jamal, meet our fourth grade class and my teaching assistant, Mrs. McKenna."

Jamal didn't have the heart to correct her and tell her he didn't go by his first name anymore. Honestly, telling Melissa that he had changed his name to Sinclair seemed a tad bit embarrassing, like he was a fake or trying to put on airs.

"You are a fake who's putting on airs," a voice in his head chided.

"Please to meet you guys," he said, looking at her students. "Welcome to the Wilson Building!"

"You're the mayor of D.C.?" one kid gushed, staring up at him, wide-eyed. "That's so cool!"

Jamal cleared his throat. "No, I'm the . . . the deputy

mayor. It's sort of like the mayor's assistant. I work for Mayor Johnson and handle some tasks for him."

The kid looked a little disappointed, but the rest nodded thoughtfully.

"What does a deputy mayor do?" another kid shouted—a little girl with braids, wearing glasses.

"Do you get a bodyguard?" another kid called out to him.

"You get paid a lot of money?" a boy yelled.

Jamal chuckled, amused by their deluge of questions. "Well, uh . . . a deputy mayor is—"

"Kids," Melissa said, cutting him off, "Mr. Lighty is a *very* busy man. We don't want to bombard him with questions and slow him down." She turned to him and smiled apologetically. "I'm sorry, Jay. We're probably keeping you from doing whatever you were about to do. I didn't mean to disrupt your morning."

He hesitated, remembering the envelope beneath his arm. Now, standing in front of her, his sense of urgency began to wane. His resolve began to falter. He told himself he could always mail the package to Phillip later today.

And if not today, maybe tomorrow, Jamal reasoned.

"Actually, my schedule is completely open! I'd be happy to answer your students' questions." He looked at the children. "I'll even give you guys a VIP tour of the building."

Excited squeals filled the gallery again, but Melissa's smile disappeared. She furrowed her brows.

"Jay, you don't have to do that," she whispered, leaning toward him.

"I know I don't have to. I *want* to."

She stared at him a few more seconds before finally nodding and gesturing toward him. "Lead the way!"

For the next hour, he dutifully took the kids on a tour of the building, pointing out the architectural details and telling them about D.C. government and its functions. Several of the kids "oohed" and "ahhed." The ones who got bored and stopped paying attention, Melissa and her assistant quickly corralled, holding their hands and dragging them along.

He ended the tour at the indoor food court next door where the kids would have lunch.

"Can I treat you?" he asked Melissa. "You have your choice between such fine dining establishments as McDonald's, Taco Bell, and Panda Express."

Melissa giggled, making his chest go warm. "Hey, I'd never turn down a free meal!"

He bought their food and they sat at one of the tables adjacent to those crowded with Melissa's students.

"Thanks for having lunch with me," he said, removing the paper wrapping from his taco.

"No, thank you for treating me to lunch and taking us on the tour!" She reached over her bowl of orange chicken and lo mein and gave his hand a quick squeeze, making his pulse accelerate. "That was so sweet of you, Jay."

He lowered his eyes to the tabletop. "It was no problem. Really."

"I still feel like we interrupted your day though. You didn't even get to mail that letter you've been carrying around with you." She eyed the envelope now sitting on the table between their food trays. "It looks important."

He guiltily yanked the envelope off the table and sat it on his lap. "It isn't . . . I mean, it wasn't important." He laughed nervously. "I mean . . . I can always mail it later."

And frankly, he was starting to wonder if Melissa showing up at the very minute he'd intended to mail the package had been a sign. Maybe it was fate interceding and stopping him from making a huge mistake. He had been self-righteously naïve about the ramifications of sharing so much incendiary information with the press. Who knows how many lives could be ruined? How many jobs could be lost? No, he had to think about this a bit longer.

"Well, it was nice to hang out with you either way," Melissa continued. "Since you and Derrick are on the outs, I don't get to see you anymore. I don't have to stock as much white cheddar popcorn at our place for game night. Besides me, you were the only one who ate it," she joked.

"Derrick won't . . . he won't mind us doing this, will he?" Jamal ventured, making her frown.

"Doing what?"

"I mean, is he gonna mind us having lunch together?" He gestured to their food. "Since he and I aren't talking."

"Derrick doesn't control who I talk to, or who I eat lunch with. We've never been like that. Besides, you and Derrick may not be tight anymore, but I still consider you one of my friends."

His eyebrows shot up. He stared at her in surprise. *"You do?"*

"Of course, I do! We've known each other since we were kids." She glanced at the tables of children, keeping an eye on a group of boys who were getting rowdy. "You knew me back when I was still in braces and a training bra, Jay. That's a deep connection."

Really? Because it never felt very deep, he mused as he watched her begin to eat her lunch, but he didn't share his thoughts aloud.

His interactions with Melissa had always been limited to when Derrick was around. In fact, this would be the first time in years that they'd ever been alone together.

"And the truth is," she continued between chews, lowering her fork from her mouth, "I've been kind of irritated with Derrick lately, so I don't give a damn if he would have a problem with us eating lunch together. Serves him right! He does whatever the hell he wants. Why shouldn't I do what I want, too?"

"Wait. What did Derrick do?"

"Well, he's been talking to my daddy behind my back this whole time, for one."

So she finally found out about that, Jamal thought as he bit into his taco.

He was wondering if she would get wind of the fact that Derrick was still regularly meeting up with her father, despite her wishes to the contrary. Jamal hadn't thought staying friends with Mr. Theo was worth alienating and pissing off your fiancée, but that was his opinion. When he'd told Derrick as much months ago, Derrick had ignored him.

"Dee wants to get married but then he pulls some shit like this? How the hell am I supposed to trust him?"

Jamal sat silently for several seconds, carefully considering his words. He didn't want to bad mouth Derrick, but he did feel his former friend had been out of line.

"I know you're upset," Jamal began, "but Dee did have good intentions. He felt bad for Mr. Theo and he thought he could find a way to get you and your dad talking again."

"Yeah, he did, but I just wish he wouldn't always assume that he knows what's best. Who died and made him the authority on everything?"

"That's blasphemy, Lissa. Didn't you know Dee, our lord and savior, died for our sins?" Jamal murmured sarcastically.

Melissa burst into laughter, clamping her hand over her mouth.

Jamal started laughing too.

"Died for our sins," she chortled. "You're funny! I

don't know why I never realized you were so funny before."

I know why, Jamal thought.

She didn't know he could be funny because she barely knew him at all. Now she had the chance to finally see the man he really was, to see him outside of Derrick's shadow.

An hour later, Jamal walked Melissa and her class back to the Wilson Building glass doors.

"Again, thank you so much for doing this today, Jay."

"Like I said, it wasn't a problem. You guys caught me at a good time," he lied. "Besides, I don't mind doing my part for the kids. And it was kinda fun."

She turned and watched as the children filed through the glass doors to the stone steps leading to the curb below where two yellow school buses awaited them.

"It was good seeing you," she said.

"It was good seeing you t—"

He didn't get to finish. She enveloped him in a hug, completely catching him off guard. He stood still for the first few seconds and then gradually wrapped his arms around her and hugged her back. Though the entire act probably lasted all of thirty seconds, it felt like time had slowed down.

He closed his eyes and inhaled, smelling the delicious scent of cocoa butter on his skin, absorbing the warmth of her body. And far too soon, she stepped out of his embrace.

"We should do this again sometime," she said.

"How about we meet for coffee next week?" he blurted out. "My treat."

When he saw the surprised look on her face, he realized that he had been too eager. She was only being polite when she said they should meet up again.

Stupid. Stupid. Stupid, he thought.

He opened his mouth to beg off but then she nodded.

"Sure! That would be nice. I'll text you to set something up." She walked toward the doors and waved. "But this time, it's *my* treat. You paid for lunch, remember? Bye, Jay!"

"Bye, Lissa," he said, gazing at her until she walked through the doors, down the stairs to the sidewalk, and disappeared onto the school bus.

Chapter 16

Ricky

It was easy to spot Simone even in the dark and the downpour. The sidewalks were mostly deserted due to the late hour and heavy rain that made murky water littered with trash and debris bubble out of storm drains and scuttle down the street in eddies and waves.

She stood alone near the bus stop, the sole figure on the deserted city block. He could see her in the hazy glow of his headlights, shivering under her black umbrella and wearing jeans that were already soaked up to the knees. The instant he pulled up to the curb, she ran to his car. He unlocked door and she hopped inside, slamming the door shut behind her.

"I'm going to kill him!" she shouted, not even bothering with a greeting. "I'm going to fucking kill him!"

"No, you're not," he said, driving through the intersection as the stoplight turned from red to green. He glanced at her. "Put your seatbelt on. You're a cop. You should know better."

He watched as she buckled her seatbelt and glared out the windshield. She bit hard on her bottom lip and shook her head. "He deserves to die for what he's doing to her. You know that! She's just a kid and he's passing her around to random strangers. You said yourself you think he's beating those girls to make them stay. Why the hell shouldn't I kill him?"

Ricky sighed as he drove.

He hadn't expected to meet Simone tonight, only a day after the party at Dolla's house, but of course, as soon as he texted her the pictures of Skylar, she sent him a rapid thread of text messages in reply.

She looks HORRIBLE.
Did you talk to her? What did she say?
Are they hurting her?

Ricky had called her back and tried to share everything he'd seen and what had happened that night, but the questions continued to flood out of her. Her words sped up and she got louder and louder on the other end of the line. She sounded one part angry and two parts hysterical. She threatened more than once to charge in there with a warrant—and if she couldn't get a warrant, she would just kick the door down and come in with guns blazing.

Ricky worried that it wasn't just bluster. Simone had said before that it was a daily struggle not to become untethered since her sister had disappeared, to hold it together. Would she really do something so reckless and put herself and her sister in harm's way?

He had to talk her out of it, so he'd suggested, perhaps foolishly, that they meet in person.

That's how he now found himself listening to her mutter as she sat in the passenger seat of his Mercedes SUV.

"Running up in there to rescue your sister ain't going to accomplish a damn thing, but getting you killed."

"So!" she yelled.

"What do you mean, 'So'? Dolla doesn't give a shit that you're a woman, Simone. He could *really* hurt you. You've got a death wish?"

"No, but I can't sit idly by either! I went to my commanding officer and told him what's happening to Skylar."

Ricky whipped his head around to face her. "*You told him that I told you?* You told him about me? Why the hell would you—"

"I didn't say anything about you," she added quickly, seeing the alarm on his face even in the darkened car compartment. "Calm the hell down! I acted like I stumbled on the info myself. Besides, he's not going to do damn thing! He said I needed proof of abuse, that she's being held against her will. He said he would need to talk to her, which I explained to him isn't possible unless we go in there and *make* Dolla let us talk to her. But he blew me off. What does he care?" She sucked her teeth in disgust. "She's just another black girl junkie runaway, one of thousands in this city that people ignore and forget. They could be alive or dead—and *no one* cares." She closed her eyes. She sniffed. "I see those blue and yellow missing flyers on the wall in our lobby and I look at all their faces. They're *so many* little black girls, Ricky. So many!" Tears flooded her eyes. "And I just . . . I just want to punch the wall because I'm so pissed. I want to cry because I think . . . I think about their families and how they may never find them. I think about Skylar. I think about what's happening to her and I . . . I can't . . . I can't imagine . . . what am I going to tell my mother? I promised her I would bring her home! What am I . . . I . . ."

She couldn't finish. Her words were engulfed by sobs that made her shoulders shake, that made her gasp for air.

"Simone," he said, reaching for her. "Simone, are you all right?"

She didn't answer him. Instead, she continued to sob,

pulled at her seatbelt, and clutched at her chest, like she was hyperventilating.

"Shit," he spat before quickly scanning the road around him. When he saw an open parking lot and pulled into it. He removed his seatbelt and turned to her.

"It's okay," he said, rubbing her back. "It's okay. Just take a deep breath."

His voice was barely audible over the sound of the rain pattering on the car roof.

He was surprising himself with his response, how gentle he was being. Derrick and Jamal would be shocked to see him like this, patiently comforting a woman. He didn't normally act this way, but then again, with Simone *none* of his behavior had been normal.

She tugged off her seatbelt, too, and leaned forward in the passenger seat, resting her forehead on his leather dashboard.

"It's okay. It's all right," he whispered into her ear.

Her sobs finally subsided. She slowly raised her head and turned to him with reddened eyes. She sniffed.

"God, I'm a mess! I'm sorry for breaking down like that in front of you. I didn't . . . I didn't mean to do that."

"Stop apologizing. You don't have to apologize for something like that."

"It's just a lot. I don't know what to do! I don't—"

"I'll take care of it. Okay? I'll take care of everything. Don't worry," Ricky assured her, still rubbing her back, wondering even as he said the words what insane impulse made him utter such nonsense.

He had already done more than enough to help Simone, definitely more than he had intended when she first showed him the photo of her sister back at Club Majesty. Just what the hell else was he supposed to do?

"Thank you, Ricky," she whispered. "Thank you so much."

"And stop thanking me," he replied gruffly.

"Never. You deserve it."

Their eyes met and he felt that old pesky tug at his groin. The temperature of the car compartment seemed to rise within seconds and a static charge filled the air. Ricky wasn't sure who leaned forward first—him or Simone. Either way, their lips collided like two cars careening on the slippery roadway outside their windows. Within seconds, lips turned into tongues, and tongues quickly morphed into hands. The next thing he knew, she was straddling him in the driver's seat and he was yanking down the zipper of her jacket, shoving the garment off her shoulders. He was hiking up the front of her T-shirt, fondling her breasts over the lace cups of her bra. Their mouths stayed connected the whole time. He sucked her tongue, enjoying the taste of her, and she did the same to him. She bit down on his bottom lip and tugged it ever so gently with her teeth, and he groaned. They kissed again, angling their heads so that this kiss was more fervent than the last. She shifted her hips, rubbing her crotch enticingly against his dick, making him as hard as a rock.

He wanted the bra gone.

He wanted her jeans gone, and if she was wearing panties—he wanted those gone too.

He wanted to take her right there in his front seat with the fogged up windows and the only noise in the car coming from the rain and their mouths as they moaned and screamed their way to sexual bliss. But something held him back. Maybe it was her tears from earlier or the fact that she wouldn't be doing this if she wasn't emotionally destroyed by what was happening to her sister. Either way, Ricky tugged his lips away from hers. He lowered his hands from her breasts.

She stared down at him, confused. "*What?* What's wrong?"

"You don't want to do this," he whispered grimly.

"Why do you think I don't want to do this?"

"I don't think—I *know*." He shifted her, easing her from his lap back onto the passenger seat. "You're all fucked up about your little sister. You're not thinking straight. You'll regret it later."

She slowly shook her head. "You don't know that, Ricky. I wouldn't do anything I didn't—"

"Well then *I'll* regret! How about that?" He glared at her. "I already feel like I'm in over my head with all this shit you've dragged me into! We don't need to complicate it any more than it already is."

Her shoulders fell. She actually looked hurt. "I didn't realize I was dragging you into it. I thought you *wanted* to help me . . . to help Skylar! If it's that much of a problem, then why are you even bothering?"

Good question, he thought.

Why was he doing any of this? Why was he sticking his neck out for her? It certainly wasn't to get a piece of ass. If Ricky wanted to get laid, he had plenty of other women he could go to. And it wasn't because she had anything on him, and could use it to blackmail him. He wasn't involved directly with any of Dolla Dolla's criminal enterprises and she knew that or she wouldn't be bothering with him in the first place. So why did he keep helping and risking his life and livelihood for a woman he barely knew?

Maybe it was because he never got to save Desiree and helping her offered him a chance to save Skylar, someone very similar to his deceased sister. Or maybe there was something else, something about Simone that he couldn't quite put his finger on. Either way, it bugged the hell out of him.

"Where should I drop you off?" he asked, not looking at her anymore. Because if he looked at her again or let her keep talking, he might lose his resolve, tug her back onto his lap, and continue where they left off. He was trying to do the right thing tonight, but he was no saint.

Don't test me, honey.

She put her seatbelt back on and turned to look out the passenger side window. "Just take me back to where you picked me up. It's only a couple blocks from my place."

Ricky shifted the car into drive and pulled out of the parking lot. He did as she asked, taking her back to the spot next to the bus stop. The rain had finally ended, so at least she didn't have to walk in that again.

She shoved open the door and climbed out, but she paused on the sidewalk. She leaned down and stared at him. "Can I still count on you, Ricky?"

He waited a bit before he nodded. "I'll call you if I see her again."

"*If* you see her? But you said you'd take care of—"

"I know what I said, but I can't promise you anything, Simone! This is the best I can do for now."

Her face hardened. The glint was back in her eyes. She let out an impatient breath and slammed the car door shut. He watched as she walked down the block, tugging her jacket closed. He only pulled off when he saw her disappear around the corner.

Chapter 17

Derrick

"So what did the vet say?" Derrick asked, typing a few keys on his laptop while he held his office phone between his ear and the crook of his shoulder.

"He said Brownie doesn't have fleas like I thought. He has psychogenic alopecia," Melissa replied tiredly on the other end of the line.

"Psycho-*whata?*"

"Psychogenic alopecia. It's just a fancy term for excessive grooming. I guess it's a condition that cats can get sometimes."

Melissa had decided to take their cat, Brownie, to the vet that morning when she realized the feline was starting to lose patches of fur and was coughing up hairballs like there was no tomorrow. Derrick hadn't considered the situation life threatening, but he knew how she felt about their pet. He wasn't going to put up much of an argument either way.

"Okay, so what's the treatment for psychogenic whatchamacallit?" he asked, already resolving himself to the prospect of paying an expensive vet bill for a cat with no job who just liked to lick himself a lot. He propped his feet up on his desk. "Does he get a few shots? Do we have to put him on pills or something?"

"No, she said the cause is probably stress. If he's less stressed out, the condition should gradually go away."

"Stress?" Derrick squinted at the light streaming in through his office window. "What the hell does Brownie have to be stressed about? He's a damn cat! All he does is eat, climb shelves, and sleep all day."

"Well, she asked if there were any changes in our household. If maybe he could be stressed out from that. I told her . . ." Melissa cleared her throat. "I, uh, told her we've been arguing a little more lately. That things have been kinda tense between us. Maybe he's picking up on that."

Derrick rolled his eyes. "So Brownie is stressed out because what's going on *between us*? You're kidding, right?"

"I don't know, Dee!" she huffed. "The vet asked a question, and that was the only thing I could think of. Don't give me shit about it. I'm just telling you what she said!"

Derrick dropped his feet from his desk and leaned forward in his chair. He told himself to count to ten, to not respond to her anger with his own anger. It would lead them nowhere; they would just stay stuck in the same cycle they had been lately.

"Okay, well, we'll just . . . just try to work on creating a calmer environment at home for . . . for Brownie," he muttered, feeling ridiculous even as he said it. "So what do you have planned for the rest of the day? You took off from school, right?"

"Yeah, Lily is subbing for me. I'm going to hang around here for another hour or so. Give Brownie some love and attention then head out. I'm supposed to meet somebody for coffee a little later."

"That sounds cool. Who are you meeting up with? Catching up with Bina? I know you guys haven't seen each other as much since she had the baby."

"Umm, no, she's still under baby house arrest. I figured I'll ask her out to lunch next month when the baby is a little older and she can take him out with her."

"That makes sense. So who are you going out with today? You still haven't said."

She paused. "Why do I have to tell you?"

"You don't *have* to tell me, baby. I was just asking." He forced a laugh. "*What?* You meeting up with your secret lover or somethin'?"

"That's not funny, Dee. And since when do you care who I have coffee with? I didn't think I had to report to you. I didn't think we were that kind of couple."

His smile faded. "We aren't. Look, where is all this—"

"You certainly don't tell *me* everything! You didn't tell me that Calvin called you a few days ago with a job offer. He wants you to be the director of development at his non-profit."

Derrick stilled. His stomach dropped. "How . . . how do you know about that?"

"He left a message today on our voice mail. He said he's willing to up the offer by another five grand if *you're* willing to change your mind."

Derrick closed his eyes.

Calvin was an old college buddy from Howard who Derrick had stayed in touch with over the years. Calvin had started a small non-profit eight years ago that had since grown. He'd hit Derrick up a few times, asking if he would be willing to quit the Institute and work for him. Though Derrick had been flattered by the offer, there was no way in hell he would take on a job like director of development, where he would spend his days tracking down grant funding and sucking up to corporation heads to get them to donate money. He didn't care how much the salary was, he wasn't interested.

"Why didn't you tell me he offered you a job, Dee?"

"Because I knew what you would say. You would tell me to take the job."

"Why wouldn't you take it? You can finally make what you're really worth! Why wouldn't you take a job that doesn't require you to break up fights or deal with parole officers and judges or—"

"You know why," he answered tightly. "I've told you about a thousand damn times."

"And it doesn't make any more sense now than the first time you told me!"

"Hey, Derrick!" he heard a female voice call out to him along with two quick knocks on his opened office door. "Can I talk to you for a . . . oh, damn, I'm sorry! I didn't know you were on the phone."

Derrick looked up to find Morgan standing in the doorway. She was wearing denim work overalls and a black T-shirt. Both were stained with paint and sawdust. Even a streak of yellow was on her forehead and chin. Her curly hair was piled atop her head in a ponytail.

He quickly shook his head, held up his finger, and mouthed, "Just a sec." He then turned around to face his window, trying his best to hide from Morgan how pissed he was at that moment.

"Look, I've gotta call you back," he told Melissa, dropping his voice to a whisper.

"Really, Dee? I ask you why you would keep *yet another* secret from me, and you want to rush me off the phone?"

"It wasn't a secret! There was nothing to tell because I'd already said no." He glanced over his shoulder at Morgan. "Look, I have someone waiting at my door. I have to go."

He heard Melissa suck her teeth on the other end. "Fine."

She hung up with a loud click, and Derrick squeezed the phone receiver so hard he thought the plastic might crack in his fist. Again, he told himself to count to ten. When he finished, he turned back around, lowered the phone receiver into its cradle, and looked up at Morgan. He wasn't totally calm, but he hoped he at least looked like he was.

"Hey, what's up?" he said, forcing a lightness in his voice that he didn't feel.

"Again, I didn't mean to barge in, but I wanted to talk to you while I was in between classes. I have another one that starts in about an hour and—"

"It's fine." He painted on a smile and gestured toward the chair facing his desk. "Have a seat. Take a load off."

She walked toward his chair and wiped the dust off her rear before sitting down. "I wanted to talk to you about Cole."

At the mention of the boy's name, Dee narrowed his eyes. "*Why?* Did he get into another fight? I figured since Tory had to go back to the juvie that he would be—"

"No, he's fine. No fighting at all. In fact, he seems to be getting along with all of the kids in class. Maybe . . . I don't know . . . maybe he's getting along a little *too* well."

"*A little too well?* What . . . what does that mean?"

"It means for a kid who just started a couple of months ago, he seems to have a lot of sway over all the other boys. It's like . . . like he's their damn leader or something."

Derrick shrugged. "Maybe he's just popular. And Tory used to be kind of a big dog around here. For Cole to step up to him in your defense, that would certainly command respect from the other boys. Maybe Cole just has a rep now."

"Yeah, rep is one thing, Derrick, but . . . I saw one of the kids actually apologize for bumping into him the other day." She made a face. "Fifteen-year-old boys don't usually do that, do they? It just seemed . . . weird."

Derrick leaned back in his office chair, now frowning. He thought back to something Tory had said during his fight with Cole in the workshop, something that had sounded odd at the time.

"I don't care who the fuck he is or who he fuck with! Nobody *disrespects me!"* Tory had said as he held the nail gun to Cole's temple.

Just who exactly did Cole "fuck with"? Did he run with some notorious crew?

Sure, more than a couple of the boys had gang affiliations, but it was part of the mandate of the Institute that they had to put all that aside when they joined the program and walked through the doors. Derrick knew Cole had a few drug charges under his belt, but only for marijuana possession and drug paraphernalia. Nothing serious. It wasn't like the boy was a big-time criminal.

Derrick shrugged again. "I'll keep an eye on it and an ear out, but I wouldn't worry about it much. Again, the other boys probably just like and respect him. I wouldn't read too much into it."

Her shoulders sank. "Okay, if you think so. I didn't mean to bother you with nonsense but I figured since my last . . . uh . . . incident, I promised you I'd give you the heads up if anything looked questionable."

"Don't call it nonsense! You did exactly what I asked you to do. If you have any concerns about the kids, I'd want to know. That's what I'm here for."

"I know and thanks, Derrick," she said with a nod.

He watched as she rose to her feet and walked toward his door. She paused in the doorway and turned back to look at him. "Hey, I've got some extra tickets to a Wizards game tomorrow. A couple of my friends had to back out. You think you might wanna go?"

He raised his eyebrows.

"I mean . . . you can invite your girl, too!" she rushed out. "I wasn't asking that you . . . well, I wasn't asking you go with me. I . . . I know you're engaged and everything."

"I'd love to, but Melissa and I have plans for tomorrow night," he lied. "And to be honest, basketball isn't really her thing. Never has been."

"Oh, well . . . I figured I should ask. Maybe I'll find someone else who can use them."

"Maybe."

Though part of him did want to tell her yes. He resented having to reject Morgan's invitation out of respect for a fiancée with whom he couldn't even carry on a phone conversation without arguing. But Derrick had to say no. It was the only responsible thing to do.

Morgan waved. "Well, let me know if you guys change your mind. See you later, Derrick."

"Bye, Morgan," he said.

Chapter 18

Jamal

Jamal could barely sit still in his bistro chair as he peered out the floor-to-ceiling windows, looking for one woman in particular among the many faces of people who walked by. He reached absently for his latte and nearly knocked over the cup, sending it flying across the table's metal surface and spilling onto his pant leg. He shouted in surprise and grabbed it before any real catastrophe could happen. Only a dime-sized spot landed on his knee.

A white-haired old woman in a thick, cable-knit sweater sitting at one of the tables next to him gave him an indulgent smile. "Good save," she said with a smoker's laugh, folding over the newspaper she had been reading.

He nodded and glanced down at the paper coffee cup he now held. "I'm all thumbs today."

"Anxious about something?" she asked, raising her gray brows.

He nodded. "I'm . . . umm . . . I'm meeting someone special today, and I'm kind of nervous. I don't want to screw this up."

"Oh, I'm sure it'll be fine, honey," she said, waving off

his fears. She then returned her attention to her broadsheet.

He nodded again and glanced at his wristwatch. Melissa should be arriving any minute now. He had come early to grab a perfect table toward the back where they'd have a relative amount of privacy for their coffee date.

It's not a date, he silently corrected himself, though it certainly felt like one. His palms were sweating. His heart was racing. The collar of his dress shirt felt too tight so he kept reaching up to undo a button or two and then redoing it when he worried that he had undone too many.

It felt like he was about to go on his first date with Melissa after all these years.

Of course, he reminded himself that Melissa was still engaged to Derrick and he was living with Bridget so anything romantic happening between them was almost impossible, but it couldn't keep a man from dreaming or hoping. And it was nice to finally be looking forward to something for once. At that moment, Mayor Johnson and all the drama that surrounded the shady politician was pushed to the back of his mind. For now, his sole focus was Melissa.

Finally, Jamal spotted her walking through the opened glass door. She made a quick glance around the shop before her eyes landed on him. When they did, her face brightened.

This time, he didn't just feel like he had been nudged in the stomach. He also felt a sharp tug in his groin like a compass needle being magnetically pulled due north.

He watched as she removed her peacoat and walked toward him, excusing her way past a woman pushing a stroller. She was wearing skinny jeans, a red V-neck sweater, and high-heeled boots.

Melissa wasn't slim like Bridget. She certainly wasn't petite either. Bridget barely reached his height, even wearing four-inch heels, whereas Melissa was probably taller than him today thanks to her boots. But Jamal didn't mind. Just watching that tall, curvy body sway and bounce as she sauntered toward him like some sexy Amazon was a reward in itself. He wondered what she looked like with all her clothes off. What would it be like to have that curvy body pressed naked against his?`

"Hey, Jay!" she said, holding her arms out wide for a hug. "What's up?"

He shot to his feet and embraced her. He couldn't feel her naked body against him, so he'd have to settle for a clothed one instead.

She stepped out of his hug and glanced down at his coffee cup. "Aww! You started without me?" she asked, poking out her bottom lip playfully. "I told you I would treat you!"

"I got here early and needed some caffeine. Don't worry. Go ahead and make your order. I won't have another sip until you get back."

She laughed. "I'll hold you to that," she said before walking to the coffee counter.

"Is that the special someone you were waiting for?" the old woman beside him asked in a stage whisper, lowering her newspaper and leaning across the aisle toward him.

He whipped his head around to face her. He had forgotten she was still sitting there. He nodded. "Yeah," he answered quietly.

"She's a cutie," the old woman said and gave him a wink. "Good luck!"

A half hour later, he and Melissa sat facing each other, laughing and talking. The old woman had left, granting the coffee shop corner entirely to the couple.

"So he squirted poop all over me—my T-shirt, my jeans! It even got on my shoes!" she exclaimed, throwing her head back as she laughed. She was telling him the story of the first time she'd changed her infant godson's diaper. "It had to have shot out about a good three feet!"

"That sounds disgusting," he muttered, slowly shaking his head and laughing too.

"It was! I asked my girl Bina why she didn't warn me that her son had projectile poops. She told me it even catches her off guard some days too. Oh, well." Melissa shrugged and drank from her venti cup. "I just know I'll never wear that outfit again."

Their laughter tapered off and Melissa inclined her head.

"I feel like I've been doing most of the talking, Jay. Talk to me! Tell me what's going on with you. How's work, Mr. Deputy Mayor?"

His smile faded. He pursed his lips. "Work is . . . uh . . . good. I'm busy."

"I would imagine! Handling economic development for a big city like D.C. can't be easy! It's gotta be pretty complicated."

It's more complicated than you think, he reflected, remembering again the dirty deals he had discovered Mayor Johnson had been engaging in for the past decade. The envelope he had planned to mail the day Melissa had shown up at the Wilson Building still sat in the locked bottom drawer of his desk.

"And how are you and Bridget? You guys planning to do anything exciting for the holidays? Are you eating Thanksgiving with her family or with yours?" she asked before taking another sip from her cup.

And here was another topic he'd rather avoid entirely. He was enjoying his time with Melissa; he really didn't want to talk about his girlfriend right now, or be reminded that he was avoiding thinking about Bridget.

"We'll probably eat with her family," he said with a

shrug. "My mom usually heads to North Carolina to have Thanksgiving, and Bridget's family is really serious about spending the holidays together. It's a big thing for them."

"You don't sound excited at the idea though." She eyed him. "*What?* You don't like her family?"

He rolled his eyes. "They're fine. They just take . . . effort, you know? Being the one black dude in the house and probably one of five black dudes in whole town of Avon for three straight days can get a little tiring."

"Let me guess," she said, peering up at the ceiling, "you get asked lots of questions about 'that hip hop music' and whether you prefer to be called African American or black."

He chuckled. "Last Christmas, Bridge's mom asked me to explain Kaepernick's NFL protests. 'What's with all the kneeling, Jamal? Can't he find another way to do it?' It dragged on for a good hour."

"Oh, man!" Melissa giggled. "I can only imagine. I've never had to deal with that when Derrick and I eat with the fam during the holidays, but we have our own brand of awkwardness now." She went somber. "My dad was much more into celebrating Thanksgiving and Christmas than Mama. And now that I don't talk to him anymore . . . well, the holidays aren't what they used to be. I can't get excited like I used to."

Jamal lowered his coffee cup. "I'm sorry, Lissa."

"Don't be sorry!" She shrugged again. "What's done is done. Dad chose to trade his old life with us for a new one. Now if Derrick could just accept that fact, I'd be a lot better off."

Their coffee date ended soon after. Jamal walked her to the coffee shop door and onto the sidewalk. By now she was wearing her coat again and had draped a scarf around her neck. Jamal exhaled, seeing mist sprout in the air. It had been almost seventy degrees outside a week ago. Now the fall weather was officially announcing itself, bringing a heavy chill with it.

"That was nice," Melissa said, turning to him and smiling. "We should do it more often."

"Whenever you want. I'm here," he replied—and he meant it.

"You know, every time we talk, I realize just how much I don't know about you," she began. "I mean . . . I know surface details. I know your mom and your girlfriend's name. I know where you grew up and what school you went to. But I never realized how much I don't know *you,* Jay, and you and I have chilled together so many times it's not even funny. Does that sound crazy?"

He slowly shook his head, gazing into her eyes. "No, it doesn't," he answered softly.

"It's so messed up!" She tossed her braids over her shoulder. "I'm glad I'm finally getting to know you though. It took too damn long!"

They stared at one another for another few seconds. His eyes involuntarily dropped to her full lips. He wanted to kiss her goodbye. He wanted to kiss her so bad he could almost taste it.

The whole time they'd sat in the coffee shop, Jamal could feel a chemistry erupting between them, an almost magnetic pull that surely she could feel, too. But he reminded himself once again that they were both in relationships. Just because he felt an attraction didn't mean he could or should act on it. So instead of kissing her, he leaned forward, and wrapped a brotherly arm around her in a half hug.

"I should get back to the office. It was good seeing you, Lissa."

"It was good seeing you too, Jay!"

And he wasn't sure, but he could have sworn he felt her

lips brush his cheek, making the skin tingle there. He leaned back and stared at her.

"Talk to you soon," she said, before turning and walking back to her car.

Meanwhile, Jamal stood mutely on the sidewalk, feeling like his twelve-year-old self would at that moment.

Melissa Stone just kissed me goodbye.

He wiped his cheek and gazed down at his fingertips to prove it to himself, amazed to find red lipstick there.

Chapter 19

Derrick

"Drinkin' the usual tonight, fellas, or are y'all switchin' it up?" Ray asked as he walked up to the table where Derrick and Ricky sat.

He had to shout to be heard over the music and the couples on the dance floor.

"Imma switch it up. A glass of Hennessey White sounds good," Ricky said, slumping back against the booth's leather padding.

"Give me a shot of Tennessee Honey, Ray," Derrick mumbled.

This was one of the few nights that more than a dozen people were at Ray's Bar and Lounge. It looked like someone had decided to throw a birthday party there, filling the space with balloons and forty- and fifty-somethings who danced to eighties and nineties hits.

Ricky was currently staring wide eyed at a man in a red pleather suit doing the cabbage patch to Bobby Brown's "Prerogative."

Though the partygoers seemed to be having a good time, Derrick was starting to feel claustrophobic. He wasn't sure if it was all the people, or the anxiety that seemed to plague him today—hell, that seemed to plague him for the past *few* days—but he felt the overwhelming urge to escape. He just wanted to get out of here, to be any place but this smoke-filled lounge.

But I damn sure don't wanna go home, he thought.

Melissa was at their apartment at that very moment grading papers with Brownie nestled in her lap. But he didn't feel at peace when he was with her anymore. Their apartment was a place of tension, filled with unspoken words and barely repressed anger. Hell, according to the vet, even Brownie felt it. He was probably grooming himself like crazy at that very moment.

Derrick wondered what Morgan was doing right now. She had mentioned she had tickets to the Wizards game for tonight. Though he had turned her down, he now wished he hadn't. It certainly would have made for a more enjoyable evening than this.

"So you gonna talk, or just keep staring into your drink?" Ricky asked after they had been sitting silently at their table for almost ten minutes. "You're the one who told me you wanted to meet up."

"Sorry," Derrick said. "I've just got a lot on my mind."

"When do you not?" Ricky asked with a chuckle before raising his glass to his lips and taking a sip. "You and Lissa still arguing?"

"That shit is like . . . constant. I can't even ask her a simple question anymore. Yesterday, I just asked her who she was meeting with for coffee and she got all defensive. Turned it around on me and it turned into another damn argument! And when we aren't arguing, it's these strained silences. I hate it!"

"But y'all have been through this before, Dee. It'll level out. It always does."

Derrick slowly shook his head. "Nah, this feels different. I don't know what it is about this time around, but it feels like we keep hitting a wall with each other."

"Again, I've heard this shit from you before. But every time you—"

"I know what I'm talking about, Ricky. Lissa and I have known each other for damn near forever, but it's like . . . like we can't communicate anymore. People grow up, and sometimes . . . sometimes they grow apart. Maybe that's what we've been doing all along. It's hard to accept it, but that shit is the truth."

"What are you trying to say? You ready to call it quits with Melissa?"

Derrick rested his elbows on the tabletop. "Shit, I don't know! I don't know if I'm ready to call it quits, but sometimes I wonder if this whole thing could be easier."

"Easier than what, nigga?"

"I wonder whether it would be . . . you know . . . easier with someone else, with a woman who gets the man I am today, and doesn't keep reminding me of the man I used to be."

"And you know for sure that this woman exists . . . that some mess wouldn't come up with her too?"

"No, I don't know that for sure, but I'm starting to wonder if it would at least be worth a try to look . . . to see what else is out there."

He wondered what type of girlfriend Morgan would be. He doubted she would see him working at the Institute as a burden or a pointless waste of time. And she didn't carry the same baggage about his work that Melissa did because of her father. He wouldn't have to explain to Morgan on a daily basis why he'd chosen his career path and why he could never walk away from the Institute. And he liked how laidback Morgan was.

Like how Lissa used to be, he thought forlornly.

Morgan was a chill, funny chick he could easily see

snuggling with on the couch on the weekends. But she had the beauty and the body that made a guy want to take it from a couch to the bedroom to do a lot more than snuggle.

Oh, man. This was the second time he had thought about Morgan tonight. This was starting to become a habit.

Ricky squinted at him and lowered the glass from his mouth. "You're not . . . you're not thinking about stepping out on Lissa, are you?" Ricky asked, like he was reading Derrick's mind.

"No! Hell, no!" Derrick shouted over the Boyz II Men ballad that now had the couples slow dancing on Ray's parquet dance floor. "I would never cheat on my girl, man. You know that's not in me!"

"People say that all the time, Dee. There's a lot of things they claim they would never do until they're faced with a hard decision—and then they do it." He took another drink from his glass. "Believe me. I know that shit."

Derrick inclined his head. "And just what have you done lately that you thought you would never do?"

"It ain't just *one* thing. That's the problem. It's a lot of stuff that has me thinking, 'Ricky, what the hell are you doing, man? Have you lost your damn mind?' "

"So don't be all cryptic. Tell me what it is."

Ricky sucked his teeth. "It's stupid. I feel dumb even saying the shit out loud."

"Come on! If you can't tell me then who the hell else can you tell? It's me—Dee. I'm not gonna judge you."

"Well," Ricky began tentatively, rubbing his thumb over the lip of his glass, "I've been . . . I've been helping out a cop."

Derrick's eyebrows shot up almost to his hairline. "*You've* been helping out a cop? Like . . . a police officer?"

"What other cops do you know who aren't police officers, Dee?" he asked sarcastically.

"But you hate cops!"

"I know. I know! But her sister went missing and she needed help finding her—"

"*She?*" Derrick grinned slyly at his friend. "Okay, now it's starting to make sense. I guess this cop is fine too, right?"

Ricky nodded. "But that ain't the reason why I helped her. She said she thought her sister might have gotten mixed up in some shit . . . that she might be turning tricks, and she thought . . ." He looked around the club at the partygoers, the men at the bar, and the couples dancing only a few feet away from their table. He then leaned toward Derrick, lowering his voice to a whisper. "She thought Dolla might be involved, that he might be the one pimpin' her out."

Derrick stared at his boy in utter shock. "Wait. Wait. Wait a minute! You mean to tell me you're helping a cop who's trying to go *after Dolla?*"

"She's not going after him! She just wants to get her sister back. And as it turns out, he *is* keeping her at his crib and he's making her—"

"But he's not gonna know the difference, Ricky. He's not gonna care. Bruh, have you fuckin' lost your mind? If he finds out what you're doing, he could kill you!"

"You don't think I know that?" Ricky exclaimed. "I told you, I know what I'm doing is stupid as hell! But she reminded me about Desiree and how I didn't help her. I thought . . . I thought this was finally a chance to . . . you know . . . do the right thing."

Derrick's face softened.

"And now . . . and now I think I'm starting to get sucked into this mess for other reasons."

"Other reasons like what?"

"I don't know what it is about her, but . . . she got into my head, Dee. And not just because of her little sister being in trouble like Desiree was. Last night, she started kissing on me, rubbing on me like she was ready to get it poppin', and I wanted to do it too, but I just . . . I just couldn't. And you know that's not me! If a girl is down, I'm down too—especially a fine ass broad like this one. But this time, I stopped myself." He dropped his eyes to his glass. "It didn't feel right."

Derrick stared at his friend in silence for several seconds, pursing his lips.

In the two decades that he'd known Ricky, he'd never seen him have any real feelings for a woman. Even Ricky's girlfriends had seemed as disposable as a five-dollar razor; he'd often move on to the next chick without any sadness or regret, with little to no afterthought. But for Ricky to risk his life and his livelihood for this cop, there had to be something more substantial between him and her, something that went beyond mere attraction.

"Well, it sounds like to me you're starting to have feelings for her, bruh."

At those words, Ricky's eyes shot up from his glass. He glared at Derrick.

"What the fuck you mean?" he asked angrily, like Derrick had just called his mama a whore.

"I mean exactly what I said. You like her so it's not easy to just separate—"

"I barely know her, Dee. I can't like her like that." He shook his head in denial. "Nah, it's probably because all the shit that's swirling around her. My dick didn't want any part of that mess! I don't want to get involved with her any more than I already am. I helped her find her sister. I can walk away now with a clear conscience. I did my part. It's time to just end this shit."

"You're probably right." Derrick finally took a sip of his Jack Daniel's. "You know I'm not a fan of Dolla, but as long as you work for him, hooking up with a cop would definitely put your ass in jeopardy—not to mention a cop who has beef with him."

"I told you I know, Dee. You're preaching to the choir, man! I made my decision. My little drama with Officer Fuller is over. I'm done!" he said, draining the last of his drink.

Derrick gazed at his friend warily, wondering if Ricky would stick to his declaration.

Derrick arrived home a couple of hours later. When he pushed open the front door, he saw the apartment was cloaked in total darkness; Melissa had already gone to bed for the night. In the past, Melissa might have waited up for him. Maybe he would've found her reclining on the bed in one of her negligees, ready to give him a little midnight lovin' before they fell asleep, but tonight that obviously wasn't the case. When he turned on the hallway light, the only person who came to greet him was Brownie who purred softly, rubbing himself against Derrick's leg.

"Hey, buddy," he said, running his hand over Brownie's ears and back.

Derrick crept down the hall to his and Melissa's bedroom. He pushed the door open, wincing as it loudly creaked, sounding like the lid of a coffin. As expected, Melissa was fast asleep on her side of the bed, curled into almost the fetal position. He walked into their bathroom and undressed before returning to the bed and finding her in the same spot where he'd left her.

He lifted the sheets and eased onto the mattress and she stirred a little. He looked at her, seeing only the dim outline of her features in the darkness: her button nose, her slender neck, her long eyelashes. This beautiful woman was capable of bringing him the most sublime joy and making him feel utterly useless. He wished they could get back to the good times. He hoped the connection they once felt hadn't been permanently severed.

Derrick eased across the bed and lightly kissed her shoulder. She shifted, turning onto her stomach. He then kissed the base of her neck and she raised her head and squinted at him.

"What are you doing, Dee? I'm trying to sleep, baby," she whispered.

"You don't want me to kiss you?"

She loudly grumbled. "Dee, please don't start. It's almost midnight and I have to be up early, okay?" she murmured, before burying her face in her pillow. "Just go to sleep."

He rolled onto his back, feeling rejected and frustrated yet again. It would take another hour until he finally fell asleep.

Chapter 20

Ricky

At the ringing of his front doorbell, Ricky stumbled out of his bedroom, bleary-eyed and annoyed.

He had fallen asleep only an hour ago, after tossing and turning for most of the night. He had been tossing and turning for several nights, unable to quiet his chaotic thoughts. He kept thinking about Simone and the last time he'd seen her. He remembered the promise he'd made and the one he'd refuse to make. In his dreams, he kept replaying their kiss in the driver's seat of his Mercedes—the way she'd tasted, the feel of her breasts against the palms of his hands, and how it would've been so easy to slide inside her, if only he'd kept his damn mouth shut. His eyes would flash open and find himself lying in bed alone, half-mast and furious.

The waking hours weren't much better. He was losing his ability to concentrate at the restaurant and Club Majesty. Throughout the day, while he walked the floor or sat at his table on the mezzanine, his gaze would shift to the restaurant or strip club's entrance, wondering if Simone would stomp through the front door to ambush him, to ask him why he hadn't returned any of her text messages or phone calls in more than a week.

But Simone didn't come to the restaurant or the club, which was good for him. He needed to put some distance between himself and her, at least until he figured out the situation between them, if you could even call it a "situation." Though he reacted strongly to her, he constantly had to remind himself that he barely knew the woman.

A few of his employees had noticed the change in Ricky—how he got more easily distracted, how he was quicker to catch a temper or reprimand someone for a mistake. Some had even questioned him about it.

"It's nothing," he'd murmur. "I'm fine. Worry about yourself."

But he wasn't fine and they all knew it.

". . . it sounds like to me you're starting to have feelings for her," Derrick had said more than a week ago, but Ricky knew that wasn't true. The only thing he felt for Simone was sexual frustration.

Maybe getting a piece might help, he now wondered as he walked down the hallway to his apartment's front door.

He hadn't had sex in almost three weeks, which was the longest he'd ever gone without smashing a chick in quite a while. Maybe cleaning the pipes was just what his mind and body needed. Maybe that could help force Simone out of his head.

Ricky knotted the belt of his robe as the doorbell rang again.

"I'm comin'! I'm comin'! Goddamn," he muttered tiredly, strolling down the hall. "Who the hell just shows up to someone's place at two a.m. anyway?"

He finally drew near the front door and looked through his peep hole into the apartment corridor. He did a double take. His mind must be playing tricks on him because he could swear he saw Simone standing out there.

He really must be obsessing about that girl.

"Ricky, you in there? Come on! Open up," she said, pounding her fist on his door.

He quickly undid the deadbolt then the bottom lock and whipped his door open.

It was indeed Officer Simone Fuller standing on his welcome mat, wearing an oversized hoodie and skinny jeans.

"What the hell are you doing here?"

She gave a small smile. "That's an interesting way of saying hello."

"Well, it's in the middle of the night and I wasn't expecting fucking house calls. Excuse me if I forgot my manners," he answered sardonically. "How did you find me anyway? How do you even know where I live?"

"If you can find me, I can certainly find you. We've got databases for those things."

He should've known.

"So you're pulling my DMV records now? *Why* are you here, Simone?"

"Because I wanted to see you, and you weren't returning my phone calls."

"I didn't return them because I had nothing to say to you. I haven't run into Skylar again. I told you that I would call if—"

"I *am* worried about Skylar. Of course, I am! But that's not why I'm here." She took a step toward him and peered over his shoulder into his living room. "Can I come in?"

He shook his head. "No, you can't! Whatever you have to say to me, you can say it right here," he insisted, pointing to the floor.

She shrugged. "Fine. Have it your way." She then wrapped her arms around his neck, stood on the balls of her feet, and kissed him.

He was caught off guard at first, wondering why her

lips were on his. But confusion was replaced with lust within seconds. He wrapped one hand around her waist and used the other to cup her bottom, grabbing a handful. He kissed her back and they quickly went from a languid pecks and nibbles, to dueling tongues and panting.

Despite his proclamation only a minute ago that she couldn't come into his apartment, Ricky practically lifted Simone off her feet, carried her over the threshold, and slammed the door behind them. They landed with a thud against the entryway wall and console table near the door where he kept his keys, loose change, and wallet. All of it went clattering to the hardwood floor.

He quickly disrobed and she did the same, tugging down the zipper of her hoodie, showing that she wasn't wearing a shirt or a bra underneath. Both his robe and her hoodie went flying in some unseen direction. She started to unzip her jeans and push them down her hips, but she didn't get to finish. He was kissing her again, fondling her breasts and rolling the hardened nipples between his thumb and forefingers.

She moaned, and that moan was like a whip being cracked over his head, urging him to go faster, to make her moan even louder. He shoved her jeans down to her knees, revealing the black satin briefs underneath. He eased his hand past the elastic waistband and delved between her thighs.

She was wet already. He could feel it against his fingertips. He began to toy with her, to stroke her there and she twisted her hips and eased her legs open in ready invitation as much as the jeans around her knees would allow. He toyed with her even more even as they kissed, increasing the speed of each stroke, playing her like an instrument.

And she sang like one too. Her whimpers and moans grew louder. She gripped onto the edge of the console but couldn't stand still, shifting her hips, backing away from him then easing forward.

"Mmm, that feels good," she whispered hotly, licking her lips, closing her eyes. "Do that again, baby."

He grinned because he knew he could do a lot better than "good." Simone was about to get the full Ricky Reynaud experience.

He stepped back and abruptly turned her around, making her face the wall and lean over the wooden console. This time *she* was the one caught off guard. She stared over her shoulder at him quizzically.

"What are you doing?"

He could hear a hint of unease in her voice. He placed a finger to her lips and shushed her.

"Trust me," he said before kissing her neck then nibbling her shoulder.

She smelled exactly like she did the night he first spoke to her: musk mixed with vanilla and a floral fragrance he could now pinpoint as lavender. The scent made his mouth water.

Ricky took her hands and pressed them against the entryway wall. "Don't move," he ordered, and like a good little police officer, Simone followed his command.

He shifted his kisses from her shoulder to the nape of her neck, running his tongue over the glossy skin. He cupped her breasts and squeezed them gently as the kiss trail descended lower and lower, past her shoulder blades, down her spine, and right above her ass where he was delighted to find a silver-dollar-sized tattoo in the shape of a purple butterfly.

Well, look at that, he thought. This woman was full of surprises—but so was he.

He roughly tugged her panties down to her knees too, getting an up-close-and-personal view of her delectable ass. He slid his hands down her hips and playfully nipped one cheek then the other, making her yelp.

"Oww," she said with a chuckle, twisting away from him. "That hurt."

"It was supposed to."

"I liked the kisses better though."

"You like me kissing your ass, huh?" he asked, doing as she requested, reverently kissing the same spots that he had just nipped with his teeth.

"Much better," she said with a smile, gazing down at him over her shoulder.

Her hands were still braced against the wall. He urged her to lean forward, to bend over the console table. He then switched from kisses to licks, teasing the junction between her thighs and her ass, alternating between the two. This time, she didn't just whimper, she groaned. She cursed and called out his name. She begged for him to stop, then begged for him to keep going. She was even wetter than before. He could not only feel it against his mouth, but taste it. Her legs started to tremble. Her thighs tensed against his mouth. She started to make a keening sound. That's when he knew it was time.

He quickly reached for his wallet and pulled out one of the condom packets inside. He had the condom on in less than a minute and quickly rose from his knees, letting his boxer briefs fall to his ankles. He arched her hips, positioned himself behind her, and entered her soon after. The feel of her around him was as good as he had anticipated, maybe better.

He cupped her breasts again, sucked her neck, and tried to start off slow, just to give her a taste—but she wasn't having any of it.

"Do it, Ricky. Give me what I came here for, baby," she whispered breathlessly.

He sped up the tempo.

"Faster! Faster! Show me what you got," she challenged between clenched teeth. "Give it to me!"

So much for measured control.

The next thing he knew he was grabbing her hips and humping for dear life, pounding her from behind like some porn star. Her hands still didn't leave the wall, but she arched her hips and back. She bent forward even more to give him better access, so that he could go even deeper and the sensation was almost overwhelming. Every nerve ending in his body seemed to concentrate in his dick. His sight started to blur. His heart felt like it might burst out of his chest. Though she shouted commands, he couldn't utter a thing, not one damn word. He was too busy gulping for air.

She came first, screaming out his name as she did it, shaking all over. Her arms went slack and she finally let go of the wall and dropped her elbows to the console table. He came a minute later.

Ricky didn't know what he yelled—more than likely something unintelligible. But it didn't matter what he said.

That was the best sex he'd had in a long damn time.

"So what's the story with the butterfly?" he asked as he and Simone lay in bed together. He trailed his index finger down the slope of her lower back.

They had already gone a second round—this time with her on top—and Ricky was simultaneously exhausted physically and invigorated from the endorphin high. Sex usually did that for him. It was better than a shot of Vitamin C and came with a kick just short of a snort of coke. He wasn't quite addicted to it, but he'd hate to imagine his life without sex. The lovemaking he'd had tonight had been particularly good though he couldn't put his finger on why. He hadn't done anything with Simone that he hadn't done with the other dozens of women he'd slept with in his thirty years on the planet. And she hadn't done anything particularly kinky or awe inspiring. But, again, there was just something about her.

Was Derrick right? Was he starting to have feelings for her?

Nah, Ricky though with a mental shake of the head, *not possible.*

Ricky Reynaud didn't fall in love—to the consternation of many women he'd dated in the past. He just didn't have the capacity for it. Besides, he barely knew Simone. And she was a cop, he reminded himself for the umpteenth time. It was just the sex euphoria talking. He hadn't gotten any ass in a while, and she'd come at the right time—pun intended.

Nothing more, nothing less.

Simone squinted at him and grinned. She pushed herself to her elbows to gaze down at him. "You making fun of my tramp stamp?"

"No, I wasn't making fun of it," he insisted, tugging her toward him and kissing her collar bone. "Just makin' conversation. You know . . . pillow talk."

She rested her chin on his chest and blew a gust of air that made her bangs flutter. "I got it when I was eighteen. I had just broken up with my boyfriend after he cheated on me, and I listened to the Emancipation of Mimi album about thirty-thousand times. Mariah Carey has that obsession with butterflies so . . . that was the tattoo I got to finally show the world I was over him."

Ricky frowned. "Wait. You got a butterfly tattoo because of Mariah Carey?"

"It wasn't *because* of her. I said she inspired it!"

He started to laugh and she grabbed one of the pillows from his leather headboard and thumped him over the head with it, making him laugh even harder.

"Stop making fun of me," she chided playfully and he wrenched the pillow out of her hands and tucked it behind his head.

Now she was laughing too. "Look, I know it was cheesy. But again . . . I was *eighteen!* Just chalk it up to the stupidity of youth. We do dumb shit at that age."

"That's true. When I think about what I was doing at eighteen, it wasn't pretty either. I did a lot worse than get a tattoo I didn't want to own up to later."

She raised her brows expectantly. *"Like?"*

He shook his head. "Yeah, no offense but I'm gonna keep that shit on the low, Miss Police Officer. I don't want my ass thrown in jail for something I did years ago."

"I'm sure the statute of limitations has already passed," she said dryly. "Besides, I'd be more worried about what you're doing now than what you did when you were a teenager."

"What does that mean? What am I doing now?"

She shifted off of him. "Come on, Ricky! You're working for Dolla Dolla. Don't play stupid."

"I'm not working for Dolla. He's my *business partner.* There's a big damn difference. We own a club together. That's all!"

"A club that's probably a front for shit that could land the average person in prison for twenty to thirty years."

"That's *his* business. It's not mine. I ain't got a damn thing to do with it!"

"That's complete crap, Ricky, and you know it."

The sex afterglow was fading. He was starting to get annoyed with her little lecture.

"By associating with someone like him," she continued, "you're setting yourself up for—"

"Do *you* take responsibility for everything the dirty cops do in this city, Simone?" He sat upright and slumped against the headboard. "Should I blame you every time a pig pulls over some poor dude and beats the hell out of him on the side of the road because he didn't show his license and registration fast enough?"

She pursed her lips. "That's different and you know it."

"No, I don't fucking know it! How the fuck is it different? If I'm responsible for Dolla, then how aren't you responsible for what they do, too?"

"You *knowingly* associate with a criminal, Ricky . . . with the man who basically kidnapped my little sister. You can't ignore that."

"And I'm trying to help save your sister!"

"Don't you get it? Saving just her isn't enough. A man like that needs to be taken down," she said, drawing close to his face.

"*Taken down?*" He barked out a laugh. "You're joking, right?"

"Do I look like I'm joking?"

He stared at her in shock. So she really was crazy, after all.

"Do you know how powerful Dolla is? How deep his connections are? *Nobody* can take him down, especially not you and me! What do you expect me to—"

"Damnit, stop making excuses and stop enabling him!" She pounded her fist into the mattress. "Stop being a front for his bullshit, Ricky. You're better than this!"

Her words cut deep. He didn't know how to respond so he didn't say anything at all.

She slowly climbed off the bed. "Look," she said, bending down to pick up her panties, "I didn't come here to argue with you."

"Then why did you come here?" he asked, watching as she slipped on her underwear.

She chuckled and reached for her jeans. "Why do *you* think I came here? To do what we just did. Next to agonizing about my sister, thinking about you and that magic stick of yours," she said, glancing down at his bare crotch, "had been keeping me up at night. I thought this would be the distraction I needed." She started to put on her jeans, tugging them up her legs.

"Glad to offer you a distraction," he muttered, trying his best to keep the bitterness he felt out of his voice.

So that's all he was to her? *A distraction?* He swore he didn't understand this woman.

"I guess it's 'peace out' then? You headed home?" he asked.

She raised her zipper and turned to him. "I didn't expect to stay the night. I figured a guy like you would be counting down the minutes until I grabbed my clothes and purse and headed out the door."

"A guy like me?"

"Isn't that usually the case?"

"You know me so well," he murmured. "A guy like me must be so easy to read."

"I'm just stating the obvious, Ricky." She paused and squinted at him. "You aren't mad, are you?"

No, he wasn't mad—he was furious. Furious that she could give him a lecture about how he should live up to his character one minute, then question his character the next. Yes, he *usually* preferred women not to spend the night, but he resented all these assumptions she was making about him. Just who did she think she was?

"*Did you* want me stay?"

He shrugged and turned away, giving the illusion of indifference even though he wanted to shout at her. He wanted to tell her that he didn't have time for this shit, and he wasn't going to apologize for the decisions he had made, and she wasn't going to make him feel guilty for being the man that he was. He wanted to tell her that she had no right to barge into his apartment and his life and stir up all these emotions and open doors he thought he had sealed off a long time ago.

She walked around the bed and sat on the mattress beside him.

"Do you want me to stay, Ricky?" she repeated.

He did, but he wasn't about to tell her that. Instead he reached for the digital clock on his night table. "It's three a.m.," he said holding up the clock for inspection. "Metro is closed and you shouldn't be driving on the road this late. It's not safe."

She looked at the clock then at him.

"You can stay tonight. Better to get some sleep and drive after the sun is up."

He could tell she was holding back a smile. She knew what he really meant, but thankfully, she pretended that she didn't. Simone nodded. "You're right. I should sleep and drive when I'm more refreshed. Good idea."

She undressed again and climbed back in bed beside him. She snuggled up against him beneath the sheets and he wrapped an arm around her shoulder. Within fifteen minutes, they both fell asleep.

Chapter 21

Jamal

"Hey, Gladys," Jamal said as he strode into the mayor's office.

He smiled down at Mayor Johnson's secretary who was sitting primly at the large desk near the entrance, typing away at her keyboard. Even though it was the end of the day, she looked as fresh and alert in her crisp white blouse and stiff snowy white bob as she had when he saw her at 8 o'clock that morning.

"Working late too, huh? I stopped by to see the mayor. Is he in?"

She stopped typing and stared at him blankly. She seemed to hesitate before she finally nodded. "Uh, y-yes. Yes, he is, but he's . . . he's busy at the moment, Mr. Lighty."

"Oh, well, Mayor Johnson asked me to stop by before I left for the day. He said it was important." He glanced at the mayor's closed office door. "I'll just wait for him here, if you don't mind."

He strolled to one of the leather sofas on the other side of the waiting area. He began to pull out his cell phone from his suit jacket pocket.

"Actually," she called out as he lowered himself to one of sofa cushions, stopping him mid-motion, "it was an unexpected meeting, I believe, and it might be a while before he's done. You'd . . . you'd probably be better off . . . umm . . . coming back tomorrow, Mr. Lighty."

Jamal realized for the first time that Gladys's smile was tight, almost forced. She looked nervous for some reason, almost desperate—like she really wanted him out of that room.

"Oh. Well . . . okay, I'll just . . . try again tomorrow then." He rose to his feet, tucked his cell back into his pocket, and began to walk back toward the waiting room entrance when a door opened behind him. Jamal turned and stared in surprise at the three men who strolled out of the mayor's office into the waiting room.

One was a short young man—even shorter than Jamal. The two others were hulking dudes who looked like linebackers on a college football team with their barrel chests and thick arms. They were all wearing jeans and T-shirts and had this menacing air about them. Jamal couldn't say for sure, but he suspected men like these weren't constituents complaining to the mayor about their electric bills. They weren't members of the neighborhood watch either.

He wondered who they were. He wondered if they were Dolla Dolla's men.

"He'll be waitin' to hear from you," the short, skinny one called over his shoulder at Mayor Johnson who stood in his doorway. "Don't make him wait too long. You feel me?"

The mayor dropped his eyes to his Florsheims and gave a barely discernable nod.

The trio gradually made their way to where Jamal stood near the waiting room's entrance.

"Hey, don't I know you, nigga?" the skinny one called

out, jabbing his index finger at Jamal. "Haven't I seen you around somewhere?"

Jamal didn't respond. He didn't know where he could possibly have run into this character. Jamal began to shake his head, but stopped when the young man snapped his fingers.

"Yeah, you tight with Pretty Ricky, ain't you? I seen you at his strip club on S Street in Northwest."

Jamal's eyes widened. If he knew Ricky then these were *definitely* Dolla Dolla's men. He couldn't believe they were bold enough to show up here at the Wilson Building.

His gaze shifted to Gladys, who was now gawking at him. When she realized her mouth had fallen open, she snapped it shut. He then looked at the mayor who was staring at him, too.

"You mute, motherfucka'?" the skinny one barked, sneering up at Jamal, baring his buckteeth. "Didn't you hear me ask you a question!"

"No, I'm not mute," Jamal finally answered, glaring right back at him. "I just don't know anybody named Ricky," he lied. "I don't know what you're talking about."

At that, the skinny one began to laugh. "Yeah, okay. My bad then." He glanced over his shoulder at the two large men standing behind him. "Come on, y'all. Let's get the fuck up out of here. I'm hungry. Y'all want some chicken wings?"

"Sounds good to me, T. J.," one of them said with a nod.

T. J. cast one more contemptuous glance at the mayor before striding past Jamal into the hallway. He was then followed by the two other men. One bumped Jamal's shoulder as he passed.

"Move the fuck out the way," he grumbled, making Jamal grit his teeth in frustration. Jamal then turned to see the mayor still looking at him.

"Thanks for stopping by, Sinclair," the older man said.

"No problem, sir," Jamal murmured before glancing at the retreating backs of the men who were now headed down the hall toward the elevators. "I got your message from earlier. You said you wanted to see me, but Gladys mentioned it was a bad time—"

"No, right now is fine." The mayor shook his graying head. "Please, come in." He gestured him into his office.

Jamal stared at him apprehensively. The mayor seemed unaffected by what had just transpired. Three thugs had just walked out of his office literally seconds ago and he was behaving as if it had never happened.

"Please come in, Sinclair," he repeated.

Jamal walked across the waiting room and stepped through the doorway into an office that was about three times the size of his and much more expensively decorated with cherry wood and leather furniture.

"Have a seat," the mayor said, gesturing to one of the leather chairs facing his desk. Just as Jamal lowered himself into the chair, the mayor shut his office door and strolled across the room. He then walked to a cabinet and opened one of the doors, revealing several liquor bottles and a row of glass tumblers. Jamal watched as the mayor removed a bottle of Jack Daniels and set it on his desk.

"Would you like some, Sinclair?" the mayor asked, twisting off the bottle cap.

Jamal blinked. "I'm . . . I'm sorry, sir?"

"Would you like something to drink?" the mayor asked again in a louder voice before gesturing to the glass he was now pouring. "I don't know what you usually drink. So many folks are all about wine nowadays. But I'm old fashioned; I like the hard stuff—especially after the day I've had. I've got it all here: whiskey, scotch, bourbon, vodka . . . I make sure I stay fully stocked."

"Uh, Jack Daniels is fine, sir," Jamal said, shifting uncomfortably in his chair.

The mayor grabbed another tumbler from the cabinet and poured Jamal a glass. He handed it to him before falling back into the chair behind his large, mahogany desk. Instead of looking at Jamal as he sipped, he stared out the window facing the busy D.C. street, staring at the people and cars streaming five stories below.

Jamal waited patiently for him to say something, to say *anything*. After all, the older man had called him in here for a reason, conceivably. When he didn't say a word, but continued to gaze out the window, Jamal shrugged and took a drink.

"Do you know those men who just left my office?" the mayor asked, still not looking at him.

"I don't believe so, sir."

"They seemed to know you though." He slowly turned his chair around to face Jamal again. "Do you know who those men were, Sinclair?" he repeated with a sharper edge to his voice.

Jamal nervously licked the last bit of Jack Daniels that lingered on his lips. He gradually nodded. "I . . . I think I do."

"You think you do," the mayor repeated. He laughed, reclined back in his chair, and took another drink. "Oh, don't be modest, son! Of course, you know who they are. You know *lots* of things, don't you? You see, I've been keeping an eye on you. You've been busy lately. I'm aware of your little . . . research project, shall we say. I know that you've been asking questions of people in other divisions in the mayor's office. You've been asking them questions about me."

Jamal swallowed. Suddenly, it started to feel very hot in the mayor's chambers.

The mayor tilted his head. "Did you think it wouldn't get back to me? My people are loyal, Sinclair. They tell me what foxes are sniffing around my hen house."

"Sir, I . . . I don't know what you mean."

The mayor narrowed his eyes. "Don't insult my intelligence, son. It's offensive."

"I . . . I'm not trying to offend you," he stuttered. "I really d-don't know what you're talking about."

"Well, let me refresh your memory."

He watched as Mayor Johnson yanked open one of his desk drawers, reached inside, and pulled out an envelope—a large manila envelope. He tossed it onto his desk and it landed only inches away from Jamal.

Jamal instantly recognized his own handwriting. He recognized Phillip's name and the mailing address to the *Washington Recorder* headquarters.

At the sight of the envelope he'd thought he'd hidden in a locked office drawer, Jamal went silent. All the blood drained from his head. He could feel the Jack Daniels that he had drank only seconds ago rise in his throat. He was dangerously close to hurling it right there on Mayor Johnson's desk and Afghan rug.

"How did you . . . how did you find . . ." His words faded as he sputtered helplessly.

The mayor shrugged. "Nothing happens in this building without me knowing about it, Sinclair."

"You went into my desk? You dug through my things and—"

"Your desk, your phone, and your computer are all the property of the D.C. government. If you want to keep something private, don't keep it here," the mayor replied icily.

How could he have been so dumb? Why had he kept the envelope at the office and not back at his place?

"Besides, don't act self-righteous like your privacy was invaded, like *you* were violated. What about me, Sinclair? How should I feel knowing that you've been slithering around here like some snake? How should I feel knowing you were about to stab me in the back?"

Jamal didn't answer him. He couldn't. He felt like he had been forced into a corner, and there was nothing he could do to get out of it.

"So when were you planning to mail this little bombshell?"

"I . . . I hadn't decided," Jamal finally said, deciding he had no other choice but to be honest at this point. "I wasn't sure if I was going to mail it at all."

The mayor cocked an eyebrow. "*Why?* Were you planning to use it for blackmail instead?"

"No! No, of course not! I would never do something like that."

"Yes! Yes!" the mayor said, waving his hand dismissively. "That's what people always say—until they're backed into a corner. But situations change, Sinclair. It happens all the time." He lowered his now empty tumbler to his desk, thumping it against the varnished wood. "So here is what I will tell you. Hopefully, it can help you determine what you plan to do with the information you gathered, since you claim to be undecided." He sat upright in his chair. "If you know who those men are that just left my office, then you also know who they work for. You know what they are capable of. They will protect their boss's interests, which, for now, are also *my* interests. If anyone gets in the way of what he and I are trying to accomplish, that person will in turn get taken care of. Do you understand me?"

"Y-yes, sir."

"I'm not issuing a threat, mind you. I'm only explaining the reality of the situation. I would hate to see anything happen to you, Sinclair. Or for anything to happen to your beautiful girlfriend, Bridget. That's her name, isn't it?"

Jamal nodded limply.

"You're a smart young man with lots of potential. I wouldn't have promoted you to deputy mayor if I hadn't known this . . . if I hadn't believed it. And people make mistakes. I know this, too. But I ask that you smarten up and do it quickly. Don't make a mistake like this ever again, or my partner will make sure it doesn't happen a third time."

Jamal felt sick to his stomach. His heart was racing.

"Can I continue to rely on your cooperation? I'm willing to accept your word on it."

"Y-yes, sir," Jamal replied, "you can . . . can depend on me."

"Good. I'm glad we understand each other. And you never know, there could be a benefit in the end for you in all of this." He slapped his desk. "I'm glad we had this conversation, but I really have some work I need to finish and a few more phone calls I have to make."

"Uh, sure. Sure. I should be heading home anyway. I'll let you get to your work." Jamal pushed back his chair and rose to his feet. He began to walk toward the closed door. His legs were unsteady with each step he took.

"Oh, and Sinclair!" the mayor called out as he tugged the door open. "Learn to use a little more stealth when you're asking questions. It's not enough to be smart. You need to learn to be cunning, too, if you really plan to have a future in this world."

"Yes, sir," Jamal whispered.

Jamal's drive home was a trying one. He almost clipped a car while changing lanes and barely missed hitting a pedestrian who had stepped into the crosswalk just as he was about to make a right-hand turn.

"You almost killed me!" the woman screamed and Jamal held up his hands and mouthed "Sorry" at her through his windshield. She gave him a sneer and kept walking.

He was distracted during the entire drive. His mind kept harkening back to his conversation with the mayor.

Though Mayor Johnson had claimed he wasn't threatening him, that's *exactly* what the older man had done. He had basically told Jamal that his life would be in danger if he decided to do anything with the info he had gathered. So would Bridget's.

What the hell have I gotten myself into?

Derrick had warned him to quit, to walk away when he still had the chance. Why hadn't he listened?

As Jamal stepped through his front door, shut it behind him, and dropped his keys in the ceramic bowl in their entry way, he heard the sound of laughter. It was Bridget's.

"Oh, come on! That's cheating," she said between giggles.

"No, it's not!" a familiar male voice answered. "I'm just better at it than you are."

Jamal closed his eyes and silently groused. Bridget's ex, Blake, was here. Of course that bastard psychically knew the worst possible day to show up at their apartment. Jamal wasn't in the mood to put up with Blake or any of his bullshit.

He yanked off his suit jacket and strode down the hall into their kitchen where he found Bridget standing at the kitchen island with a wineglass in her hand. Blake was sitting on one of the stools with a half-filled glass at his elbow. They were both huddled over Bridget's iPad.

"Oh, honey, you're home!" she said, looking up from the screen and grinning ear-to-ear. "I didn't hear you come in!"

"I can see that," Jamal replied dryly as he loosened the knot in his tie and walked toward them.

"Blake was in town this weekend and decided to stop by. We were wasting time on the goofiest app game until you got home."

"You're only calling it goofy because you're losing," Blake chided before sipping white wine from his glass and tapping the iPad screen.

"Anyway," Bridget said, playfully slapping Blake's shoulder, "he wants to take us out to dinner at this new Greek place downtown I've been wanting to try for months. We have to leave here in the next fifteen minutes to make our reservations."

"My treat, bro! It's my way of saying thanks for you guys taking me to that Creole place with Bridge's parents last month."

"I appreciate that, Blake, but . . . uh . . . not tonight. I'm beat. I had a . . . a pretty rough day. Sorry, but I'm gonna have to skip dinner."

"I understand." Blake shrugged. "Well, maybe you and me could go, Bridge. No point in the reservations going to waste. I'm sure Sinclair won't mind—would you, Sinclair?"

Actually, I would mind, Jamal thought. *I've had the worst fucking evening and I'd like to talk to my girlfriend about it.*

But he didn't say the words aloud. He didn't want to come off like the overbearing boyfriend. Instead, he turned to Bridget, hoping that she would pick up on the mental vibes he was sending her way, hoping she would pick up on the fact that he needed her desperately at that moment.

"It's up to you, sweetheart," he said, trying to sound casual. "I won't hold you back if you really want to go."

He watched as Bridget glanced between him and Blake. "Well, okay, I'll go to dinner. But only because you already made the reservation. I just won't stay out that late."

"*Why?* Is it a school night?" Blake asked with a snicker.

She set down her wineglass, walked around the counter, and stood in front of Jamal. "Thanks for being such a great guy, sweetie!"

"No problem," he whispered.

She looped her arms around his neck, rose to the balls of her feet, and gave him a quick peck. "I'll bring you back some baklava." She then released him and turned to look at Blake. "Guess we better head out."

"Guess so," he said with a nod before finishing the last of his wine.

"Bye, honey," Bridget called as she grabbed her coat off the back of one of the stools and strolled toward the front door.

"Catch you later, bro," Blake said, slapping Jamal hard on his back, making his jaw clench.

Chapter 22

Derrick

"Are you ready?" Morgan asked, poking her head into Derrick's office.

"Yeah," Derrick called back, glancing at her over his laptop screen, "just give me a couple more minutes to finish up. I'll meet you downstairs in the lobby."

She nodded before disappearing back into the hall. He could hear her receding footsteps and the squeak of tennis shoes from the boys who ran up and down the corridor. Most of them were headed to the courtyard to hang out with their friends or play ball, or they were on their way downstairs to the cafeteria to get in line for dinner.

Derrick and Morgan were about to grab dinner themselves.

They had dinner at least twice a week now, walking to one of the local carry-outs or driving to a restaurant or bar downtown. They'd started doing it after he'd stayed and worked late one night. Metro delays had left Morgan stranded at the office, too.

"Might as well grab something to eat if we're stuck

here. Or am I being inappropriate again?" she had chided playfully.

The truth was he liked having dinner with Morgan. He liked her easy conversation and how she made him laugh.

It was an alternative to what it was like to eat dinner with Melissa nowadays—when they *did* manage to eat dinner together. Most of the time he ate alone at the dinner table or in front of the television while she ate in their home office, grading papers or going over her lesson plans while handing over bits of food to Brownie.

He suspected hiding in her office was her excuse to avoid having to eat dinner with him in silence. After a while, he started to eat dinner before he got home so he could avoid the whole awkward situation. At least, when he ate dinner with Morgan, he wasn't eating alone.

Derrick finished the last email and shut down his laptop. When the screen went black, he rose to his feet, grabbed his satchel, and walked toward his office door. He stepped into the hall and noticed one of the boys walking past. He recognized the young man's lanky build and his confident gait.

"Hey, Cole!" he called out and the young man turned around to look at him.

"Oh, hey, Mr. Derrick!" Cole said, halting in his steps.

Cole was only a few inches shorter than Derrick but had to weigh about fifty pounds less. Maybe he would fill out in the future, but for now he was all bones and wiry muscle. Derrick still marveled at the fact that Cole had bucked to Tory, who had to be about two hundred pounds of pure muscle, in order to defend Morgan.

"How's it going, Cole?"

"It's all good. No complaints." Cole shrugged.

They both stared at one another awkwardly.

Since the fight in Morgan's workshop class and since Morgan had told him about Cole's status among the other boys, Derrick had been keeping a closer eye on the newest addition to the Institute. He had asked Cole's other teachers how he was doing in his classes, and they all said he was doing fine.

"He's a smart kid. Everybody likes him," the English instructor had told Derrick only last week.

Derrick observed how the other boys behaved around Cole, and while it was true that Cole seemed to command respect from most, if not all, of the other boys at the Institute, Derrick still couldn't find anything so out of the ordinary about it that it warranted his intervention.

He was just a well-liked kid.

"Where you headed?" Derrick now asked him.

"To get in the dinner line," Cole said, pointing to the stairwell. "I heard they're serving corndogs tonight. I was trying to get down there early before they run out."

"Sounds like a plan. I was gonna head out and grab some dinner, too. Mind if I walk down with you?"

Cole shook his head. "Nah, I don't mind."

They walked to the end of the hall and Cole pushed open the stairwell door. He took the lead and Derrick brought up the rear as they walked down the stairs to the floor below.

"So how are things going for you, Cole? Settling in okay here?"

Cole nodded absently. "Yeah, everyone's cool. I thought coming here might suck, but it's better than I thought it would be. Everybody here seems chill. Well . . ." He paused and glanced over his shoulder at Derrick. "Almost everybody."

"Yeah, I'm sorry about your run-in with Tory."

"It's nothin'. He didn't scare me none. Besides, I wasn't going to stand by and let him disrespect Miss Owens like that. She don't deserve that shit . . . I mean, stuff," the young man quickly corrected.

Derrick eyed him as they reached the next landing. "Sounds like you think highly of Miss Owens. She's your favorite teacher here?"

"Oh, yeah! She told me she could help me apply for colleges next year if I wanted. Miss Owens is straight up dope!"

Derrick fought back a smile, amused to realize the young man seemed to be just a bit smitten with his workshop teacher.

He watched as Cole shoved open the lower level steel door. They emerged into another hallway. At one end was the lobby. At the other end was a small cafeteria where the smell of tonight's dinner wafted toward them.

"Hey, Derrick! There you are," Morgan said, turning away from the waiting desk and smiling at him. "Hey, Cole!"

Cole didn't respond to her greeting. Instead, he frowned and glanced at Derrick. "You're going to dinner with Miss Owens?"

Derrick nodded. When the young man's unnerved expression didn't budge, he raised his brows. "Is that a problem?"

"Nah, it ain't a problem." Cole swallowed, making his protruding Adam's apple bob in his skinny neck. "Just make sure you treat her right, okay?"

Now Derrick was frowning. He opened his mouth to respond, to tell Cole that he and Morgan were just coworkers. They weren't dating. But Cole abruptly turned around and headed in the opposite direction to the cafeteria. His easy, self-assured stroll was gone. His posture looked stiff. His head was bowed.

Morgan walked toward Derrick. "What's up with Cole? He looked pissed for some reason. Did something happen?"

Derrick turned to her. "Not much. I told him you and I were headed out to dinner."

"And that made him mad?"

"I think he has a crush on you."

"What?" She looked at the young man again and laughed. "No! He's just a sweet kid. I told him I'd help him apply for college next year if he wanted."

"If you say so, Miss Owens," he murmured as they walked back toward the lobby, making her punch his shoulder playfully.

A half hour later, Derrick strolled into a noisy sports bar in Northwest, holding open the glass door for Morgan as she stepped in front of him.

"Why thank you, sir," she said, pausing to tug off her jacket.

They were immediately met by a waitress who ushered them to one of the high boys along the far-right wall.

Considering Derrick had never heard of this place before, he was surprised to see how crowded it was. The voices of all the patrons even eclipsed the rock music playing on the restaurant's speakers.

"It got a profile or a good review in the Washington Post or somethin', I think," Morgan explained after climbing onto her stool and throwing her jacket over the back. "Anyway, the last time I was here, the food was bomb so I wanted to come back."

He nodded as he looked over the menu. "I can't vouch for the taste but it sounds good based on what I'm seeing here."

They ordered their meals soon after and fell into a familiar and easy conversation that he was quickly getting used to falling into with Morgan. They talked about the boys at the Institute, her class, and the petty drama among some of the instructors. They even talked about the basketball season.

He noticed they studiously avoided any conversation

about Melissa or Morgan's ex. They hadn't agreed not to talk about them but for some reason their names never came up. It was a relief, actually. He was tired of complaining about how bad his relationship with Melissa had gotten lately; it was nice to talk to someone who didn't know her and seemed to have no interest in hearing more about her.

When their food arrived at the table, they quickly dug in. They'd ordered a platter with an assortment of buffalo wings. He'd also gotten a basket of nachos while Morgan had ordered fried pickles. As he watched her eat the pickles, closing her eyes and moaning in almost orgasmic delight, he grimaced.

"I'm glad you like them, but those fried pickles look nasty as hell," he said, reaching for his beer.

"Don't judge until you've walked in my shoes!" She shoved the basket of pickles toward him. "Go ahead. Take a bite."

"Hell naw!"

"Oh, come on! How do you know that you don't like it if you don't try it?"

"I don't need to jump off a building to know I won't like hitting the ground," he replied sarcastically before taking a drink.

She laughed, making her pretty face light up. It was almost arresting, seeing her smile like that.

"Derrick, are you really comparing eating a damn fried pickle to jumping off a building?"

"Both seem the same amount of crazy." He shrugged and reached for one of the wings sitting in the plastic basket at the center of their table. He took a bite. "Why not compare 'em?" he asked between chews, licking the sauce off his lips.

"Come on, just try it!"

He shook his head and took another bite of chicken wing. "Nope."

"How about if I dip it in some Ranch?" she asked, dunking it into one of the plastic cups.

"That makes it worse."

"Come on!" she said, playfully waving the fried pickle in front of his face. He tried to shove it away but she did it again, smearing Ranch dressing on his lips. She started to cackle and he couldn't help but laugh too as he grabbed her hand, trying to wrestle the pickle away from her.

"Dee," he heard someone say behind him.

He turned, still grinning, and looked over his shoulder to find Mr. Theo standing behind him, staring at him quizzically.

Derrick's grin withered at the sight of Melissa's father.

The older man's eyes shifted from Derrick to Morgan who was still holding a pickle to Derrick's mouth.

"Hey!" Derrick said, dropping Morgan's wrist like it was on fire. He quickly reached for one of the table napkins so he could wipe the dressing smeared on his bottom lip. He then hopped off his stool. "Uh, hey, how are you doing, Mr. Theo?"

He embraced him stiffly.

"I'm . . . doing okay. Me and Lucas were just grabbing something to eat," Mr. Theo said. His gaze still lingered on Morgan. He broke it to point off into the distance at one of the booths across the restaurant. "Lucas was in the mood for some buffalo wings."

"This is a good place get them," Morgan volunteered. "They're really good here. I'd recommend the blackberry jalapeño wings."

"Is that so?" Mr. Theo asked, staring at her again with unmasked interest.

"Uh, this is Morgan. She's the new woodshop instructor

at the Institute," Derrick muttered, feeling embarrassed for some reason, like Mr. Theo had caught him in the middle of doing something wrong or unseemly. But he wasn't doing anything wrong. He and Morgan were simply eating dinner—that's it.

Nothing wrong with that, he told himself.

"Morgan, this is Mr. Theo Stone. He used to be director of Boys' Institute before I came on board."

"Oh!" she exclaimed, leaping to her feet, offering her hand for a shake. "Oh, man! It's so good to meet you! Derrick has told me so much about you."

"Has he now?" Mr. Theo asked, shaking her hand and giving a side glance at Derrick. "Well, what did he say?"

"He said you had a big influence on him. He's worried he can't fill your shoes, but I told him he's got nothing to worry about," she said, rubbing Derrick's shoulder and gazing up at him. "He's a good guy. Stuff like this comes to him naturally."

"Yeah, Dee is definitely a good guy—an *honest* one, too," Mr. Theo said.

At those words, Derrick blanched a little.

Was Mr. Theo calling him out, right in front of Morgan? She knew she was talking to Derrick's mentor, but Derrick had neglected to mention that Mr. Theo was also his fiancée's father. All of Morgan's smiling and touching couldn't be making the best impression on the older man. It had to be leading him to the wrong conclusion about what was going on between Derrick and her.

"Well, I'll leave you two to your dinner," Mr. Theo said, pointing to the baskets at the center of the highboy. "Dee, I'll see you around, son. Okay?"

"Okay," Derrick said with a nod then watched as Mr. Theo walked toward the men's room.

"He was so nice!" Morgan gushed, hopping back onto her stool. "Glad I got to finally meet him."

"Yeah," Derrick said absently, taking his seat. "Glad you did too."

Derrick tried to enjoy the rest of his meal and Morgan's company, but he couldn't. His eyes kept drifting to the booth where Mr. Theo and Lucas sat, focusing on the back of Mr. Theo's head and Lucas, who was so intent on chowing down on his basket of buffalo wings and waffle fries, he was unaware that Derrick was staring at them the whole time. But Morgan noticed the difference in his behavior.

"Are you okay?" she asked while sucking sauce from her fingertips.

He blinked, shifting his gaze away from Mr. Theo's booth back to her. "Yeah, I'm good. Why?"

"Because I've basically been having a one-sided conversation for the past fifteen minutes. Something on your mind?"

"No. Well," he glanced down at his wristwatch, "I should probably get our waitress and ask for the check. I've got to get in the office a little earlier than usual tomorrow."

She nodded. "Okay, let's get the check then."

Ten minutes later they were walking to the restaurant's doors when Derrick abruptly halted. Morgan realized he was no longer following her. She turned around and looked up at him in surprise. "What's up?" she asked. "Forgot something?"

"Go ahead outside," Derrick said, shrugging into his coat. "I just want to ask Mr. Theo a question right quick. I'll be out in a couple a minutes."

"Yeah, no problem." She pushed open the glass door and stepped into the cold night, buttoning her jacket as she did it. After she did, he turned back around and headed straight to Mr. Theo and Lucas's table.

"Mr. Theo!" he called out, making Mr. Theo stare up at him in surprise. "Lucas, hey! I just wanted to come over and say what's up," he said, thumping Lucas on the back. "I didn't get a chance to earlier."

"Well, hey, Derrick!" Lucas said, smiling and wiping his mouth with a napkin. "Theo told me you were here with a friend and—"

"Not a friend," he rushed out, quickly correcting Lucas. "Just . . . just someone I work with at the Institute."

"Really?" Mr. Theo asked, biting into one of his waffle fries. "Y'all looked pretty friendly to me."

Derrick's brows lowered. His anxious smile disappeared.

So Mr. Theo had been thinking what he'd suspected all along.

"Yeah, well, things can look one way, but in reality, they're very different."

"That's true," Mr. Theo said between chews. "Melissa met her yet? Your coworker, I mean."

Derrick shook his head. "No, no reason to. Anything about the Institute leaves a sour taste in her mouth, anyway. The less I talk to her about it, the better off she seems."

Mr. Theo shrugged as he reached for another waffle fry. "It's up to you."

"Well, uh . . . I should get going. Morgan is waiting for me. It was nice seeing you guys."

"Nice seeing you, too, Dee," Lucas said.

Mr. Theo didn't respond.

"See ya'," Derrick said, shoving his hands in his coat pockets. He walked toward the restaurant door and had been about to push the door open, but paused when he heard Mr. Theo call out, "Dee! Dee, hold up!"

He turned to find Mr. Theo standing behind him.

"Can I talk to you for a quick sec, son?"

Derrick nodded. "Of course."

"Look, you're a grown man. What you do is your business," Mr. Theo began.

He was giving him the same look he'd given him in the old days when he found out he'd broken curfew or gotten into a fight with one of the other boys at the Institute.

"And Melissa may not be talking to me anymore," Mr. Theo continued, "but she's still my daughter and she is still *your fiancée*. So whatever you're doing with that girl—"

Derrick loudly groused. "Mr. Theo, there is nothing . . . I mean *nothing* going on between me and Morgan! I told you, she's—"

"Look, just remember the last time we talked and what I told you. Figure out what you really want, and be willing to make the sacrifices to get it. But don't lie, and definitely don't try to have it both ways. You can end up hurting people. I speak from experience."

He then thumped him on the shoulder and turned away, leaving Derrick to stare mutely at his retreating back.

Chapter 23

Ricky

Ricky hadn't smashed this much in years, maybe in his whole life—certainly not with one woman, the *same* woman. But he and Simone were burning up the sheets on the regular in the past few weeks like two horny teenagers with no parental supervision. At his apartment in Brookland . . . at her efficiency near Eastern Market . . . while they were parked in deserted lots at one in the morning . . . in the back office at Reynaud's after closing, they made love like their lives depended on it.

He got to know her body and her smell. He knew what she tasted like and what took her from a whimper to a soft moan to screaming out his name in ecstasy.

Of course, it was reckless. They shouldn't . . . *couldn't* be seen together. Ricky didn't want to consider what the aftermath would be if Dolla Dolla found out he was screwing Simone. He also wondered what the other officers at Simone's police department would say if they found out she was sixty-nining with the business partner of one of D.C.'s highest-profile criminals. But Ricky and Simone rarely spoke about the repercussions of what they were doing. Instead, they talked about other things.

When the sex was over and they stared tiredly at the bedroom ceiling, they would lie in each other's arms and share stories about their childhood, past loves, and old favorites. He talked about things he hadn't spoken about in years, including Desiree. He told her about teaching his little sister to ride a bike. He thought she would get good momentum by doing it on a hilly roadway near their old apartment. But soon, he'd figured out his mistake when his screaming sister almost rolled into oncoming traffic when she couldn't brake. He'd had to rescue her.

"At least that time I saved her," he muttered forlornly.

He told Simone about the blackberry cobbler his dead grandmother, Mama Kay, used to make every Christmas and how he used to pair it with vanilla ice cream. He was sure if ambrosia of the gods ever existed, it would taste like Mama Kay's blackberry cobbler.

Simone told him stories, too. She shared one about a favorite pair of shoes she had when she was eight-years-old.

"They were pink, glitter jellies with little buckles on the side," she told him. "I loved those damn shoes."

She'd worn them all summer almost exclusively, and during the fall and winter with socks. When it was snowing outside, her mother had put her foot down and told her she wasn't going out the house with those jellies, even if she had socks on. But Simone had snuck out the house and worn them anyway.

"I don't know if you realize it, but I can be a bit stubborn when I want to do something," she'd admitted.

"No, *really?*" he'd deadpanned, earning a thump with her pillow.

Simone said she had walked to school and arrived with toes almost blue from frostbite. The school nurse had called her mom and told her to take her to the doctor to get her feet checked out.

"That was the end of my jellies," Simone had told him with an almost whimsical sigh. "Mama threw them in the trash after that."

He listened to her stories with fascination, wanting to learn more about her. The sex wasn't enough. He wanted to understand this woman who occupied so much of his thoughts. And with each story he felt like he was peeling away another layer of her. Simone was thoughtful but stubborn. She respected rules, but was also a risk taker. She fought to hold onto the reins of control in her personal and professional life, but a passion and fire burned inside her that refused to be contained—hence, her hooking up with someone like him. When they were alone, she was his total focus—but he wasn't hers. Inevitably their conversations would always veer back to Skylar, a topic he wished they could avoid.

"Mama's doctor put her on antidepressants. She's taking Skylar being gone so badly," she'd told him last week. "We've got to get her out of there, Ricky."

We? When exactly did this turn into a "we," he thought, but didn't say it aloud.

Skylar wasn't his sister. And yet, he found himself keeping an eye out for Skylar whenever he was summoned to Dolla Dolla's apartment. He had even gone wandering down the hall in search of her after he'd made up a lie that he needed to use the bathroom. When he'd gone to another one of Dolla Dolla's parties on his property in Virginia, he even tried to sneak upstairs again but he'd been stopped by T. J.

"Nah, nigga," T. J. had sneered, blocking his path up the stairs, "paying customers only."

Ricky had rolled his eyes and shrugged. "Well, how much then?"

T. J. had laughed coldly. "Too much for you!"

He'd told her the next night in bed what had happened, how T. J. had turned him away.

"We just have to try something else. Another chance will come along," she'd insisted. "I know it will."

"I've looked for Skylar. I've asked about her. Even when I tried to get her to leave, she wouldn't do it! What more can I do?"

"She wasn't thinking straight. You said so yourself that they keep her locked in that room, strung out on who knows what! She didn't realize what she was saying!"

"Simone, come on! She—"

"Ricky," she'd said, clasping his cheeks and gazing into his eyes, "*please* don't give up. You're all I've got!" She'd given him one tantalizing kiss then another. "Don't give up, baby. I *need* you," she'd whispered as she wrapped her hand around his dick and kissed him again, sliding her tongue into his mouth. He instantly hardened in her warm palm. "If anyone can do this, I know you can."

Sucker, he'd thought with disgust even as she began to stroke him and he closed his eyes, letting the blissful sensation take over him. He was officially a sucker—a slave to the pussy.

Months ago, he had warned Jamal against something similar, about being brainwashed by his girlfriend, Bridget.

"No pussy is worth half the shit she makes you do," he recalled lecturing his former friend.

Ricky found great irony in the fact that he was doing a lot more for Simone than Jamal had ever done for Bridget. Jamal wasn't risking his life for his girl, while Ricky ran the serious risk of catching a bullet to the head if Dolla Dolla figured out what he was doing. But for Simone, it was worth the risk.

He realized now that when men like himself did stupid things for a woman, it wasn't just for a "piece of ass." He could get that anywhere. No, if you were willing to put your life on the line, you did it for something of higher value, you did it for love.

He could admit it after a few months of knowing her; he was in love with Simone, though he would never tell her that. He also didn't have the heart to tell her that he'd probably never run into her sister again since Dolla Dolla seemed to be going out of his way to keep her under lock and key now.

That's the thing about love, Ricky realized. You could love someone so much that sometimes you wanted to protect them from everything—including the truth.

Ricky stepped out of the elevator doors and walked down the carpeted hallway to Dolla Dolla's apartment on Wisconsin Avenue. He hadn't told Simone he'd gotten the text from the drug kingpin about an hour ago, ordering him to come here tonight. He knew she'd be on edge until she heard from him, until she discovered whether he'd seen her sister again.

When he approached the door at the end of the hall, he rang the gilded button, listening to the chime of the bell on the other side of the door. He patiently waited for the front door to open. When it did, he saw one of Dolla Dolla's bodyguards, Melvin, frowning down at him quizzically.

"What you doin' here, Ricky?"

"Dolla called me and told me to come here." He paused and leaned to look around Melvin's wide shoulder. "He's here, ain't he?"

Melvin nodded his bald head. "Yeah, he's here. But he's asleep."

Asleep . . . or passed out, Ricky wondered.

Dolla Dolla had been partying pretty hard lately, doing rails of coke, smoking weed, and drinking enough alcohol for three men. He was in a celebratory mood, though

Ricky wasn't quite sure why. Ricky suspected that all the partying was starting to catch up with him, though.

"You sure he told you to come here . . . tonight?" Melvin asked again.

"Yeah!" Ricky loudly grumbled. "Can't I just wait for him, Mel? If his ass wakes up and I'm not here, he's gonna be pissed—and I don't wanna get cussed out."

Melvin nodded, opening the door farther and waving him forward. "Come on, man. Just wait for him in the living room, I guess."

Ricky made his way to the living room, like Melvin said, descending the stairs.

"You okay in here by yourself?" Melvin asked.

Ricky nodded absently. "Yeah, I'm cool. I'll keep myself occupied. Don't worry about me."

Melvin nodded then walked off, strolling down the corridor and disappearing into the one of the rooms.

Ricky looked around him and sucked his teeth. He could be home right now in bed sleeping, maybe even sleeping next to Simone, but instead he was here waiting for a grown ass man to wake up from a nap.

He strolled to one of the sofas—a chinchilla-covered piece that looked vaguely like a decapitated Muppet—and sat down. He glanced at his wristwatch. He'd give it an hour. If Dolla Dolla didn't wake his ass up by then, then he was leaving.

Ricky settled back onto the sofa and pulled out his cell phone. He brought up one of his sports apps and started to check the basketball scores, but paused a few minutes later when he heard a thump behind him. He turned slightly to find someone standing in the kitchen. One of the stainless steel doors to the industrial-sized refrigerator stood open and Ricky could hear someone rummaging around the shelves, like they were looking for something. Slowly the door closed, revealing a young woman ripping open a pack of deli meat. She shoved one slice into her mouth then another, gobbling them with a ravenous zeal, like she hadn't eaten in days. Ricky stared at her in shock.

"*Skylar?*" he called out to her.

She jumped at her name, almost dropping the package of deli meat to the tiled kitchen floor. She stared back at him mutely.

He didn't know it was possible but she actually looked worse than the last time he'd seen her, a couple months ago at Dolla Dolla's fight night party. She looked skinnier; her cheek bones were more prominent and her eyes were more sunken. The luster in her skin was gone. Her hair was matted to her scalp. She looked like she'd aged about ten years.

Seeing her made him stick to his stomach. She reminded him so much of Desiree, of the last day he'd seen her alive.

"Skylar?" he said, rising from the sofa and walking across the living room to the kitchen.

She didn't recognize him from the last time they'd spoken—or at least, if she did, she didn't acknowledge it. As he drew closer, she took one hesitant step back, then another, almost bumping into the refrigerator.

He glanced over his shoulder, on the lookout for the bodyguard or Dolla Dolla himself. He saw neither of them so he rushed toward her.

"Come on! Let's go. I can get you out of here but we've got to do it now," he said, reaching for her.

She shrank back. "No! No! I don't want to go with you!"

"Skylar, listen to me. I'm a friend of your sister's . . . of Simone's. She sent me to look for you. She asked me to bring you home."

"*Simone?*" she repeated through dry, cracked lips. She blinked up at him. "My . . . my sister, Simone?"

"Yes, your sister Simone has been looking for you for . . . for *months*. She figured out what happened to you and asked me to look for you here. I can take you home, but you have to leave *now*. You understand me?"

He glanced over his shoulder again when he thought he heard footsteps. Luckily, no one was standing there. He yanked the package of deli meat out of her hand and tossed it onto the kitchen's marble island. Ricky did the math in his head, calculating how much time they had, how much of a lead he had to give her before he told one of the guards that he'd seen her run out the door. He figured she'd need at least five minutes in her dazed state, maybe a bit longer to make it downstairs and out the door before Dolla Dolla's bodyguards ran after her.

He grabbed her shoulders.

"When I open the front door, run to the elevator down the hall. Take it to the first floor and go through the lobby, straight to the revolving doors. Don't stop for anybody. You hear me? I'll call an Uber now and have him pick you up at the corner of Friendship and Montgomery. It's only a couple blocks from here. The driver can take you to—"

"I'm not going anywhere! I like it here," she said, cutting him off and making him furrow her brows.

"What the hell do you mean you like it here?"

He looked her up and down with a mix of disbelief and disgust. Maybe Simone was right. Maybe her sister had been brainwashed.

"Skylar, they're not treating you right. They're not feeding you! Look, I know you're scared to leave, but when you get home, your sister will make sure you'll—"

"I don't want to go home to her! I don't want to go home to Mama either! They're always telling me what to do," she mumbled petulantly. "They treat me like a baby. But he doesn't treat me like a baby." She gave a smile. "He treats me like a woman. He says I'm sexy. That he can get me in videos with Lil Yachty and the Migos. He said they like girls like me."

Ricky slowly shook his head, now bewildered. She was still hanging onto the dream that Dolla Dolla would make her famous? After all this?

"None of that shit is gonna happen, sweetheart. You have to know that."

"Yes, it is! Because when I meet them, I'll do *all* the things that Dolla taught me so they can't say no. They won't be able to resist me." She reached out to Ricky and ran her hands over his chest. She saucily licked her dry lips. "You want me to show you what he taught me? Want me to show you what I can do?"

Ricky cringed. He yanked her hands away and shook his head again. "He turned you out. He's never gonna get you in fucking music videos! He's just pimping you! He's going to use you up until there's nothing left, Skylar. You have to get out of here."

At that, her face changed. The sultriness disappeared and her blank expression returned. "What do you know?" She reached for the deli meat on the counter and shoved passed him. "You don't know anything. Just leave me alone."

"It's the drugs talking; it's not you," he called after her. "Once you get out of here—"

"You don't know me!" she hissed. "This is where I want to be. Tell my sister to leave me alone. I don't need her to save me. I don't *need* saving. Just leave me the fuck alone!"

He then watched as she strode back down the hall.

Chapter 24

Jamal

The gospel choir, clad in purple velvet robes adorned with gold tassels, reached its booming crescendo and the choir director raised his arms dramatically before clapping his hands over his head, bringing the song to an end. He turned to face the crowd and did a deep bow to a round of applause.

Jamal was one of many in the crowd politely clapping at the performance. Bridget was too.

"Well, that was interesting," she said dryly as she stood beside him. She leaned toward his ear. "I could have done without all the booty shaking and shouting though."

Jamal shrugged. "It was meant to be festive."

They were attending the pre-Christmas celebration held at the Wilson Building. The main gallery had been converted into a party space filled with Yuletide decorations, from the twenty-foot-tall Christmas tree near the staircase to the tinsel and twinkling lights hanging from the banisters and scaffolding near the glass ceiling.

Jamal hadn't wanted to attend; he hadn't been in the holiday mood frankly. Whatever Christmas spirit he had toward his colleagues was completely lost a few weeks ago in Mayor Johnson's office when he realized that, all along, he was being spied on by many of those very same colleagues. It was hard to get excited about the holidays when the mayor basically threatened his life. He had the sinking feeling that by agreeing to keep the mayor's secrets—even to protect his own hide—he had become part of the conspiracy. He was now entwined with the older man's twisted lies and corruption. Jamal was no longer an innocent bystander, but an accomplice to a crime.

He was no better than Ricky.

Hell, I practically am *Ricky*, he thought with disgust.

"Are you all right, sweetheart?" Bridget asked, taking a sip from her wineglass.

She had worn a deep green velvet gown tonight that complemented her red hair. She looked like an upscale Poison Ivy.

"I'm fine," he muttered before glancing down at his wristwatch. "I was just wondering how much longer we have to stay here before we can leave without looking rude. I'm just not feeling it tonight."

"You're kidding, right?"

He shook his head. "Why would I be kidding?"

"Look," she began, lowering her glass from her lips, revealing a smear of ruby red lipstick on the rim, "I can understand why you'd want to escape my business functions. Professionally, it doesn't benefit you to be there. But here, it's a completely different story, Sinclair. You need to get some face time with these people." She leaned toward him and dropped her voice down to a whisper again. "Who knows what potential donors you could meet lingering near the buffet table."

Jesus!

Did everything with his girlfriend have to turn into

some discussion about strategic career moves or running for office?

Melissa would never talk this way, he thought unhappily, finishing the last of his wine. She wouldn't give a damn that he might be messing up the chance to hobnob with potential donors. If he said he was tired and ready to go home, she'd laugh and say she was thinking the same thing, link her arm through his, and steer them to the exit.

He had been thinking a lot about Melissa lately. He hadn't talked to her in a couple of weeks even though they had exchanged a few inane texts. He wondered if she and Derrick were still fighting. He wondered if she was finally ready to throw in the towel and accept that the two weren't meant for each other.

"So whatever bad mood you're in, snap out of it." Bridget then glanced over her shoulder. Her face brightened; she pasted on a grin. "Don't look now," she said between her clenched pearly whites, "but the mayor and his wife are headed toward us."

Jamal flinched.

With a room filled with a few hundred people, he'd hoped to avoid having to talk to the mayor tonight. He had avoided talking to him directly for the past couple of weeks. He knew they'd have to do a few photo ops at tonight's party, but they only needed to exchange glances—not words. It didn't look like that would be the case though.

"Vernon . . . Bernice!" Bridget shouted. "It's so great to see you again!"

The mayor's wife, a plump woman in a too tight fuchsia gown, air kissed Bridget's cheek. "Why hello, honey, I thought I saw you standing here from across the room. You're hard to ignore in such a stunning dress!"

"Why thank you, Bernice! You look amazing too!" Bridget gushed. "I absolutely love you in that color."

Jamal locked eyes with the mayor, who was gazing at him like a cat watching a mouse skirt around its cage.

"Sinclair," Mayor Johnson said with a slow nod.

"Mayor Johnson," Jamal replied, dipping his chin stiffly.

"So how are you two enjoying the evening?" the mayor asked, turning to look at Bridget. "Having a good time?"

"Oh, we're having a fabulous time!" Bridget said.

"What did you think about the choir?" Bernice asked. "They're from our church. The choir director has been working with them for weeks to perfect their performance."

"Oh, it was amazing!" Bridget gushed. "I was just telling Sinclair that I haven't seen something so . . . so uplifting!"

Jamal side-eyed his girlfriend. *Laying it on a little thick, aren't we, sweetheart?*

"You two should come to our church," Bernice insisted, gently patting Bridget's arm. "See the choir perform again. And our minister is one of the best. He just fills you up with the Holy Ghost with his sermons! Why don't you come with us this Sunday?"

Bridget's green eyes widened eagerly. "Oh, we would love to—"

"I don't think we can make it this weekend," Jamal interjected, cutting off Bridget. "We're . . . uh, meeting up with my parents," he lied.

"Oh," Bernice said. The smile on her round face disappeared. "Maybe . . . some other time then."

"Absolutely. Thanks for the offer though," he added.

Bernice nodded and turned to her husband. "It was lovely catching up with you two, but we should probably circulate around the room, shouldn't we, Vernon?"

The mayor nodded. "You're right, honey. I've been meaning to catch Harry before he leaves." He thumped Jamal's shoulder then shook Bridget's hand. "You two enjoy the rest of your evening."

"Th-thank you, sir," Bridget called out weakly just as the mayor and his wife turned away.

When Jamal settled behind the wheel of his Audi less than an hour later, he could practically feel the anger radiating off of Bridget's petite frame.

"I'm sorry," he said as he shifted the car into drive and pulled onto the roadway. "I know I rushed you out of there. I just want to head home. I'm just . . . I'm just tired."

She didn't respond but instead glared out her passenger window at the pedestrians on the sidewalk.

He loudly exhaled. "Honey, don't give me the silent treatment. Not tonight, okay? I said I was sorry."

She mumbled something in reply.

"What did you say?"

"I said you're *always* sorry, Sinclair. You *always* do this. We go to these events and you completely blow it and humiliate me—"

"*Humiliate you?* How the hell did I humiliate you?"

"We went there to help your career!" she shouted, making him wince. "The mayor's wife was nice enough to invite us to their church and you were so . . . so rude. You actually turned her down! Who does that?"

Jamal lurched to a stop at the stoplight and stared in shock at his girlfriend who was fuming beside him.

"First of all, you're not religious. You don't even fucking go to church! Secondly, if we were there to help *my* career, then what the hell do you care if I turned down Bernice's offer? What does any of that have to do with you?"

Bridget blinked. "I care because . . . well, because I can't believe you would waste this opportunity to get closer to Johnson. I want to see you succeed, Sinclair. As your girlfriend, I have a right to be mad!"

"And thirdly," he continued, accelerating through the green light, "I didn't want to go to church with the mayor and his wife because I don't want to have anything to do with him outside of city hall. He's a corrupt asshole, Bridge!"

She loudly grumbled. "Oh, you don't know that for sure! Just because you saw him with—"

"I know it! I confirmed it and he confronted me about it. He practically threatened my life and your life if I didn't keep what I knew about him to myself."

The car compartment fell silent. Only the drone of NPR on the car radio filled the space. Bridget shifted in her chair so that she could look at him.

"What do you mean *he threatened you?* When the hell did this happen?"

"A few weeks ago," Jamal murmured. "I saw him in his office with Dolla Dolla's men and he knew that I realized who they were. The mayor also knew that I'd been . . . I'd been . . ." His voice drifted off.

"You'd been *what,* Sinclair?" she asked impatiently.

"That I'd been asking questions about him and his business dealings. Someone told him I'd been asking around. And he saw . . . he saw some papers that I had planned to send to the press."

"You were going to talk to the press?" she screeched. "Are you fucking insane? Why would you—"

"Look, none of that matters now! What matters is that he knows that I know how corrupt he is, Bridge. He knows and he's going to have me fucking killed if I tell anyone."

"Goddamnit," she said through clenched teeth, balling her fists in her lap. "Goddamnit! I told you to leave it alone. Didn't I tell you? I told you to mind your own fucking business!"

"Yes, you did, but I didn't, and this is the situation that we're in. So what the hell do you want me to do about it?"

"After we worked so hard," she mumbled, like she hadn't heard him, "after all this time . . . I can't believe you would completely destroy what we've built by being so . . . so stupid. Mayor Johnson could've been a huge asset!"

"*An asset?* Didn't you just hear what I said? He threatened to kill me . . . to kill *you* if—"

"Oh, stop being so fucking melodramatic! You're from the ghetto, aren't you? You've had people threaten you before."

Jamal was struck speechless.

"Besides, I don't care what threats he made. I only care about how much of my time you've wasted! I cannot believe this. Blake was right," she snapped, making him squint at her.

"What did you say?"

"I said Blake was right! He told me I had way too much confidence in you, that you probably weren't up to snuff. He said you weren't my equal. I just thought he was touting some racist shit—or he was jealous I'd moved on from him, but now I realize he was telling me the truth. We aren't equals, Sinclair! And I can't keep dragging you along. I need a man with goals and follow through, and frankly, you're not it!"

Jamal's hands tightened around the steering wheel.

Part of him was stupefied at what had just come out of Bridget's mouth, but the rest of him wasn't really surprised. He realized now why Bridget had hooked up with him in the first place. He was her little project she could show off to the world, the ghetto boyfriend who cleaned up nicely whom she could nurture and fuck on the side. She didn't love him as much as she loved the man she wanted him to become. And in the course of their relationship, he had changed nearly everything to be what she'd wanted. He had busted his ass to get the appointment to deputy mayor. He'd changed his clothes, dropped his friends, and had even changed his name.

How could he have been deluded for so long? Why should he stay with a person who only loved everything he wasn't—not what he was?

"Get out," he said as they drew to a stop at another red light.

"Ex-excuse me?" she sputtered.

"I said get the hell out of my car! I'm not listening to any more of your shit. You consider me a deadweight you've gotta drag along? Well, I'll make it easy for you—we're over! You don't have to drag my ass around anymore."

"You can't kick me out of this car, Sinclair!"

"I just did," he said icily, glowering at her. "And my name is Jamal, not Sinclair."

She unbuckled her seatbelt. "Fine! Fine, I'll get out then. Have it your way!"

He watched as she shoved open the car door and stepped onto the nearby sidewalk, almost tripping in her stilettoes. She leaned down and shoved her hair out of her face.

"By the way, that night that I came home late after having dinner with Blake wasn't because of a car accident near Union Station like I told you. It was because I had too much wine, and let him fuck me! I felt guilty about it, but not anymore, you fucking asshole!"

Jamal turned away from her. "The light's green. Could you please shut my door so I can drive?"

At first, she didn't respond. Out the corner of his eye, he could see her face go from pink to almost a bright shade of red in a matter of seconds. Veins bulged near her temples. "Fuck you, Jamal! Fuck you! Fuck you! Fuck you!" she yelled before slamming his door shut.

She was still screaming at him as he drove down the roadway.

Chapter 25

Derrick

I am not cheating on my girl.

Derrick repeated it like a mantra to himself almost daily. He did it when he and Melissa stood in front of the bathroom mirror every morning: she doing her hair or applying her makeup, he brushing his teeth or shaving—and both pretending like they didn't notice the other. He did it when he went out to dinner or to bars with Morgan at night. Every time he heard Morgan's laugh, gazed into her big green eyes, or tried not to stare at her breasts or her ass when she walked, he told himself that his feelings for her were completely platonic.

Cole had been wrong. Mr. Theo had been wrong. There was nothing going on between him and Morgan.

No, he still hadn't mentioned his friendship with Morgan to Melissa. And sure, he did lie occasionally and claim he was doing something else when he was really hanging out with Morgan after work, but that didn't mean anything. It certainly didn't mean he was cheating. He just didn't know if Melissa would understand the situation. He and Melissa already were going through some stuff. Why make it worse by giving her a reason to be suspicious or jealous of his relationship with Morgan?

That evening, he and Morgan decided to try a new place, an Italian restaurant in Northwest with soft lighting and leather booths. After they gave their orders to the waiter and asked for a bottle of Brunello, Morgan's phone buzzed. She looked down at her screen and sucked her teeth in disgust.

"You gotta be fuckin' kidding me," she mumbled before her fingers started flying. She furiously tapped the screen, making Derrick stop mid-chew.

"What's up?"

"My ex," she snapped, slamming her phone down on the tabletop. The table wobbled slightly as did the wine inside their glasses, swirling around and around. "He was supposed to come by last week to get the last of his shit, and *now* he's saying he wants me to bring it to him. Like I've got nothing better to do! He's lucky I don't just chuck it out my apartment window!"

"Didn't y'all break up a few months ago?"

"Yeah, but he keeps trying to drag this shit out. It's annoying as all hell!" She grabbed her glass and took a drink.

Derrick leaned back in his chair and gazed at her under the low lights of the restaurant. He cleared his throat. "So how did you . . . I mean . . . when did you . . . you know . . . when did you know it was over?" he asked, making her lower her glass from her lips and frown at him quizzically.

The question was out before he could take it back. Part of him wondered why he had asked it, but then the other part knew damn well why he had. It was a dilemma he also faced, one that he still didn't have the answer to.

"What do you mean?"

"When did you know it was time to break up with your man . . . that it was time to go your separate ways?"

She shrugged. "Well, I wouldn't say it was one moment or one day when I suddenly woke up and decided the shit wasn't working anymore. It just . . . well . . . built up over time. I knew it. And I'm pretty sure he knew it too, but one of us had to have the balls to say it out loud."

He nodded thoughtfully and took a drink too.

"Is there a reason why you're asking?"

He looked up from his glass, startled. "Huh?"

"Is there a reason why you asked me that question?" She tilted her head and cocked an eyebrow. "You and the bride-to-be having issues?"

He quickly shook his head. "No! No, we're not having issues . . . I mean, everybody goes through things. We've been through them before. I mean . . . couples have rough patches and it feels a little different this time but we . . ." His words drifted off. They sounded hallow and forced. He set down his glass and exhaled. He closed his eyes. "I'm just . . . I'm just fucking tired. I'm tired of being pissed off. I'm tired of seeing her pissed off at me. I'm tired of the silence. I am fucking tired of talking about the silence between me and her! I am just . . . I'm just *tired,* Morgan!"

"I was too. That's when I knew. That's when I knew it was time to end it."

He opened his eyes.

"When trying to make it work doesn't seem worth it anymore, it's just better to walk away, Derrick. Life is too short to be miserable!"

"That's easy to say, but it ain't that easy to do," he muttered. "We're engaged! We've got almost twenty years of history together and—"

"*So what?* What does any of that matter if it's not working out for you two *now*?"

"I love her," he said, and he meant it with every fiber of

his being. Melissa frustrated the hell out of him, but he still loved her. After all these years and all those moments they had shared, how could he not?

"And I love my ex too . . . sort of, despite all the shit he did! But it doesn't mean we should've stayed together. It doesn't mean our relationship was healthy or right for us, Derrick."

He pursed his lips.

"Let me ask you something. If you found a genie in a lamp . . ."

He narrowed his eyes at her. "*A genie in a lamp?* Come on, girl!"

"I'm serious! I'm making a point here. Just stick with me. If you found a genie in a lamp who could grant you only one wish, and the choice was between breaking up with your girl today, or continuing your relationship for the next five years in the same state it is now, which would you choose?"

He shook his head. "But I don't know if it'll stay the same. Things could get better."

"And you don't know if things will get *worse* either. Besides, that wasn't my question," she said, leaning forward. Her curly hair almost skimmed the top of her wine glass. "My question was, if he gave you a choice, which would you choose?"

Derrick held up his hands in surrender. "Break up, I guess."

"Then that's your answer."

"How is it—"

"It's where your head space is. I bet you've tried, right? To talk . . . to compromise . . . to love up on her. But it didn't work?"

He gradually shook his head.

"So now you're waiting around for things to get better,

but you gotta accept they may never get better again. If you're willing to accept that, then stay with her. If you're not, then it's time to bounce."

He pursed his lips, letting her words sink in. The waiter arrived soon after with their food. Their conversation drifted to other topics. He even laughed a few times, but in the back of his mind he kept thinking about what Morgan had said. His life as it was right now would be unbearable; it would be like a prison sentence if he had to do this with Melissa five more years. He'd be serving time all over again, much like he had when he was twelve-years-old. Did he really want that for himself? Did he want that for Melissa?

A couple of hours later, Derrick pulled up to the curb in front of Morgan's apartment building. He drew to a stop and gazed through the window at the brick exterior and its cement front stoop. A few young men milled about near the entrance, leaning against the railing, making him frown.

"You sure you don't want me to walk you inside?" he asked, peering over her shoulder.

She laughed. "I'll be okay. I know half of those dudes. They won't bother me."

He nodded. "All right. If you say so. I'll just sit here until you get inside though."

"You don't have to do that . . . but thank you."

He watched as she unbuckled her seatbelt and reached for the door handle. But she paused before pushing the door open and turned to face him again.

"I really had fun with you tonight—despite the heavy conversation."

Derrick gave a half smile. "Sorry for dropping that stuff on you, but I needed to talk about it, I guess. And I had fun with you too."

He always did.

"Just know that I've been where you are, okay? It's scary to try something new, especially when you've known the same situation for so long. But sometimes . . . *sometimes,* it's for the better. You don't know what else could be waiting for you."

He squinted at her. "Like what?"

"Like someone new. Like me."

He blinked. "Uh, Morgan, I'm real . . . umm . . . flattered but I don't . . . I don't know about that."

"Oh, I think you do." She placed a hand on his cheek, catching him off guard. "I think you've felt something between us for months now but you've been holding back, like I've been holding back. Because you're that kind of guy. And I respect you for it. But now that I know you're ready to move on, I think I should show you what could be waiting for you on the other side."

She then leaned forward and brought her mouth to his. It took him a few seconds to realize she was kissing him, that she was toying with his bottom lip.

Instead of pulling his head back or easing her away, which is what he should've done and what every alarm bell in his head screamed for him to do, Derrick did the opposite. He placed his hand at the base of her neck and leaned her head back so that the kiss could deepen. He slid his tongue inside of her mouth and she moaned and met his tongue with her own. The toying with his bottom lip became full on nipping. Morgan dropped her hand from his cheek to his chest, fisting the fabric of his sweater in her hand, dragging him closer to her.

After a few minutes, she ended the sultry kiss. They were both breathing hard, like they had just run a ten-miler and finished first and second place.

He gazed down at her, at her kiss-swollen lips and the

hungry gleam in her green eyes. He realized with both fascination and horror what they had just done.

"I'll see you tomorrow," she whispered before giving him a quick peck.

He then watched, dumbfounded as she shoved the car door open, slammed it shut behind her, and strolled up her apartment stairs, excusing her way through the crowd of young men who shouted greetings to her.

"Shit," Derrick whispered as the apartment door closed behind Morgan.

He was officially a cheater now.

Chapter 26

Ricky

Simone didn't want to hear the truth. He knew she wouldn't.

"Skylar doesn't want to leave," Ricky said. "I asked her and she told me outright that she wants to stay."

He watched as Simone shook her head, folding towels on her bed as he spoke. "No. That's not possible."

"Simone," he began as she shifted and turned her back to him, "listen to me, baby. She's just—"

"No, Ricky!" she yelled. "This is bullshit! It's bullshit!"

They were in Simone's apartment. He had stopped by with no notice, only to find her in a tank top and shorts, knee deep in housecleaning and doing her laundry. He could have told her by phone what had happened yesterday at Dolla Dolla's place, but he knew that breaking news like this had to be done in person. It was like hearing a relative had just died. He wanted to be there to hold her, to help her through the full cycle of grief: denial, anger, bargaining, despair, and then finally, acceptance.

"Why the hell would she want to stay there?" she cried. She was furiously folding clothes and towels again like she was some possessed housemaid. "It doesn't make any sense! He's keeping her prisoner! He's brainwashing her and—"

"He may have brainwashed her, but he's not keeping her prisoner. She could've walked out that front door that day. She could've done it at any point—no one was watching! But she didn't want to. She *told* me she didn't want to." He took a deep breath and loudly exhaled. "She told me too that she wants you to leave her alone . . . to stop trying to rescue her."

"She didn't mean that," she said, making him close his eyes and groan. "She didn't, Ricky! I *know* my sister. She said that the last time, but when I found her and brought her home—"

"Wait." He eyed her. "What do you mean 'the last time'? She's done this before?"

Simone didn't answer him. Instead, she folded a shirt then a skirt; her movements didn't pause. She stacked them neatly in the laundry basket.

"Don't act like I'm not talking to you. Answer me, damn it! Has she done this before?"

She didn't respond and Ricky stared at her, silently fuming. He wanted to yank the clothes out of her hands, to shake some sense into her. He was reaching his breaking point with Simone . . . with Skylar . . . with this whole damn drama. He grabbed her shoulders and whipped her around to face him.

"Damnit, will you stop fucking folding shit and look at me?"

"*What?*" she yelled.

He could see her denial had shifted to anger, but he was angry, too.

"Has she done this shit before, Simone?" he repeated slowly.

Simone pulled her arms out of his grasp and crossed them over her chest. She dropped her eyes to the carpeted floor. "Yes, she's run away a couple of times. But . . . but never like this. She'd be gone a few days with friends or a boy, but . . . she never just . . . just . . ." Her words drifted off.

"Why didn't you tell me this before? You made it sound like this was some—"

"Because I knew you'd be more willing to help when you believed she was some angel," she said, raising her eyes to glare up at him. "You'd help me save her when you believed she was an innocent Catholic school girl. If I told you she'd been expelled for giving blow jobs to the track team in the bathroom at her last high school, would you have helped me? If I told you I'd found a baggie filled with coke in her dresser drawer a month before she disappeared, would you have even listened to what I had to say?"

"To hell with that shit! Don't try to turn this around on me. You should've been honest with me. I put my neck out for you. The least . . . the *very fucking least* you could've given me was the truth!"

"Fine!" She flapped her arms. "I'll be honest. Skylar isn't perfect—and neither am I. She called me a pig sometimes, and I called her a snotty little bitch. She slapped me once when we argued about her bad grades, about her skipping school . . . and we fought—fists and all. She got high. She got drunk. She hooked up with boys *and* girls. She was a fucked up kid before this even happened. But that doesn't mean I can just leave her to this . . . this *nightmare,* Ricky. You know that! You remember what happened to Desiree and—"

"Will you stop fucking bringing up my sister?" he shouted. "Of course, I know what happened to her. I'll never forget that shit!"

"Well, if you know what happened, then you understand that—"

"Listen to me! Clean out your fucking ears and really

hear me, okay? I can see how Skylar's situation is just like Desiree's. I'm not stupid! When I looked into your sister's eyes, I saw my sister, all right?" he said, feeling his throat tighten. "I saw the same stubbornness. I saw that the drugs and the little soundtrack of delusional bullshit she had playing in her head were talking a lot fucking louder than me. Skylar blew me off the same way Desiree did. She doesn't want to be saved. You *cannot* save her, Simone. You can't!"

The fury disappeared from her expression. She dropped her hands from her hips.

"She has to want to do it . . . and right now, she doesn't. Maybe she will later, but for now please, just . . . just let this go. Just *stop!*"

She pursed her lips. He could see tears flooding her eyes. He reached out to her and tried to draw her close, but she shoved his hands away, refusing to let him comfort her. She turned her back to him and dropped her head, weeping silently. It pained him to see her cry, to see her so broken, but he couldn't lie to her anymore.

"I'm sorry," he said. "I didn't want to disappoint you or hurt you. I wanted to . . . I wanted to bring her home for you."

"I know," she whispered, wiping her eyes with the back of her hands and finally turning around to face him again. "I know."

"Can you do it? Can you let her go?"

She didn't answer him at first. Finally, she raised her reddened eyes to look at him. "I'll let her go . . . if you let *him* go. If you walk away and break all ties with Dolla."

Ricky frowned. How did they get on the topic of his business situation with Dolla Dolla? What did that have to do with any of this?

"He may not be forcing her to stay but he's enabling her . . . he's *abusing* her. He's doing it to all those girls! I can't turn a blind eye to that, and I don't see how you can either." She took several steps toward him. "Don't do business with him. Break off ties, Ricky—before it's too late."

"I told you before. Doing business with Dolla is how I make my bread. My restaurant is legit. People depend on me, on me keeping the restaurant and the club open. Do you know how many folks would lose their jobs . . . who wouldn't be able to pay their bills if I—"

"That money is dirty. His business is dirty, and it's only a matter of time before he ends up behind bars. I'm not saying you have to do it, but if you want anything . . . *anything* to do with me, you'll walk away."

"Oh, I get it. I couldn't save your sister so now you're done with me? Is that what you're saying? You were okay with me working with Dolla if it could help you get closer to Skylar, now me working with him is a problem?"

"I'm saying that if you insist on working for scumbag criminals, I don't want anything to do with you. That's what I'm saying."

He clenched his fists at his sides. He'd wondered if this would happen. If she would finally give him an ultimatum.

"So what is it? Are you going to keep working with him?"

"No. No, I won't do business with him anymore," he said, shocked to hear the words on his tongue.

"You mean it, Ricky?" She squinted up at him. She grabbed the front of his T-shirt and dragged him towards her. She gazed into his eyes. "You better not be fucking lying to me!"

He linked his arms around her waist, drawing her close so she was flush against him, so they were nearly heart to heart. "I promise that's what I'll do, if that means you'll let your sister work through her own shit."

"It's a deal then?"

"It's a deal," he said, leaning down to kiss her.

Ricky was a man of his word. He'd made Simone a solemn promise, and he would keep it. Besides, she was right. Dolla Dolla was taking his criminal empire in a direction Ricky didn't want to go. Sex trafficking? Drugging up teen girls and pimping them out to men? He didn't want a damn thing to do with that.

He planned to tell Dolla Dolla when he saw him that he appreciated everything he had done for him in the past, but he wanted out of the game for good. He wanted to finish paying the last he owed him for the seed loan to start Reynaud's. He'd tell him he didn't want to manage Club Majesty anymore. For the first time in his life, Ricky Reynaud was going completely straight; no more money under the table, stolen goods in the back room, and suitcases filled with drugs in the basement.

When Ricky arrived at Dolla Dolla's McMansion in Virginia for another fight night bash, he mentally rehearsed the words in his head as he walked up the gravel driveway. He didn't know what the drug kingpin's response would be when he told him his plans to go full legit, but he suspected it wouldn't be good. Dolla Dolla would probably get angry. He might even get violent.

Ricky just hoped he made it out of here tonight with all his fingers still attached—or at least, his limbs.

Ricky strolled through the French doors and made his way past the columned foyer to the great room where most of the partygoers were. Men laughed and shouted around him, but he wasn't remotely in a partying mood. He hoped Dolla Dolla was though. Maybe if Ricky caught him while he was drunk, high, and jubilant, his response to Ricky asking to get out of their business relationship would be a lot more tempered.

"Hey, Pretty Ricky, what you up to nigga?" Dolla Dolla

boomed from behind him as he stood in the great hall entryway.

Ricky turned to find the hulking, dark-skinned man striding toward him down the hall. A blunt was in one hand and a cognac glass was in the other. "You just getting here?"

Ricky nodded. "Yeah, I had a couple of things to do at Club Majesty first. Hope I didn't miss much."

"That's what I'm talkin' bout! Always workin' hard!" Dolla Dolla said before taking a hit from his blunt and thumping Ricky on his shoulder. "That's why I like you, man. That's why I depend on you! You always about making that money and getting the job done. You don't give me bullshit like some other niggas around here."

Ricky cleared his throat. "Actually, Dolla, I kinda wanted to talk to you about that. You see I was thinkin'—"

"You was thinkin' you finally ready to take me up on that offer I made you awhile back, right?" Dolla Dolla snickered, blowing a stream of smoke out the side of his mouth. "I was wondering how long you was gonna take to make up your mind! You better not have made my ass wait too much longer or you were about to hear about it."

"What offer?" Ricky asked, confused.

"What the hell you mean, 'What offer?' To start my real estate business, nigga! I told you I needed a CEO to front it. I need a dude with class to handle that shit . . . a smooth nigga like you who I can trust."

Ricky shook his head. "Dolla, I can't just—"

"Yes, you can! And you'll get a mil a year to do it, with a half mil up front, like one of those . . . whatchamacallit . . . a signin' bonus or some shit. I worked it out with my partners. That's what we gonna pay you."

Ricky stared at him, dumbfounded. "You . . . you serious?"

"Hell yeah, I'm serious! I got a hookup with the city so I can start building some major projects, but it ain't gonna work with me front and center. I need someone like you, Ricky. You did a bomb ass job with Club Majesty. I know you would do the same with this."

"A million a year?" Ricky repeated in disbelief.

"A million a year, nigga!" Dolla Dolla grinned and handed him the blunt. "So you saying yes?"

Ricky stared down at the blunt in Dolla Dolla's hands. He could keep his promise to Simone, decline Dolla Dolla's offer for a hit and to become the fake CEO of a fake company, and try to go legit for real. Or he could take a hit from his blunt, accept Dolla's offer, and become a millionaire overnight—but become further entrenched in Dolla Dolla's dirty business dealings.

I promised Simone, he reminded himself, *but a million is* a lot *of money.*

He had worked hard his whole life, hustled his entire childhood just to keep food in his belly and a roof over his head. He didn't have a father and barely remembered his mother. He'd lost his grandmother to cancer and his little sister to the streets. Life had dealt him a bad hand, but he'd always managed to make it work. Now it was finally offering him a windfall, after *all* these years.

If Ricky had that much money, he could build a good nest egg that could last him into his old age. If he had that much money, maybe Simone would forgive him for the decision he was about to make.

Ricky grabbed the blunt and took a puff, letting the smoke float through his nostrils. He slowly nodded. "Okay! Sounds good to me."

"That's my nigga!" Dolla shouted, slapping him on the back again. "Let's celebrate this shit!" He threw his arm around Ricky's shoulder and steered him into the room. "Get this nigga a drink, y'all!"

An hour later, Ricky sank back in the arm chair, feeling the glasses of champagne he'd just downed and hits of weed starting to kick in. He tried not to think about what he'd done, what he'd just agreed to. He tried not to think about Simone and how disappointed she'd be.

He'd made her a promise—and broken that promise, and all it had taken was for Dolla Dolla to wave a million in front of his face. He was swept undercurrent by a wave of self-loathing.

His eyes began to droop and so did his head. His mind felt sluggish, like the room and everyone in it were moving in slow motion. For a good hour, he sat in the same spot. People passed his chair and he only gave them a scant glance. A pair of long legs strode several feet in front of him. His lethargic brain vaguely recognized that the legs belonged to one of the waitresses at Dolla's party.

"Hey," he called out. He was high now, but he wanted to get blackout drunk too. He wanted a bourbon. "Hey . . . hey, you. Honey!" he slurred, snapping his fingers.

She didn't seem to hear him over the din, but continued to walk toward a group of guys sitting on the sofa across the room.

"Damn," he muttered. He guessed he would have to wait until she turned around. Maybe then he could get her attention.

He watched as she bent over and set a couple of glasses and a beer in front of a group of men staring up at the fight on the sixty-inch flat screen TV on the adjacent wall. One man nodded his thanks to her. Another winked at her. "What's your name, baby?" Ricky heard him shout.

She murmured something in reply then she shifted slightly. When she did, the waistband of her skirt lowered by an inch and Ricky could see a purple butterfly tattoo at the base of her spine.

He blinked. He recognized that tattoo.

Nah, Ricky thought. *No, that's not right.*

The drugs and alcohol must be messing with his head, making him see things that weren't there. His guilt was making his weed-addled mind manifest Simone out of thin air. But when the waitress turned, he realized it wasn't the drugs playing tricks on him. His eyes landed on Simone's smiling face. She looked different but he still recognized her—he would anywhere. She wore heavy makeup, false eyelashes, and a long auburn wig that swept her shoulders to mask her appearance. She had also donned the same uniform as the other waitresses at Dolla Dolla's party: a black push-up bra, pleated skirt, and stilettoes. He watched in shock as she casually strolled back across the living room, now carrying an empty tray.

"Oh, shit," he said aloud, sobering up within seconds.

If Dolla Dolla caught her here, if he recognized who she was—there would be hell to pay. Ricky didn't know what that man would do to her and didn't want to consider the possibilities. He had to get her out of there.

Ricky shoved himself up from the arm chair, feeling vertigo as soon as he did it. When the world around him steadied, he followed Simone. She was already headed out of the living room. He jogged the distance between them and caught up with her just as she passed another of group of waitresses who were stepping out of Dolla Dolla's kitchen. They were carrying more trays loaded down with drinks and hors d' oeuvres.

He grabbed her arm and yanked her against his side, making her drop her tray to the floor.

"Hey!" she yelled, whipping around to face him, screwing up her lips. "What the hell do you think you're d—"

Her words died when she realized who he was. Her eyes widened to the size of saucers.

"No, what the hell do you think *you're* doin'?" he

hissed as he dragged her in the opposite direction of the kitchen, down a deserted hallway.

She didn't fight him. She still looked stunned.

He tried the handle of the first door he saw and threw it open. He turned on the light switch, revealing a pantry closet filled wall-to-wall with shelves and dry goods. He shoved her inside and followed behind her. He slammed the door shut.

Simone obstinately crossed her arms over her chest and pursed her lips. "Why are you here?"

"Why the fuck are *you* here?"

"You told me you weren't doing business with him anymore. That you'd have nothing to do with him! You said—"

"So that's why you pulled some shit like this?" He gestured to her outfit and wig. "Because you thought I wasn't going to be here tonight?"

"You lied to me, Ricky," she said tightly.

"I lied to you? *I lied to you?* What about you? Huh? You told me that you were going to let this shit go! What the hell do you call this?" he asked, feeling panicked and furious all at the same time.

She uncrossed her arms and lowered her eyes. "I tried. I really tried. But I couldn't get it out of my mind. I couldn't stop worrying about her. I had to at least see her, to talk to her myself!"

"To talk to her? *Are you crazy?* Have you lost your fuckin' mind?"

"I just need a few minutes alone with her, to talk some sense to her. I know I can!"

"Be honest, Simone. You came here to save your sister—the *same* sister who doesn't want to be saved. Damn it, we've been through this shit!"

"You don't know that for sure," she argued, making

him suck his teeth in frustration. "Look, I know she said she doesn't want my help, but . . . but Skylar could just be suffering some . . . I don't know . . . some form of Stockholm syndrome or—"

"*What?*"

"It's not unheard of with sex trafficking victims. I told you, maybe the problem is that she needs to *see* me. If she saw me . . . if I could just . . . just talk to her, I know she'd—"

"You're going to get yourself killed! If Dolla sees you—"

"So what if he does?" she snapped impatiently. "So what if he fucking does? I'm willing to risk my life for her. I made that clear in the beginning. Besides, I didn't come in here unprotected." She pointed to her thighs. "There's more under here than a pair of panties. Okay?"

She lifted the front of her skirt, revealing a red lace thong and a Smith & Wesson M&P Shield pistol strapped to her thigh.

He tiredly shook his head as she lowered her skirt again. He scrubbed his hands over his face, wondering why he wasn't getting through to her. "I don't care what you've got under your skirt. You won't be able to shoot your way out of this! Don't you realize that? He's got bodyguards. He's got—"

"I *don't care!* I'm doing what I have to do. I'm tired of sitting on my hands! I asked for your help. I asked my own department for help. I've waited week after week after week—and nothing fucking happened. So I'm gonna do it my goddamn self." She tried to walk around him and reached for the door knob. "Don't worry. I'm putting my neck out, not yours! I've got—"

"You're damn right I'm worried!" He grabbed her shoulders, shaking her hard. "Of course, I'm fucking worried! I *care* about you, girl. I love . . ." He hesitated. He loosened his grip on her shoulders and gazed down at her, at the "disguise" she was wearing. She looked ridiculous and desperate—exactly how he felt at that moment. "I love you, Simone."

She stared at him blankly.

"There. I said it! I love you, and it's going to fuck me up if something happens to you. So please . . . *Please* don't do this."

She lowered her head again and closed her eyes. Ricky drew her against him and wrapped his arms around her. She rested her head on his shoulder.

He could still hear the party going full throttle on the other side of the door. The heavy base of the music and the muffled laughter and shouts were the only noise that surrounded them as he held her close, offering her his protection, offering all he could give.

But after a few seconds, he felt her tense against his chest. She pushed back and looked up at him. When she did, he could see tears in her eyes and a steely resolve. She stood on the balls of her feet and kissed him. But it wasn't a passionate kiss; it was like she was kissing him goodbye.

"I love you too, Ricky—and I love my sister," she whispered. "If you care about me as much as you say you do, then you know why I have to do this, why I will have her back even if she says she doesn't want me to." She eased out of his arms and his heart sank. "I don't have any other choice. I'm sorry."

He then watched, dismayed, as she opened the pantry door and stepped back into the hall.

He stood alone in the closet for several minutes, clenching his fists, trying to slow down his racing heart and his hysterical mind.

She was going to do it anyway, despite his warnings, despite his fears. There was no stopping her—or whatever might happen tonight.

He raised his shirt and reached into the back of his

jeans, pulling out the Glock 43 he had tucked in his waistband. He checked the gun's magazine to make sure he had a full clip then popped it back in again. He tucked it back into his waistband, lowered his shirt, opened the pantry door, and stepped back into the hall, wiping her lipstick from his mouth with the back of his hand.

Ricky would take Simone's words to heart. She said that when you really cared about someone, you had their back—even if they said they didn't want your help. Well, he'd have her back tonight. If some shit went down, he guessed he was going down with her.

Chapter 27

Ricky

For the rest of the night, Ricky tried to stay, at most, twenty feet away from Simone at all times. He was her ever present shadow, following her as she went room to room, observing her as she served drinks and food while charming and flirting with Dolla Dolla's guests. He didn't stand over her shoulder like a bodyguard, exactly. He tried not to be *that* obvious, but it didn't take her long to catch on to what he was doing. More than once, she gave him an annoyed glance. She even angrily mouthed "Back off," to which he mouthed back, "Hell no." She stalked off. He didn't care. If she wasn't leaving the party, he wasn't either.

And the longer she stayed, the more his anxiety ratcheted up. Ricky wasn't sure if it was the weed, but he felt increasingly paranoid. He felt an overwhelming sense of dread, too. It was like an invisible clock was winding down, drawing them closer to some cataclysmic event. Maybe the guy managing the waitresses would realize that Simone was only pretending to work there and call her out, drawing attention to her. Maybe Dolla Dolla would finally recognize Skylar's big sister in her half-hearted disguise and deduce why she was there. Or maybe Simone would finally come face-to-face with Skylar and their reunion would be as much of a failure as Ricky suspected it would be. He didn't know. Either way, it made him nervous.

A little before midnight, Simone finally made her move. He watched from an alcove in the foyer as she walked toward the staircase leading to the bedrooms upstairs where Dolla Dolla usually kept his girls. She carried two champagne glasses on her tray. When she reached the stairs, one of Dolla Dolla's bodyguards held up his hand.

"Nah, baby," he said, shaking his bald head. "Where do you think you're going?"

Ricky watched as Simone pasted on a sparkling smile. "Oh, I'm sorry! A guy asked me to get champagne and strawberries for him and bring it upstairs."

The bodyguard shook his head. "You can't go upstairs, sweetheart."

Her smile disappeared. She pretended to look confused. "Why not?"

"Cuz those are the rules," the other, larger guard answered. "Give him his champagne and strawberries when he comes back down, but you can't go up there."

Simone groaned and pivoted on her heels. She tossed her fake hair over her shoulder. "Oh, come on y'all! Don't make me have to take this back. I'll have to throw it out," she said with a pout. "This champagne ain't cheap! My boss is gonna take it out of my tips!"

Ricky bit back a laugh. He had to hand it to her; it was a good lie.

"Then drink it yourself," the bodyguard replied dryly.

"Don't be that way, y'all. Just let me take it to him. It won't take long."

"Look, sis, you can't go upstairs. It is what it is," the first bodyguard insisted. "*Okay?*"

Simone inclined her head and gave them a wink. "How's about this? How about you let me go upstairs for just a itty-bitty minute—just long enough to give this to him, and I'll bring you two a glass of champagne each. You'll like it. It's—"

"What the fuck did he just say?" a male voice barked. "You hard of hearing?"

Ricky leaned out of the alcove and spotted T. J. jogging down the stairs toward Simone and the two bodyguards. At the sight of him, Ricky's brows lowered. His hands tightened into fists. If T. J. laid one finger on her, he was going to lose it.

"You can't go upstairs!" T. J. shouted. "Just take that shit back to the kitchen."

Ricky could tell that Simone was pissed. Hell, so was he, but to her credit, she hid it well. She stayed in character and lowered her head, shuffled away from the staircase, and headed back toward the kitchen like T. J. ordered.

Good, Ricky thought, exhaling. She'd tried to get upstairs and it didn't work. Maybe this waking nightmare was finally over. But when Simone passed him and he saw the steely resolve in her eyes again, his shoulders slumped. He knew she hadn't given up yet.

Ricky got evidence of this an hour later when the guards had wandered off—one to flirt with one of the other waitresses, and the other had disappeared somewhere else.

Probably to go take a piss, Ricky presumed.

He watched from a distance as Simone crept to the staircase again. She glanced over her shoulder, checking to see if she was being watched. With the exception of him, there was no one else in the foyer. She began to climb up the wooden stairs and had nearly reached the second floor when a voice boomed over Ricky's shoulder. "Hey! Hey, where the fuck you think you're going?"

She jumped, startled.

T. J. roughly shoved passed Ricky and walked across the room. The young man raced up the stairs, toward Simone who opened and closed her mouth helplessly. She couldn't come up with a lie this time.

"What the fuck did I tell you?" T. J. shouted, reaching for her. He seized her wrist and yanked her toward him, making her stumble off one of the stairs. She had to grab the handrail to keep from tumbling to the floor below.

"What the fuck did I tell you?" T. J. shouted again.

Watching the scene unfold, Ricky didn't think. He went on instinct.

He raced up the staircase after T. J., taking the stairs two at a time. He closed in on them in less than a minute, right at the moment when T. J. grabbed the back of Simone's neck, making her wince in pain. He shouted into her ear, "You bitches never listen! I told your ass to—"

That's when Ricky swung at him.

The first punch connected with T. J.'s mouth and Ricky immediately heard the crunch, signifying that T. J. was about to be short one bucktooth. Maybe two. The other connected with his jaw, making T. J. release a loud squeal of agony.

T. J. held up his hands to protect his face as one punch connected, then another. A spray of blood hit Ricky's cheek, then his right eye as his fists continued to fly.

"Ricky!" Simone screamed, tugging at his shirt. "Ricky, stop, damnit!"

But he couldn't stop. He kept swinging, making it his personal mission to beat the shit out of this little punk. All the anger, all his frustration at Dolla Dolla . . . at Simone . . . at Skylar . . . at what had happened to Desiree years ago, he took out on this shit-talking, pint-sized, doo-rag-wearing bully.

He didn't know how long it was before the guards finally dragged him off of T. J., or when Dolla Dolla came into the room, but by then, T. J.'s face was so bloodied and bruised, it was barely recognizable.

"Ricky, chill! What are you doin', man?" the bodyguard yelled, gripping him around the chest, pulling him back. "You tryin' to kill him?"

Ricky blinked as if waking up from a dream. He stared down at T. J. The little punk was slumped back against the stairs with rolling eyes, gurgling through his bloodied mouth and blowing red bubbles through his busted nose.

"Goddamn!" Dolla Dolla yelled, strolling into the room. His booming voice echoed to the ceiling. "I thought the fight was on TV. I didn't know y'all motherfuckas was fittin' to give us a live show tonight!" His chest rumbled as he laughed. He then turned to the crowd of onlookers huddled near the stairs and the foyer entryway. "Okay, y'all! Go back to doin' whatever the fuck you was doin'! Shows over!"

It took a few minutes but they gradually dispersed.

"T. J., what the fuck did you do?" Dolla Dolla shouted, still laughing. "Why Ricky beat the shit out of you?"

T. J. didn't respond. Instead, he continued to glare silently at Ricky, wiping at the blood on his face with the hem of his shirt. The other bodyguard tried to help him to his feet, but he angrily shoved his hand away.

"Ricky, what got into you, nigga?" Dolla asked, squinting as he approached the stairs. "You do too much coke? Got your fire up?"

"No," Ricky said, shrugging out of the bodyguard's grasp. He flexed his now swollen, bloodied knuckles. He gave a withering glance at T. J. "This nigga was just long overdue for an ass whuppin'. That's all."

"That may be. That may be." Dolla chuckled again then abruptly stopped. His face went serious. He eyed Ricky coldly. "But nobody . . . and I mean *nobody* is supposed to beat anybody's ass in *my* house without my permission. You know that, Ricky."

Ricky lowered his eyes.

"Least of all beat the ass of one of my men. I can't have that. It's disrespectful. I don't like it when folks are disrespectful."

"Sorry, Dolla," he said. "I wasn't trying to disrespect you."

"I'ma kill you!" T. J. growled, pausing to spit blood over the banister. He shoved himself to his feet and reached for his waistband. "I'ma kill you, bitch! I'ma shoot this—"

"Shut the fuck up!" Dolla boomed, making the young man go still and silent. "Y'all better listen! I told you nobody does shit in my house without my say so! You hear me? Now you *all* just better slow your roll!"

T. J. looked on the brink of tears from how incensed he was, but he kept silent like Dolla Dolla ordered.

Dolla Dolla's eyes suddenly swung up to Simone who stood a few feet away. He pointed up at her. "Hey, don't I know you, girl?"

She blinked then shook her head, causing her wig to whip around her shoulders. "I-I don't think s-so," she stuttered.

He slowly climbed the stairs and leaned against the railing, scratching his goatee. He nodded. "Yeah, I know you. I know you! I've seen you somewhere before but I can't—"

"I used mess with her," Ricky blurted out. "She used to be one of my girls a couple of years ago. I may have brought her around a few times. Or . . . or maybe you saw her at the restaurant."

Dolla Dolla squinted and frowned at Ricky. "*You messed with her?* Then why she say I never met her?"

Ricky shrugged, keeping his tone blasé. "You probably didn't. You saw her but I didn't introduce her to you."

Dolla Dolla's frown deepened. His gaze returned to Simone. He still looked troubled.

"She was just a girl I used to smash, Dolla. One of many," he continued, feeling desperate. The situation was getting dangerous again. He was feeling cornered and he could tell she was too. Her hand was shifted to her skirt. He knew she was reaching for the Smith & Wesson strapped to her thigh.

No, don't do that. Don't be stupid, he thought as he locked eyes with Simone.

"She's nobody," Ricky claimed. "Don't worry about her, man!"

"The bitch was trying to go upstairs," T. J. argued, holding his hand below his chin to catch the dripping blood. "She knew she couldn't go, but she was headed up there anyway. I was trying to stop her before this motherfucka over here sucker punched me!"

"I punched you because you grabbed her," Ricky said menacingly. "And I'd do it again!"

"So then she ain't nobody," Dolla Dolla murmured, tilting his head. "Because if she was 'nobody,' you wouldn't have cared what the fuck he did to her. Right?"

Ricky licked his lips—at a loss for what to say. He glanced up at her again. Her hand hovered over the same spot on her leg. If he messed this up . . . if he said the wrong thing and Dolla Dolla realized he was lying and started to remember *exactly* where he had seen her before, they might have to shoot their way out of here.

"So you beat T. J.'s ass over some bitch?" Dolla Dolla continued, raising his bushy eyebrows. "Is that what you sayin'?"

Now put on the spot with no idea what was the right or wrong answer, with what could put both him *and* her at risk, Ricky decided to roll the dice. He forced a smile and shrugged. "Hey," he drawled, "I'm drunker than a motherfucka', Dolla! Maybe! You know how I get."

Dolla Dolla's frown disappeared. His wide chest started to rumble with another chuckle that erupted from his mouth like a thunderclap. He slapped Ricky jovially on the back. "You crazy, bruh! That's why I keep your ass around."

Ricky laughed too and inwardly sighed with relief when Simone's hand shifted from her thigh back to her hip.

A half hour later, the party ended. Ricky hung back, letting the trickle of guests leave first. The waitresses headed out last, huddled in groups as they made their way to their cars. Simone broke off from the rest, stomping down the driveway. She walked down the gravel road where several cars were parallel parked along the shoulder. When she drew near her Nissan, he caught up with her.

"Wait up!" he shouted.

She glared over her shoulder at him and shook her head in disgust.

"Damnit, wait! We need to talk about this shit. You can't just—"

"I have *nothing* to say to you!" She raised her key to press the button that would unlock her car door. She swung the driver's side door open. He strode in front of her and slammed it shut before she could climb inside, stopping her in her tracks, catching her by surprise.

"*You have nothing to say to me?* After what I did in there for you?"

"*After what you did?*" she shouted, screwing up her face. "After what you did? Ricky, you really think you did me a fucking favor tonight, running up the stairs and beating the shit out that asshole? You think I should thank you for following me around all night, and drawing attention to me? If it wasn't for you, I could have found my sister!"

He slammed his fist on the car roof. "Oh, come on, Simone!"

"I could be bringing her home!"

"Are you fucking kidding me? If it wasn't for me, they could be doing a train on you right now in one of those upstairs bedrooms!" He gestured to Dolla Dolla's McMansion in the distance. "And when they were done, they'd put a bullet in your head and dump your body!"

"I was this close," she said, holding up her index finger and thumb like she hadn't heard him. "*This* close—and you ruined it!"

He slowly shook his head. "You really are crazy, aren't you? This shit has driven you nuts, because there is no way you could think—"

"No, *you're* the crazy one," she said, staring up at him. "You're crazy for smiling in that son of a bitch's face, pretending to be loyal to him when you know what he does . . . when you know who he is!"

"Just what the hell did you expect me to do? To spit in his face? To kick the damn door down and—"

"I expected you to be the man I thought you were! I didn't need your protection! If you weren't going to help me get the job done, then you should've gotten the fuck out of my way! Instead, I'm no closer now to Skylar than I was four months ago. I'm not going to thank you for that, Ricky!"

His head was pounding. His heart ached. He had done so much for this woman and it still wasn't enough. All the anger and fight drained out of him. "Just what . . . *what* do you want from me?" he asked, honestly bewildered.

"Nothing," she snapped, yanking open her car door again and climbing inside. "Not a goddamn thing! Because I was pretending to be someone I'm not tonight but you've been pretending for a lifetime—and you're never gonna change! I recognize that now. As far as I'm concerned, you're *worse* than he is. You're just a criminal who doesn't like to get his hands dirty!"

She slammed the car door and shoved her key into the ignition. Ricky stepped back when he heard her rev the car engine. A few seconds later she pulled off and he watched her brake lights recede as she drove down the road. He watched them until they disappeared.

Chapter 28

Jamal

Jamal watched from his perch on the stool at the kitchen island as Blake hoisted a cardboard box off the floor, carefully balancing it in his arms.

Blake had been carrying out boxes and bags from Jamal's and Bridget's apartment for the past hour to a moving van that waited in the parking lot downstairs. The whole time the two men had studiously avoided making eye contact, pretending like they weren't in the room together.

Good, Jamal thought as he chewed his sandwich. Because if Blake said one word to him . . . if he even *sneezed* in his direction, he'd probably punch him in the face. He had already broken up with Bridget; it's not like he had anything to lose if he did hit him.

"Is this the last of it, Bridge?" Blake called over his shoulder.

"Yeah, that's it," she said, striding into their living room, tucking something into the tote bag on her shoulder.

"All right. I'll take it to the van and meet you downstairs," he called as he walked to the apartment's opened front door.

"I'll be down in a sec," she called back.

It hadn't taken Bridget long to pack all of her things. She'd yelled two nights ago that she didn't want any of the stuff they'd purchased together during their year and a half as a couple.

"I just want my things! You hear me? *My* stuff. That's it! I don't need any of the rest of this shit!" Bridget had shouted, gesturing to their living room.

He hadn't cared enough to argue. Besides, her taking that stance meant he got to keep all the furniture and their televisions. But she'd made one exception to her declaration; Bridget was taking their Crate & Barrel stoneware and wineglasses with her, which was why he was eating his dinner off a paper plate and drinking wine out of a Styrofoam cup. He looked up from his panini when Bridget tossed her set of keys on the granite countertop in front of him with a clang.

"I won't be needing these anymore," she said, dropping her hands to her hips and raising her chin defiantly.

Jamal nodded, took the keys, and tucked them into his jean pocket. "Okay."

"*Okay?* Okay? That's all you have to say to me?"

"What more am I supposed to say? You gave me your keys. You're headed out the door." He shrugged. "Leave me your forwarding address and I'll send you whatever mail that comes here that's addressed to you."

Her freckled face flushed crimson. She balled her fists at her sides. "Fuck you, Jamal Lighty! Fuck you!"

He loudly exhaled. He could yell back at her. He could bring up that she had no right to be angry at him, considering she had cheated on him with her ex, but he figured it wasn't worth the energy.

"Goodbye, Bridget," he said flatly instead, then watched as she stomped to the front door and slammed it shut behind her.

He sat on the stool for another minute and surveyed his now quiet, empty living room. A few pictures of he and Bridget as a smiling couple still sat on their end tables. On the sofa was a shawl he had given her for her birthday. On the fireplace mantle were a set of pewter bookends she'd picked up for him while on a business trip in Chicago. He waited for a sense of loss or melancholy to overwhelm him, but it didn't come. Instead he felt invigorated. His breakup with Bridget had ended one chapter, but had also opened another. He could finally try something new. He could finally take a chance.

He rose to his feet and walked into the living room. He grabbed his cell phone, which sat on one of the end tables. It was the third Saturday of the month. Derrick and Ricky likely would be meeting up for drinks at Ray's. It would be the perfect time . . . the perfect window for Jamal to do what he'd secretly been longing to do for weeks.

Just broke up with Bridget. Really need to talk to someone.

He pressed send and waited for a text response, but his cell phone rang instead fifteen minutes later.

"Oh shit, Jay!" Melissa shouted on the other end of the line as soon as he answered the phone. "I'm so sorry to hear about you and Bridget! Are you okay?"

"I'm getting through," he said, hoping that he sounded sad, not eager—which was how he really felt at that moment. "I'm just . . . I'm just a little shell-shocked, I guess. I mean . . . I thought we were okay."

"Did you guys have a fight or something? What the hell happened?"

"We argued a few nights ago, and she . . . well, she admitted she cheated on me."

"*What?* That bitch! I can't believe she did that to you!"

"I just keep replaying everything in my head, wondering what happened. What did I do wrong?"

"No, you can't do that. Don't do that. Okay?" she insisted. "You didn't do a damn thing! She's the one who cheated. You didn't cheat on her!"

"Yeah, I know. I know. It still sucks though. I've been trying my best not to sit around feeling sorry for myself."

"So don't! Get out of your apartment. *Do* something."

"Easier said than done, Lissa."

"Well, I refuse to leave you alone to a pity party. You're going to make me drag you out tonight, aren't you?" she joked. "Fine. I will! I'll be at your place in a half hour. We're doing something fun. I don't know what that will be, but I'll figure it out when I get there."

Jamal grinned. Those were the words he'd been secretly waiting to hear all along. But he quickly wiped the smile off his face. Again, he knew he had to sound wistful, not excited.

"You don't have to do that. Besides, Dee probably won't be cool with—"

"I've told you a hundred times—don't worry about him. I'm grown! Besides, he's off doing his own thing tonight anyway! Why shouldn't I do mine?"

Jamal didn't know if he was projecting, but he thought he detected a flirtatious note in her voice. "Okay, well . . . if you're down, I'm down."

"Oh, I'm definitely down! See you in a bit!" she said, before hanging up.

Jamal gazed down at his phone for several seconds after, staring at it in awe. He was finally going to have a "date" with Melissa Stone, after all these years, after all this time.

"I gotta get ready," he whispered, looking down at himself, at his clothes. "Shit! I've gotta get ready!" He then rushed down the hall to his bedroom, unbuttoning his shirt as he ran.

"Oh, my God! That was so fun!" Melissa exclaimed, trailing behind him into his living room. She shrugged out of her wool coat and handed it to him. "Come on! Admit it. You had a good time, right?"

Jamal chuckled and nodded. "Yes, I had a good time."

He'd thought they would go out to dinner, maybe share a good meal and a bottle of wine over candlelight, but instead she had dragged him to a bowling alley. They'd spent the past two hours stuffing their faces with pizza, nachos, and waffle fries, and going head-to-head in a few rounds of bowling. Despite the unconventional setting, Jamal had thoroughly enjoyed himself, momentarily forgetting about Bridget and his drama with Mayor Johnson. He'd even been able to put aside those flare ups of guilt about being alone with Melissa. In his heart, he knew he hadn't agreed to come out with her tonight just to ease his mind. He had finally decided to steal Derrick's girl.

Every time she smiled at him or threw back her head and laughed at one of his jokes, he felt a spark, a charge that bounced between them. He told himself that he was the right fit for Melissa, not Derrick. Derrick had had almost twenty years to make Melissa happy, to make things work—and he still hadn't gotten it right. She was obviously unhappy with him.

What's that old saying, Jamal now thought as he opened the door to his coat closet and hung his and Melissa's coats. *That the definition of insanity is doing the same thing over and over again and expecting a different result.*

Maybe it was finally time for Melissa and Derrick to stop the insanity and try something different. Maybe it was finally time for her to give Jamal a chance.

"Would you like something to drink?" he asked as she sauntered to his sofa and flopped onto one of the cushions, giggling drunkenly and bouncing as she did it.

"Not unless it's a glass of water!" She tossed her braids over her shoulder, kicked off her tennis shoes, and tucked her feet beneath her bottom. "I think I had too many beers at dinner. I'm starting to feel lightheaded!"

"A glass of water, it is." He then opened one of the overhead cabinets and pulled out two glasses, before grabbing a pitcher from the fridge to pour water for them both.

He would've wanted to pour himself a whiskey or bourbon instead for what he was about to do next, but water would have to do. He took a deep breath and pushed back his shoulders, working up the courage. Jamal carried the glasses over to where she sat on the sofa. He took the spot beside her and handed her one of the glasses.

"Thanks again for making me go out tonight," he said.

She laughed and waved a hand at him. "No problem, Jay. I just didn't want to see you sad and stuck in here all day. I wouldn't give the bitch the satisfaction."

"I don't think she cares either way. I bet she and Blake are pretty . . . well, preoccupied . . . right now," he mumbled dryly with raised brows before taking a sip from his glass.

Melissa reached out and gave his shoulder a quick squeeze. "I'm so sorry, Jay. What she did was really fucked up. You deserve better."

He shifted slightly and met her dark eyes. When he did, the muscles in his stomach tightened. His pulse quickened. "You think so?"

"I *know* so! You shouldn't have to put up with that shit. You deserve a woman who will appreciate you, and love you for the great guy that you are."

"You do too," he whispered, making her squint in confusion.

"Huh?"

It's now or never, he thought before setting down his water glass, clearing his throat, and slowly reaching out to grab her hand, clasping her soft palm in his own. The action seemed to catch her by surprise, but she didn't pull away. He took that as a positive sign.

"I said . . . I said, you do too, Lissa. You deserve a man who . . . who will appreciate you and love you for exactly who you are," he began. "And I know for a fact, that's not Derrick."

"What . . . what are you talking about, Jay?"

"Look, part of the reason why you guys argue so damn much, why you break up and make up over and over and *over* again, is because you don't match! You can't see it, but I can! He's an idealist. You're sensible. He's emotional. You're rational. You're always gonna butt heads. He doesn't get you—but . . . but *I* do. I always have. I love you for who you are!"

"*You love me?*" Her mouth fell open. She barked out a laugh. "Jay, I don't know if it's the alcohol from earlier talkin' or—"

"It's not the alcohol. I'm not drunk. I love you, Lissa! I've loved you for as long as I can remember, since I was twelve years old. I couldn't tell you back then because . . . well, because you started dating Derrick first. I never really got a chance . . . *we* never really got a chance. But now that Bridget and I aren't together anymore, and you and Derrick are . . . well, now that you are going through your own thing, maybe you can finally, *finally* see me as something more than just a friend. Maybe you can see me for the man that I am."

She slowly shook her head, looking utterly mystified.

"I could make you happy, Lissa. I know I could. Just . . . just give it a chance."

He waited for her to say something—to say *anything*, but instead, she stared down at their clasped hands, opening and closing her mouth silently like she was at a loss for words. So he took another chance. He leaned forward and kissed her.

She breathed in audibly when their lips met. He felt heady and overwhelmed by her smell, by her softness, by the new sensation of Melissa's full, luscious lips against his mouth. He let go of her hands, wrapped his arms around her, and tried to draw her closer, to taste more of her, but she began to tense against him. She squirmed. She shoved hard against his chest.

"Stop, Jay! Goddamnit, I said stop!" she yelled against his mouth.

He let her go and she jumped back from him. She roughly wiped her lips with the back of her hand and shot to her feet.

"What are you doing?" she shouted. "What the fuck are you doing?"

Now he was the one at a loss for words. He stared up at her blankly.

"I trusted you! I didn't come here for this shit! Is that why you invited me up to you place? Because you thought I would . . . you thought we were gonna . . ."

She didn't finish. Instead, she shook her head in revulsion and ran out of his living room, almost tripping on the Afghan rug as she fled.

"Wait!" he yelled, rising clumsily from the sofa. "Wait, Lissa!"

"Dee said you weren't a real friend. That you didn't have his back or Ricky's," she muttered as she pulled open the door to his coat closet and tugged out her wool coat, sending metal hangers flying and clattering to the hardwood floor. "He said you weren't worth the time and effort—and I told him he was wrong! I made him feel like shit! I *defended* you, Jay!"

"Look, I'm sorry," he said, grabbing her arm. "I didn't—"

"Don't touch me!" she screamed, jerking her arm out of his grasp, making him hold up his hands and take a step back. "Don't you ever fuckin' touch me again! Do you hear me?"

He watched helplessly as she put on her coat. "Lissa, I just wanted to . . . I-I was just trying to tell you—"

"You were just trying to make me cheat on my fiancé, to get me to be a low-down, shady fuck like you! You're not Dee's friend. You never were, were you? You're not my friend either, Jay, because a real friend wouldn't do some shit like this!" She yanked open his front door. "Don't ever fuckin' call me again."

She then strode into the hallway and slammed the door shut behind her.

When she did, something in him crumbled. He staggered back and bumped into the closet door, feeling a mix of devastation and humiliation.

Chapter 29

Derrick

"Ricky is getting a little crazy tonite," Derrick typed as he sat at Morgan's kitchen island sipping red wine while she made him a home-cooked meal of yams, collard greens, and fried chicken.

"The Southern girl special," she'd boasted.

It was the third meal she had cooked him that week. As it turned out, he preferred her home cooking to the restaurant meals they used to enjoy. He preferred her place to the restaurants too, the feminine intimacy of her studio apartment that was filled with furniture she'd crafted herself and was decorated in vibrant splashes of color.

I'm gonna be home a little late. Don't wait up.

He pressed send.

The last sentence hadn't been necessary. He knew Melissa wouldn't wait up for him. But he had to send her at least a few texts. Melissa thought he was out at Ray's with Ricky; he had to keep up the farce.

Derrick tucked his cell into his pocket before Morgan

could see the message on the screen. She paused from her cooking to lean over the counter and give him a kiss that was as sweet and fiery as her honey and cayenne biscuits he'd been nibbling on for the past fifteen minutes.

"Who were you texting?" Morgan asked when she pulled away.

"Nobody. Just checking scores from a couple of games tonight."

She didn't question him further. Instead, she started humming, turned back around, and returned her attention to the chicken frying on the stove.

Frankly, Derrick was getting tired of the lies. Mr. Theo was right: he couldn't have it both ways. Not anymore. It wasn't right to lie to Melissa or Morgan. He had to be honest with them both—and with himself. He just wasn't sure when the right time to do that was.

After dinner, they settled on her sofa, and it didn't take long for things to get steamy again. Now, when they were alone together, it always did. He didn't know if it was the pent up desire they had tried to hold back during all those meals and seemingly playful conversations, but each caress, lick, and nibble only left him wanting more. They hadn't had sex yet, but they damn sure had come close a few times in the past couple weeks. Tonight was no different. It took almost Herculean strength to pull Morgan's hand away when she straddled him and dragged down his pants zipper, shoving her hand inside his boxer briefs.

"What? What's wrong?" she whispered.

"It . . . it doesn't feel right," he said, shaking his head.

"Why?" She leaned forward and nipped his ear. "It feels damn good to me. I bet we can make it feel even better," she said, wrapping her hand around his dick again.

"Come on, Morgan!" He tugged her hand out of his pants once more. "You know I'm still living with Melissa. We're still engaged."

Her face changed when he said that. The sultry look in her green eyes instantly evaporated. "So I guess you *still* haven't talked to her yet?"

"I've been waiting for the right time . . . the right moment."

She loudly grumbled before falling back onto her sofa, closing her eyes, and dropping her face into her hands. "There is no right time or right moment, Derrick! I thought we talked about this. You just have to suck it up and do it."

"I know that," he'd answered tightly.

"Then what the hell are you waiting for?" she exclaimed, dropping her hands. "Do you still want to try to make it work with her? Because if you do, just tell me! If you don't wanna be here with me, I'm not gonna—"

"I do," he said, reaching out to her, rubbing her neck, "I want to be here with you. I know Melissa and I are well past working things out. I know what I've gotta do, and you're right . . . it's finally time to do it. I can't put it off any longer. I'll do it—tomorrow. I'll tell her in the morning that we need to talk."

"You promise?" She looked doubtful.

"I promise. I swear," he said, cupping her face.

At that, Morgan leaned forward to kiss him again, to wrap her arms around him and press her body against his. It was if she was reminding him what waited for him on the other side if he finally manned up and told Melissa the truth. He had to tell her it was time to put each other out of their mutual misery.

Derrick eased open his apartment door, surprised to see one of the table lamps burning bright in his living room. It was a little after midnight. He'd thought Melissa would be fast asleep by now. He quietly shut the door behind him, locking it before dropping his keys onto the wooden console near the door.

He licked his lips as he shrugged out of his coat, still tasting Morgan and her biscuits. He wondered if the smell of her perfume still lingered on his clothes. He hung his coat on the coatrack near their door.

"*Lissa?* You up?" he called out.

"Yeah, I'm . . . I'm in here."

He hadn't planned to talk to her about their relationship tonight, but they were both awake. Now was probably as good a time as any.

Derrick took a deep breath and pushed back his shoulders, bracing himself for what he was about to do, practicing the words in his head.

I love you. I always will love you, baby, but we can't do this anymore, he thought.

When he reached the end of the hall and rounded the corner, he stopped in his tracks.

Melissa was sitting on the couch with her head bowed. Brownie was in her lap and a wad of Kleenex was in her hand. When he walked into the room, she looked up and he could see that she had been crying. She blew her nose and sniffed.

Seeing the state that she was in, Derrick's stomach dropped. His legs felt weak.

"She found out about Morgan!" a panicked voice in his head yelled. *"Mr. Theo warned you. He told you to be careful and you didn't listen. Now do you see what happens?"*

Melissa had somehow discovered that he'd been cheating on her for weeks. All those nights that he claimed to be hanging out with Ricky or with "the boys" . . . that he claimed to be working late at the Institute, he'd really been going out or loving up on Morgan. Melissa had finally found out the truth.

Not like this. Shit, don't let it go down like this, he pleaded.

She opened her mouth and he prepared himself for the screaming, for her accusations and condemnation, but instead she said, "I am *so* sorry, baby."

He watched, stupefied, as she slowly stood from the couch, making Brownie hop onto their rug. She then crossed the living room with arms outstretched. Melissa crashed into him, making him take a few steps back. She threw her arms around him and held him tight.

"I'm so sorry for being so goddamn stupid!" she cried before dropping her head onto his shoulder.

Derrick didn't know how to respond. This wasn't at all what he'd expected for her to say or to do.

"I've been so wrong." She hiccupped. "I've been so fucked up to you, and I . . . I feel awful about it. I love you more than anything, Dee. More than anything, baby!"

He gradually wrapped his arms around her, too stunned to do more than that. She leaned back her head and gazed into his eyes.

"Work at the Institute if you want. I won't pressure to change jobs anymore."

"*What?* But I thought you didn't—"

"Not anymore," she said before he could finish. "It's what you believe in. I know now that you keep trying to get me to talk to my dad because . . . because you want me to be happy. I get it now. Just be the man that you are, Dee, because who you are is so amazing. I love you so much," she said, blinking through her tears. "I'm so sorry I forgot that!"

Derrick stared down at his fiancée and was overwhelmed with relief—and guilt. She finally got it. She finally understood why he couldn't leave his job and why he had tried so hard to reunite her with her father. She was apologizing and professing her love to him—meanwhile, he had just returned from another woman's apartment. He had been kissing and caressing Morgan less than an hour ago, promising that he was ready to leave Melissa, that he was ready to finally move on. And he had been ready to move on—until this very moment. His old misgivings disappeared. He finally had his baby back.

"Do you forgive me, Dee?" Melissa asked, gnawing her bottom lip, staring at the tear stains she'd left on his shirt. "Can we start all over again?"

He nodded without hesitation. "Of course, baby."

She stood on the balls of her feet and kissed him.

An hour later, when they lay in bed under the covers, wrapped in each other's arms, Derrick heard his cell phone buzz on his night table.

He removed his arm from around Melissa and rolled onto his back. He picked up his phone and saw a message on the screen from Morgan.

Was thinking about U and missing U. Let me know how it goes tomorrow.

She then signed off the message with a heart emoji.

"What is it?" Melissa murmured dreamily, turning to face him.

Derrick quickly deleted the message and shook his head. He lowered his phone back to his night table. "Nothing, baby. Just some stupid shit from Ricky." He kissed her cheek. "Sorry I woke you up."

She chuckled. "Ricky needs Jesus. Night, baby," she

muttered before smacking her lips and turning back onto her side. She closed her eyes.

"Night," he whispered. He wrapped his arm around her and closed his eyes too, but he knew he wouldn't get a wink of sleep.

His guilt would have to be his companion until the sun came up.

Chapter 30

Ricky

Ricky gazed listlessly at the stage, watching as two of Club Majesty's dancers twirled around the main stage's stripper poles then simultaneously dropped into splits. Some of the men on the floor began to holler. A few even tossed bills into the air to show their appreciation for the performance. But Ricky watched the scene with a bland detachment.

He felt numb.

He'd been this way since he'd last seen Simone at Dolla Dolla's house. She hadn't called him or texted him since that night, and Ricky had just enough pride left not to reach out to her—but it was a struggle. He had to fight the impulse to pick up the phone, dial her number, and cuss her out, to tell her that he'd only wanted to protect her, and that she should thank him rather than give him the cold shoulder. But he knew it was pointless. They'd just have to go their separate ways. She was a bull-headed cop who claimed he was nothing more than a criminal that didn't like getting his hands dirty. Maybe it was best to just forget her.

He watched as one of the dancers—Ronnie, a small-town girl from Tennessee who had only started stripping a year ago—rose from her split and started to twerk on the side of the stage. A man wearing a Chicago Bulls jersey tossed more dollar bills at her and shouted something unintelligible before bursting into laughter.

Ricky saw Ronnie's face change; her seductive smile disappeared. She shifted to the opposite side of the stage, like she wanted to get as far away from that joker as possible. The man suddenly lunged forward, grabbing her ankle. Ronnie shouted out and gave a kick, sending the man careening back. But he quickly regained his footing and lunged for the stage again.

"Shit," Ricky muttered, finishing the last of his drink and shoving himself to his feet, ready to intervene. But two of the bouncers beat him to it. They came at a near run from the dark corners of the club to Ronnie's rescue.

Ricky watched as the man struggled in the bouncers' arms, shouting and cursing as they dragged him off the floor. Ronnie and the other dancer had stopped their routine. Both women looked badly shaken, like they weren't sure what to do next.

Ricky walked toward the mezzanine stairs. He was headed to the DJ booth to tell the DJ to cue the next set so the girls could exit the stage, when his cell began to vibrate in his pants pocket. He ignored it and motioned to get the DJ's attention. The young man quickly removed the headphones from his ears.

"What's up, Ricky?" he asked.

"Cut the set! Bring on Lisa and Carla *now!*" Ricky shouted, cupping his hands around his mouth so he could be heard over the music.

The DJ quickly nodded then reached for his mike. "Thank you, ladies. And now we're about to get a sample of some hot-hot-hot chocolate, fellas! Get ready! Brace yourselves for the heat, or you gonna get burned."

Ricky turned back to the stage just as Ronnie and the other dancer made their way behind the velvet curtains and the opening lyrics to a Drake song began to play. He started to head back toward his table on the mezzanine when his phone vibrated again, like he was getting another phone call.

"Who the hell is calling me?" he muttered, reaching into his pocket and pulling out his cell in irritation. When he stared down at the screen and saw the number, his eyes widened. He quickly pressed the green button to answer.

"*Simone?*" he shouted over the heavy bass of the speakers only a few feet behind him.

"Ricky?"

She yelled something else though he couldn't hear her over the music.

"*What?* What did you say?" he shoved a finger into the opposite ear.

He hadn't expected her call. He hadn't expected to hear from her ever again. Just the sound of her voice sent his heart racing. It made him feel almost high.

"I said, where are you, Ricky? Are you at Club Majesty? Are you at the restaurant?"

"Yeah, I'm at Club Majesty. Why? Do you want to meet me here?" he asked, hoping that the excitement that he felt wasn't transparent in his voice.

"No! No, I need you to get out of there. Leave now! Okay?"

His sense of euphoria began to wane and was quickly replaced by confusion.

"What the hell are you talking about? Why do I need to leave?"

"Just go! Go out one of the back doors, if you can. I

don't know if they'll be waiting there, but it's worth a try. They might not be. Please, Ricky! Leave now!"

"Wait . . . *who* is waiting for me? What the fuck are you talking about?"

There was a pause on the other end of the line. "I'm sorry. I thought . . . I thought they were just going to do it at his house. I had no idea. I didn't . . ." Her words drifted off.

As she spoke, Ricky looked around the club, watching as a new set of dancers began to strut on stage, as the bouncers returned to their stations after tossing out the rowdy patron. The whole scene looked so mundane—like any other night at Club Majesty—and yet, he could feel something in the air now. Something was about to happen.

"We're about to get raided, aren't we?" he asked, feeling his stomach drop. "You told the cops who I was. You told them what I told you. You told them everything, didn't you?"

She didn't respond, and he knew then. He knew the truth.

"Are they raiding Reynaud's too?"

"I'm so sorry, Ricky," was all she said.

Just then, the front and side doors flew open and more than two dozen police officers streamed into Club Majesty with weapons drawn, shouting orders. The music on the overhead speakers abruptly stopped. The dark club suddenly blazed bright, and patrons started to scatter like cockroaches when the lights are turned on. Most didn't get far. They were stopped by police officers who placed everyone in handcuffs.

Ricky watched the chaos with a mix of shock, dread, and hurt. He couldn't get out of here even if he tried. He thought about the stolen goods in the storage room. He thought about the suitcases Dolla Dolla kept in his basement. There was enough shit here to send him away for decades.

"Ricky?" he heard Simone shout. "Ricky, are you still there?"

He had fallen in love with Simone, and she had betrayed him. And she had done it on such a grand scale.

"You did this," he murmured, slowly shaking his head, watching as everything he'd built was being ripped apart in front of his very eyes. The strippers onstage and backstage scrambled. Most were still in their G-strings and pasties, screaming as the officers lunged and grabbed for them. A few were openly sobbing. "You did this! I *helped* you, Simone. I risked my life for you! I did all I could for you, and you did this shit to me?"

"I didn't want this to happen! You have to believe me! I just want my sister to be safe. I didn't . . . I didn't want to get you tangled up in this, in any of it. I just wanted—"

"Fuck you! Fuck you, you lyin' bitch!" he shouted, feeling his hurt flip to rage. "I swear to God, when I get my hands on you, I'm gonna—"

He didn't get to finish. One of the officers yanked his cell phone out of his hand and shoved him down against one of the tables, pressing his face into the marble tabletop.

"Ricky Reynaud, you have the right to remain silent," the officer began.

Ricky closed his eyes and accepted his punishment for being so trusting and so stupid.

"*You dumb son of a bitch,*" a voice laughed in his head.

As he listened to his Miranda rights and was escorted out of the club in handcuffs, he made a promise to himself that if he made it out of jail, if he made it out of this, the first person he was paying a visit to was Simone Fuller.

Chapter 31

Jamal

Jamal sat at his desk, staring out the office window at the busy street below, watching the cars and the metro buses drive by, as pedestrians strolled along the sidewalk and walked through the intersection. This was his town, his city. It had been for most of his life and yet, he felt no more a part of it today than he had when he arrived here from North Carolina when he was nine years old.

He had tried for years to be a part of D.C., to make his mark. It was why when he was eleven years old he had tagged the wall behind his apartment building with spray-paint and wrote in bright white letters, "JAY L IS DA BOMB." It was the first time he'd gotten caught tagging, and it had landed him a beating with a shoe on his backside from his mama, but it'd been worth it. He'd finally had something tangible to show the world that he existed, that he meant something in these streets. It was why he had gone to law school and gotten a job in D.C. government, working long hours for low pay in the hopes of moving up the ladder. It was why he had eagerly accepted the position as deputy mayor when Mayor Johnson offered it to him. He'd wanted to be something that people could look up to and respect.

I just wanted to be somebody.

But now the whole enterprise felt pointless, like a complete waste of time. His job as deputy mayor was full of obligation, but short on prestige. He'd lost his girlfriend. He was no longer friends with Derrick and Ricky, who he'd damn near considered his brothers. But the hardest blow had to be how things had turned out with Melissa. She'd called him a "low-down shady fuck" and she'd obviously meant it; she no longer wanted anything to do with him either.

Jamal tiredly closed his eyes.

Maybe it was time to stop living for other people. Maybe he should finally put even Melissa's judgment of him aside. All these years, he had been pretending to be something that he wasn't, putting on a mask to please and earn the love and respect of those around him. Maybe he should finally just embrace who he really was and do whatever the hell he wanted. If he really was a "low-down shady fuck," he might as well own up to it and embrace it.

Why the hell not?

He slowly opened his eyes, exhaled, and pushed himself to his feet. He then walked around his desk to his office door, buttoning his suit jacket and mentally preparing himself for what he was about to do next.

"Yes?" Mayor Johnson called out, slowly raising his eyes from the stack of papers assembled in front of him. When he saw Jamal striding into his office, he raised his eyebrows and leaned back in his chair. "Why hello, Sinclair! I wasn't expecting to see you today. Did we have a meeting scheduled? Certainly not this early."

Jamal shook his head. "No, no meeting. I'd like to talk to you though. I know you're an early riser like me and I wanted to talk to you when no one else was around."

"What did you want to talk about?"

Jamal closed the door behind him and strolled toward the mayor's desk.

"I want to talk about the little conversation that we had a few weeks ago," Jamal said, lowering himself into one of the chairs facing the mayor's desk, "when you asked me what I planned to do with the information I gathered."

The mayor's polite smile disappeared. His bushy gray brows drew together. "And what exactly did you want to discuss regarding that conversation?"

"Look, you saw what was in that envelope. I know about the hundreds of thousands of dollars in campaign contributions Dolla Dolla had funneled to you. I know for the past five years you've been getting kickbacks for building contracts."

The mayor barked out a caustic laugh. "You don't know a damn thing! I don't care who you talked to or what they told you, but you can't prove any of it. And if you even breathe a word of this to the press, it's your funeral! Do you understand me?"

There he was, threatening his life again. But Jamal wouldn't be scared off this time.

"Even if you kill me, you can't kill every reporter in town. And they'll all pick up the story. You know it, and I know it. The mayor who claimed to be anti-corruption is really working with a dude like Dolla Dolla? They'll be *salivating* over it, and my paper trail shows—"

"I don't give a shit about your paper trail! No judge or jury in this town would ever find me guilty," Mayor Johnson said, leaning forward in his chair. "But you can be sure that you won't have the same luck if I decide to sue your ass for slander. When I'm done with you, you won't have a dime left to your name! You'll *wish* you were dead—if my partner hasn't killed you already!"

"And everything I can already prove about your dirty financial dealings . . . your questionable business relationships, there's probably twice as much that an industrious reporter or the FBI could discover," Jamal continued, undaunted. "That's the stuff that could land you with those scary federal charges. That's the stuff that could put you in prison for a very, *very* long time."

The mayor quieted.

"But," Jamal said, inclining his head, "I'm a reasonable man, Vernon. You mentioned before that if I kept your secrets, if I was willing to work with you, there could be something to benefit me in the end. So . . . I have a proposition for you."

The mayor's stony visage softened. He sat back in his chair, narrowing his eyes with interest. "I'm listening."

"I don't want any part of your side businesses—whatever it is. But I *do* want a pay increase by about thirty percent . . . no, make that *fifty* percent."

"Sinclair, I can't just arbitrarily decide to—"

"I don't care how you do it; just do it," Jamal said firmly. "Get it from your dirty kickbacks, for all I care. And I'm tired of toiling in the shadows. No more grunt work. No more bullshit. I bust my ass as deputy mayor. I want to be more at the forefront from now on. When you get invited to New York or overseas or Congress to represent our fair city, I want to be at your side. I want my face in front of those cameras. The people of this city are going to know who the fuck Jamal Sinclair Lighty is from now on."

"So money, power, and fame," Mayor Johnson said with a chuckle. "That's what you want?"

Jamal nodded. "That's what I want."

The mayor's chuckle became a full rumbling laugh that made his chest shake. "Well, if that's your price of cooperation, I believe it can be arranged, Sinclair."

"Please, Vernon . . . call me Jay," he said, his face widening into a Cheshire cat grin. "And I'm glad we could reach an agreement."

Chapter 32

Derrick

It had been a sleepless night like he'd thought it would be, though Melissa had slumbered contentedly beside him. Her soft breath—its rhythmic inhale and exhale—had been the symphony he'd listened to during the most of the night as he stared into the darkness.

He'd thought he was going to break up with Melissa, had even promised Morgan that he would, and now the situation had flipped. He faced the task of ending things with Morgan instead, and the prospect felt even worse.

At least with Melissa, he had felt justified in walking away. They had been fighting for months. Though they had known each other for decades, she'd been treating him like a total stranger; she'd behaved like a woman he no longer recognized. But Morgan had done nothing wrong. She had offered him friendship and affection. He could find no justification in what he was about to do to her besides the fact that he was still madly in love with Melissa and wanted to make it work now that she was willing to do the same. They were going to start all over again, and he couldn't let this chance pass him by.

When his alarm clock sounded, Derrick felt like he was recovering from a hangover. His head was pounding. His muscles felt tight and worn. Even his stomach hurt.

"You okay, baby?" Melissa asked him worriedly as she put on her bathrobe. "You don't look well."

He shook his head. "I'm fine. I'm just . . . I don't know. Maybe I'm catching a cold or something."

She looped her robe belt around her waist and knotted it. "Well, if you don't feel good, then stay home. Call in sick."

He threw his legs over the side of the bed and stretched, listening to the crack of his muscles and joints in his back. "I can't."

She laughed. "*Why not?* You're allowed."

"I just can't," he said firmly, and then looked up at her.

She wasn't smiling anymore. Her brows were furrowed.

He rose to his feet and hugged her, not wanting to argue—not after they finally seemed to be back on track after all these months of being derailed as a couple.

"I just . . . I've got something important to do. I gotta go in today, even if I don't feel up to it. It has to be done."

She leaned back and raised her hands to his face. She ran her nails through the hairs of his goatee, rose to the balls of her feet, and gave him a lip-smacking kiss.

"Okay, Mr. Miller, do what you have to do. But if you still feel shitty after you get there, just leave early. I'll make you some soup when you get home, and, if you're strong enough," she wrapped her arms around his waist and gave him another kiss, "I'll have something *else* waiting for you when you get back home."

He smiled. "I'd like that."

She took a step back and walked into the bathroom.

"Gotta go take my shower. You can hop in with me if you want," she called over her shoulder to him.

It was an offer she hadn't made in months.

"I'll join you in a bit," he said.

When she strolled into the bathroom, he reached for his cell phone. On the screen was another message from Morgan. He didn't even read it; he instantly deleted it.

"What the fuck am I doing?" he whispered

"You comin', Dee?"

"Yeah, I'm comin', baby," he said, before lowering his cell back to his night table and yanking off his boxer briefs. He then strolled into their bathroom.

An hour later, Derrick walked down the hall toward his office.

"Derrick!" he heard Morgan call out.

He saw her waving and striding toward him, hallowed by the light from the other end of the hall. Even from this distance, he could see the adoration in her eyes. He halted in his steps, took a deep, fortifying breath, then continued in the direction he was headed.

Of course, he had to bump into her as soon as he arrived at work, or maybe he wasn't bumping into her. Maybe she had been lingering near his office door, waiting to hear how this morning had gone when he told Melissa that they were breaking up. He was about to disappoint her.

"Good morning," she said when he finally stood less than a foot in front of her. She made a quick glance over her shoulder and his, as if to see if anyone else was in the hallway with them. She raised her lips to his, as if to kiss him, but he pulled away before she could, making her squint.

"*What?* What's wrong?"

He shook his head. "Don't do that, okay? Especially don't do it here."

"Don't worry," she said with a wink. "I checked. No one saw us."

"That's not what I meant."

She took a step back, now frowning suspiciously. "Then what did you mean, Derrick?"

"Look, Morgan, I'm . . . I'm sorry."

"Sorry about what?"

"I fucked up. I . . . I lied to you."

She took another step back from him, then another.

"I told you that it was over between Melissa and me," he pressed on, "and I . . . and I thought it was but, last night . . . last night she and I—"

Morgan shot up her hand, stopping him midsentence. She shook her head, sending her curls whipping around her shoulders. "Stop! I don't want to hear anymore."

"I didn't want to hurt you. I really—"

"I said, shut up!" she yelled, then caught herself when she realized her voice projected down the length of the hall. "I should've known something was up when you didn't answer my texts. I thought maybe you wanted to be alone for a bit and didn't wanna talk. I thought you were working through some shit. You'd just broken up with your girlfriend, so you needed some space. But I gave you too much credit. Didn't I, Derrick?"

He dropped his eyes, unable to bear the look of hurt and anger marring her face.

"So what was all that shit you were telling me about, how I'm too good to be somebody's side chick? Huh? Because that is exactly what you fucking made me! I was the rebound bitch who patted you up and flattered your ego until your ball-busting fiancée was ready to give you your nuts back!"

She was going below the belt now, but Derrick accepted it silently. This was his punishment for how he had treated her, for what he had done. She was using her words to whack at him like a piñata. He'd let her get her hits in. He wouldn't fight back. He wouldn't say a word.

"Fuck you! Fuck you and your lies!" She turned away from him but then paused and faced him again. Her eyes were red and bright, threatening to spill over with tears at any second. "You know I was with an asshole for almost three years. I thought I could spot one from a mile away, but turns out, I can't. You fooled my ass, Derrick Miller. You fooled me good!"

She then stomped away from him.

"Morgan!" he called. He started to follow her, but then stopped.

He wanted to defend himself, to explain why he had done what he had done, but there was nothing to explain. He had lied to her like she'd said, though he hadn't meant to do it. He had behaved like an asshole. Everything she'd ranted about was true.

One of the stairwell doors swung open and the hallway filled with a stream of boys headed to their morning classes.

"Hey, Miss Owens!" a few of them called to Morgan as she walked by.

She didn't respond but instead dropped her head and sniffed, turning away from their eager gazes and ready smiles.

"What's up, Miss Owens?" Cole said, holding the stairwell door open for her as she approached him. When he saw her face, he stared at her with concern. "Hey, are you all right?" Cole asked.

Morgan gave one last glance over her shoulder at Derrick who stood mutely several feet away. She quickly nodded at Cole before a lone tear spilled onto her cheek. She then eased past him into the stairwell, letting the door slam shut behind her.

Cole stared at the closed door for several seconds. He

turned around and looked at Derrick. "Why was she crying? What happened?"

Derrick began to tell him that it was not his concern and to just head to class when Cole charged at him. Derrick barely had time to brace himself before the young man gave him a hard shove, almost sending him flying into the wall behind him.

"What did you do to her?" Cole shouted.

All the others boys stopped in their tracks. Conversations and laughter halted, like the volume had been turned down in the hallway. They stared in shock at Cole and Derrick. Even a few were gawking.

"Oh, shit," one murmured before letting out a nervous laugh. "Did he just buck to Mr. Derrick?"

It was one thing to pick a fight with another boy at the Institute. It was a completely different matter to pick a fight with the director himself.

Cole tried to shove Derrick again, but Derrick was ready for him this time. He caught the boy's scrawny wrist, stopping him before he could.

So Cole *did* have a crush on Morgan, after all, as Derrick had suspected in the beginning. And Cole was willing to go to great lengths to defend his lady love. Derrick could respect that. But he couldn't let this get out of hand, either.

"Don't be stupid and end up in juvie like your friend, Tory, Cole," he said.

The young man still glowered up at him like he wasn't going to back down, like he wanted to take a swing.

"I repeat, don't be stupid. I let you get one shove in, but don't think I'll let you do it again. Come at me and I'll come right back at you, son, and it's gonna hurt. Trust me."

He squeezed Cole's wrist in an iron-like grip to illustrate his point, and the young man winced.

"Go to class," Derrick growled.

He finally let go of Cole and the young man still glared up at him but didn't say anything else. Instead of walking toward the classrooms though, Cole turned and headed toward the stairwell where Morgan had gone.

"Cole!" Derrick shouted after him. "I told you to go to class!"

"Kiss my ass!" Cole yelled as he pushed the steel door open, darting into the stairwell. Derrick followed him, now both frustrated and pissed that he was chasing down a disobedient sixteen-year-old. As he shoved open the door, he could see the top of Cole's head as the young man thundered up the stairs.

"Cole! Boy, you better come back here!" he yelled as the third-floor stairwell door slammed shut.

Derrick emerged through the same door ten seconds later, to find an almost empty corridor. This was the dormitory floor, where the boys' bunk beds were arranged in large rooms with stark white walls and metal lockers, where they could store their clothes and personal items.

He walked into the room where Cole usually stayed. Though the young man was nowhere in sight, a couple of other boys lingered on their bunkbeds, lounging on their mattresses.

"What are y'all doing in here? Get to class!" Derrick barked, making one of the boys hurriedly close the magazine he was reading and the other yank earbuds out of his ears as they both scrambled to the door.

Derrick made a beeline to the bathrooms and checked each stall, but still didn't find Cole. He cursed under his breath, and began to walk back across the room, wondering if maybe Cole had just come up here to shake him off. Maybe he was already headed back down the stairs to the workshop in search of Morgan. He walked back through the dorm room but paused when he spotted something. He squinted.

Under the bottom bunk where Cole slept were two large suitcases barely hidden by the blanket Cole had thrown onto his bed. The boys weren't allowed to keep suitcases, duffel bags, or boxes. Each was issued a milk crate and locker to store his stuff. Derrick didn't know how Cole or his bunkmate had managed to get these suitcases past room inspection, which the Institute did daily. Something like this would have to be confiscated.

Derrick bent down and reached beneath the bunk to remove the suitcases, but was caught off guard by how heavy they were—like there was almost a hundred pounds worth of bricks in each. Why hadn't the bags been unpacked?

He tossed one suitcase onto the bed and yanked open the zipper, prepared to find a stack of tennis shoes and T-shirts or maybe even some contraband like video games or candy bars. But he wasn't prepared for what he discovered instead. Inside were at least a dozen bags of neatly stacked white powder. When Derrick saw them, he staggered back as if Cole had given him another hard shove.

"What the fuck," he whispered, still in disbelief.

He quickly wrestled the other suitcase out from under Cole's bunkbed and dropped it onto the mattress. With shaking hands, he pulled open the zipper. He stared in shock. There had to be at least a quarter of a million dollars here.

"Oh, my God," he whispered again.

Don't miss the next installment in
The Branch Avenue Boys series
Coming soon from
Shelly Ellis
and
Dafina Books

A READING GROUP GUIDE

IN THESE STREETS

Shelly Ellis

ABOUT THIS GUIDE

The suggested questions are included to enhance your group's reading of Shelly Ellis's *In These Streets*.

DISCUSSION QUESTIONS

1. Is Jamal wrong and selfish for separating himself from Ricky and Derrick, or is distancing himself from his old friends a smart move?

2. Derrick suspects that the reason his fiancée, Melissa, doesn't like him working at the Boys' Institute, is because she's projecting her feelings about her father onto him. Do you think his assumption is correct?

3. Should Jamal listen to his girlfriend's advice to ignore what he suspects about Mayor Johnson? Why or why not?

4. Why do you think Ricky decides to help Simone? Is it in some way connected to his own deceased sister, Desiree?

5. Derrick suspects he's starting to develop feelings for Morgan. Do you think it's legitimate attraction, or is it just a reaction to how Melissa has been treating him?

6. Ricky, at first, decides to put distance between himself and Simone, but later changes his mind. Do you think he should have other concerns about their relationship besides Dolla Dolla finding out about it?

7. After Jamal is confronted by Mayor Johnson, he decides to keep the mayor's secret. Should he have done so, or taken the risk and told the press about the mayor's corruption?

8. Derrick begins a romantic relationship with Morgan, despite still living with Melissa. Do you think his behavior is justified considering how badly his relationship with Melissa has deteriorated?

9. Ricky suffers a huge betrayal. Do you think this was Simone's intention all along, or was it out of her control, like she claims?

10. Jamal makes a huge shift of mindset at the end. Were you surprised by his change of heart/decision?